Eric Malpass was born in Derby in ⟨...⟩ bank after leaving school, but his ⟨...⟩ become a novelist and he wrote in h⟨...⟩ years. His first book, *Morning's at Seven*, was published to wide acclaim. With an intuitive eye for the quirkiness of family life, his novels are full of wry comments and perceptive observations. This exquisite sense of detail has led to the filming of three of his books. His most engaging character is Gaylord Pentecost – a charming seven-year-old who observes the strange adult world with utter incredulity.

Eric Malpass also wrote biographical novels, carefully researched and highly evocative of the period. Among these is *Of Human Frailty*, the moving story of Thomas Cranmer.

With his amusing and lovingly drawn details of life in rural England, Malpass' books typify a certain whimsical Englishness – a fact which undoubtedly contributes to his popularity in Europe. Married with a family, Eric Malpass lived in Long Eaton, near Nottingham, until his death in 1996.

AT THE HEIGHT OF THE MOON
BEEFY JONES
THE CLEOPATRA BOY
FORTINBRAS HAS ESCAPED
A HOUSE OF WOMEN
THE LAMPLIGHT AND THE STARS
THE LONG LONG DANCES
MORNING'S AT SEVEN
OF HUMAN FRAILTY
OH, MY DARLING DAUGHTER
THE RAISING OF LAZARUS PIKE
SUMMER AWAKENING
SWEET WILL
THE WIND BRINGS UP THE RAIN

ERIC MALPASS

Pig in the Middle

HOUSE OF
STRATUS

This edition published in 2001 by House of Stratus, an imprint of
Stratus Books Ltd., 21 Beeching Park, Kelly Bray,
Cornwall, PL17 8QS, UK.

www.houseofstratus.com

Typeset, printed and bound by House of Stratus.

A catalogue record for this book is available from the British Library
and the Library of Congress.

ISBN 0-7551-0193-6

Chapter 1

Gaylord certainly had his full enjoyment out of the family's visit to the circus.

He sat entranced, spellbound by the swirling movement and colour. He laughed himself nearly sick over the clowns. He looked with some disappointment at his baby sister, fast asleep on her mother's knee. "Amanda doesn't seem to be enjoying it much," he said disgustedly. "Fancy sleeping through those clowns."

May Pentecost, rather more sophisticated than her son, nuzzled the baby, thinking Amanda had got exactly the right idea. She wouldn't have minded dropping off to sleep herself. But she knew she would outrage her son. So like a good mother she made herself stay awake.

But now she saw her son's mood had changed. Gaylord's eyes were no longer on the clowns. The bright eyes were even brighter, and had been joined by a pair of burning cheeks. "Momma," he cried. "Isn't that lady *beautiful?*"

"Which one, dear?"

Silly question! "That one, Momma. The glittering lady on the trapeze."

"She is, isn't she, darling."

Gaylord stared. "Momma?" he asked hesitantly.

"Yes?"

"Momma, she couldn't be Auntie Becky, could she?"

"I don't think so, dear."

"Well, she looks like Auntie Becky."

Jocelyn said unkindly, "A lot of young ladies in circuses look like your Auntie Becky." Fond though he was of his younger sister, he did feel she carried around a whiff of grease paint.

Gaylord, who had been in love with his Auntie Becky before she married Uncle Peter, sighed. What chance had he of marrying this beautiful Circus Lady? None. He resigned himself to the shelf.

Yet Gaylord was enjoying himself: lions, tigers, horses; even the sad evanescent love of seven-year-olds had its sweetness. But then, suddenly, the show was over. The tigers roared for the last time, the smiling trapeze lady bowed her supple waist, the lights dimmed, the excitement and emotion were over.

But they weren't. Next morning Gaylord had a wonderful surprise. A knock on the door and a visitor walked into the classroom: a most intriguing visitor: none other than Police Constable Harris, wearing his helmet, walking to attention, saluting Teacher. And Teacher said, "Now children, Constable Harris has something serious to tell you. And I want you to listen to him very, very carefully."

Constable Harris cleared his throat, took off his helmet, and laid it on Teacher's desk, and looked around the class. His heart sank. His eyes had fallen on that Pentecost kid. And Constable Harris regarded the words *That Pentecost kid* and *Trouble* as synonymous.

Well now, began Constable Harris, he didn't want anybody to be frightened. Everything was under control. Just a case of being a bit careful going home from school.

Gaylord thrilled. What could it be? His little mind reviewed the current possible excitements: one, his friend Henry Bartlett said someone or something had knocked a big hole in the sky over the South Pole and the sun would come rolling through, or we should all tumble out, Henry wasn't sure which; two, Reuben Briggs claimed one of his sheep had got the scrapie, and might run amok; for Gaylord, the rich tapestry of life was wholly made up of such exciting disasters. He sat with bated breath waiting for the good Constable to announce which particular one was about to engulf them all.

And Constable Harris produced something more wonderful than even Gaylord's fertile mind could have thought up: Oh frabjous day! A man-eating tiger had escaped from the Circus!

Then Constable Harris spoilt *everything* by saying that a bus was being arranged to take home any children living more than a mile out of the village.

Well you couldn't expect Gaylord to know how far a mile was, could you now. They hadn't done Measurement yet – had they? He would just assume a mile wasn't very far.

But trust the suspicious grown-up mind to spoil things. "Now Gaylord, you *will* go on that bus, won't you?" That was Teacher, when four p.m. came.

He nodded. He had a theory that breaking a nod wasn't as bad as breaking a spoken word.

"Go and get in the queue, then," said Teacher.

"Yes, Miss," said Gaylord. He went and got in the queue.

The bus arrived. Teacher gave the driver a list.

Then she cycled off, throwing back another suspicious glance at Gaylord as she left. Gaylord, though a kindly child, hoped the tiger would eat her. He didn't like suspicion in people. He found it depressing.

It was no good. The idea of going on a bus when there was a chance of meeting a real live tiger was unthinkable. At this precise moment in time both Gaylord's shoelaces came undone. By the time he'd fastened them all the other children were on the bus.

Gaylord, still bent double, ran round to the near side and moved forward, taking time from the bus until he had to fall back away from the shelter of the bus. But by this time he was out of sight of anyone who mattered. He went on his way rejoicing.

His first daily port of call on his way home was the lonely cottage of Mrs Fisher, a lady of nervous temperament who always gave him a biscuit to keep him going till tea time. "Mrs Fisher, Mrs Fisher, guess what! A tiger's escaped from that Circus. Isn't it exciting! I reckon it'll come this way."

Mrs Fisher nearly dropped the biscuit barrel. Was it April 1st? No it wasn't. Could a tiger climb the elm outside her window? Yes it could. Gaylord, for Mrs Fisher at any rate, had murdered sleep as efficiently as Macbeth.

He made a detour to bring the good news to his second daily caller: Reuben Briggs.

Gaylord had never thought to mention these detours to Momma. He suspected that, if Momma ever stepped inside Reuben's cottage, it would immediately be placed Out of Bounds. Gaylord didn't think Momma and Reuben would quite see eye to eye about washing up and things.

"Mr Briggs, a tiger's escaped. I reckon you ought to round your sheep up."

Briggs slowly put down his book, worked an empty mug out of the hearth with his right welly, reached down and picked it up, wiped his handkerchief round inside it, ladled in a spoonful of condensed milk, lifted the teapot off the hob and poised it over the mug. "Strong, thick, stupefying? Or wishy-washy?"

"Strong, please Mr Briggs." Gaylord thought Reuben's tea was the most wonderful brew in the world. To sit, one on each side of Reuben's grate, sipping the old STS was the most manly thing he knew.

He raised his mug and took a deep and satisfying swig.

They clinked mugs. "Tigers," said Reuben. "What about 'em?"

"It escaped from the Circus."

"Nonsense."

"It *did*, Mr Briggs." Gaylord was very disappointed in his old friend.

"Don't be daft, lad. Have another STS. Help you to think straight."

"No thank you, Mr Briggs," Gaylord said politely. He was eager now to find another, less sceptical, audience. Momma!

"Tiger, tiger, burning bright," murmured Reuben. "Shut gates," he called. "Don't want him getting in and eating my old ladies." Gaylord heard him chortling. He was, frankly, a little hurt. He ran down the woodland path. He opened the gate into the field. And as he turned to pass through, something in his vision turned his legs to water. A hundred yards away, heavily camouflaged by leaves and branches, and camouflaged again by his own stripes, was an unmistakable Bengal Tiger!

As a country boy, Gaylord had always known about shutting gates. But no-one had said anything about gates and Bengal Tigers. A Bengal Tiger, he felt instinctively, must override the normal conventions of English country life.

So, not stopping to shut the gate, he ran and dodged and leapt through the field of sheep like a rugby threequarter weaving through the opposing players. Not until he was safely in the next field did he look back. The outraged sheep were carrying on no end. But of the tiger there was no sign; though Gaylord thought perhaps he could hear him roaring.

Gaylord didn't think he'd go back and warn Reuben. He might disturb the sheep. Perhaps he'd go home and ask Grandpa what to do,

And on the way he ran slap into Constable Harris, with guns and minions. "Constable Harris, he's up there, near Mr Briggs' cottage. I bet he's eaten him by now."

"I bet he has," said the Constable sourly. He muttered to his minions: "It's that Pentecost kid again. Come here, boy."

Gaylord approached a warily. Harris said, "Quite an expense, putting that bus on for you lot, *Master* Pentecost."

Gaylord looked impressed, though he said nothing. There didn't really seem anything to say.

"But I see you decided to walk," said Harris.

"Sort of," admitted Gaylord.

"Oh, go home, sonny," said the Constable. "And don't talk to any strange tigers." In a sudden burst of irritation he growled, "Hang around, and we'll use you for bait."

Gaylord couldn't help wondering whether perhaps Constable Harris didn't like him very much. He found it rather a depressing thought. But by the time he had reached home he was working on another problem. He was longing, yearning to tell Momma he'd seen the tiger at such close quarters. Yet he had an instinct that it would be better not to. He had a lot of instincts where Momma was concerned. And they were usually right, he found.

He pulled his schoolbag from his shoulders. He was flushed, breathless and his dark eyes shone with delight. "Momma, you know that circus? Well one of the man-eating tigers has escaped."

May Pentecost looked at him thoughtfully. She knew Gaylord's imagination. "Did you meet him on the way home?" she asked cautiously.

"Not exactly," said Gaylord. "But I helped Constable Harris and some policemen search for him with guns."

"I bet they were glad of your help."

"They were, rather. But we didn't see him," he admitted sadly.

May was intrigued. If Gaylord had been making it all up, he would probably have wrestled with the beast single-handed. But you couldn't be sure. Her son didn't lack subtlety. She sat down, pulled him to her. "Gaylord, how did you know about this tiger?"

"Constable Harris told us. This morning."

"And what did Teacher say then?"

"She taught us a poem. 'Tiger, tiger, burning bright, in the somethings of the night!' Then a bit about a cemetery."

"And a very positive contribution too," said May bitterly. She stared at her son. "And they didn't send you home on a bus or anything?"

"Momma! That would have spoilt *everything*," Gaylord said reproachfully. Oh dear, he'd never understand the adult mind.

May said, "Right. Now you sit there and eat your tea. And don't you dare stir from this room." She went up to her husband's study two at a time. She marched in. "There's a tiger loose," she announced.

Jocelyn Pentecost, caught in mid-paragraph, made himself think hard. Tiger! Tigers didn't fit in with the novel he was writing. Nor did they inhabit that real countryside where he lived with his testy old father and his dear wife and family in a big Victorian farmhouse. Cows, yes. Sheep and horses, yes. Even the occasional bull. But tigers, no. Was Blake apposite here, he wondered. He couldn't see how.

May exploded. "And all Teacher could do was make them

learn that thing of Blake's."

"It's a damn good poem," he said thoughtfully.

"Jocelyn! You know Gaylord. If he'd met a tiger he'd have chatted him up and shared his Mars Bar with him. Yet they let him walk home alone. Good Lord, where's your father?"

"Snoozing in his orchard like Hamlet's father if I know him. Why?"

But she'd gone, clattering down the stairs and out at the back door. She glanced en passant at her son, happily and messily dunking soldiers into his egg. Then she hurried out to the orchard.

There, surrounded by trees behind any of which might lurk a man-eating tiger, in a deckchair set in a warm pool of afternoon sunshine, lay her father-in-law, breathing softly, rhythmically, bubbling occasionally and benevolently like a good stew. An elderly gentleman, the world forgetting by the world forgot, a man consciously revelling in the peace of his world, unperturbed by the knowledge that the peace of the next could not be too far away.

"Father-in-law," she cried, "you must come indoors. I'll tell you why as we go. Come on." She snatched at the travelling rug that swathed his legs.

It was a mistake. No one, not even his admired May, could hustle John Pentecost and get away with it. One baleful eye opened. It regarded her with venom. "Don't 'come on' me," he growled. "How *dare* you, woman?"

She said, "A tiger's escaped from that wretched circus. It might be anywhere."

"Not in my orchard," he said coolly.

"Oh, don't be so smug," she cried. She gave another heave at the travelling rug.

He looked at her in surprise. His voice became friendlier. "May, May! It's not like you to be as jumpy as this."

No, it wasn't. She pulled herself up short. What had happened to that cool, mocking approach to life that had seen her through so many crises. She said, "Oh, I'm sorry, Father-in-law. But it's this disintegrating world – muggers, terrorists, disasters of every kind." She laughed unsteadily. "Somehow a tiger seemed the last straw."

"Pull me up," he said holding out both arms. She tugged, he came up, smooth and steady as a piece of machinery. He slipped an arm into hers. They strolled towards the house in the long, golden afternoon. He said, "I know what you mean, May. The world isn't shaping well. Not well at all." He looked at her thoughtfully. "But even a tiger can only be in one place at once. Which means it's not likely to be both on Gaylord's way home and in my orchard."

"But he could be in one of them," she said quickly.

"Yes." He sighed. "He could be." He squeezed her arm. "I think what we both need is a nice dry sherry, my dear."

How sensible, how reassuring the old man was! They settled down in the drawing room with their wine. Through the open windows came the sounds of summer: the buzzing of bees: the assertive thrush (yet how strange, she thought, that if he is only concerned to establish his territory, he should have chosen so sweet a song: and how typical that it was left to my cynical generation to decide that that liquid loveliness means only aggression): the distant lowing of the cattle, the shout of a man in a far meadow. And so firmly had the old man dismissed her fears that she did not even listen for the outlandish roaring of a tiger.

What had Momma said? "Right. Now you'll sit there and eat your tea. And don't you *dare* stir from this room."

Gaylord had to admit it was a pretty watertight injunction. But Gaylord could have found a few holes in the Ten

Commandments if he'd given his mind to it. So he began to consider Momma's orders, word by word, sentence by sentence.

"You'll sit there and eat your tea." Well, he'd done that, hadn't he, and not a crumb left. Even Momma couldn't fault him on that.

"And don't stir from this room." That, on the face of it, was pretty definite.

But for how long? It could mean, "don't stir from this room while you eat your tea." If so, he'd obeyed her orders to the letter. And if it didn't mean that, what did it mean? "Don't stir from this room for ever?" But that was absurd. He'd die, wouldn't he, if no-one came to feed him. The more he looked at it, the more obvious it became. He'd eaten his tea without stirring from the room. He'd done exactly what Momma said. Both logically and morally he was now a free man, he told himself. But just to be on the safe side and to avoid any wearisome moral and logical red herrings being raised, he crept silent as any Sioux Indian out of the back door. Sitting Bull would have been proud of him.

Lest one should think Gaylord motivated by any hint of self, it should be pointed out that his sole reason for leaving the room was to help his fellow man.

In a crisis like the present, one thing above all was needed: one thing which neither the Police nor Momma, those twin bastions of law and order, seemed to have thought of: one thing he'd never heard mentioned, yet which any village headman in India would have had in working order by now: a tiger trap! No use sitting indoors when you alone had the answer (and the expertise) to solve the problem that had got Momma into such a tizzy.

He knew exactly where such a trap should be: in Polly Larkin's Pad.

Polly Larkin's Pad ran down to the river: one of the innumerable grass tracks of England, overhung by box and elder, tight-flanked with nettles, its air close and heavy with the sweet scents of the box and acrid nettle, and with the dank, pervading smell of the river: just the place to catch a tiger on its way to its waterhole! He took his trowel and began digging in the middle of the path.

But you couldn't dig a tiger trap on your own between tea and supper. He needed his friend Henry Bartlett's help.

Five minutes later, led by some strange osmosis of thought, Henry Bartlett appeared, trowel in hand, and began digging, without a word, at Gaylord's side.

Henry Bartlett was all pink and bland and spectacles. If his friend Gaylord had asked him to throw himself fully dressed into the river he would have done so without a moment's hesitation. Yet Gaylord never asked or commanded anything. Henry was just his willing slave.

They went on digging. Henry said, "That tiger escaping. Fancy."

"Yes," said Gaylord, "I reckon I saw him when I came home from school."

Henry looked impressed. "You digging to Australia?" he asked hopefully.

" 'Course not," said Gaylord.

"What you digging for then?"

"A trap for tigers," said Gaylord.

Henry cogitated. "I don't reckon I should like to catch a tiger. They eat you."

"Not if they're in a trap they don't."

Henry looked unconvinced. They went on digging. Gaylord said, "When it's big enough you cover it with palm fronds."

"You got any palm fronds, Gaylord?"

11

" 'Course," said Gaylord. He'd no idea what palm fronds looked like. But he knew he'd recognise them as soon as he saw some.

They went on digging. Gaylord looked at the hole critically. It would, he had to admit, accommodate no more that a decent-sized cat so far. But he was really getting rather worried about Momma's possible reaction to his absence. He thought he'd just slip home and get those palm fronds and give a general impression of being around the house.

"I'm just going to get some palm fronds, Henry. Shan't be long," he said.

Henry, digging away, said, "Gaylord?"

"Yes, Henry?"

"I've just had funny idea, Gaylord." Henry gave an unusual chortle. "Gaylord, I was thinking. Wouldn't it be funny if that escaped tiger fell in *this* hole?"

"It would, wouldn't it Henry," Gaylord said kindly. He liked is friend Henry very dearly. But he did sometimes wish he had a little more imagination.

May always held that domestic crises might come and go and Jocelyn, writing away in his study, would never hear a thing. The only sound, she maintained, that brought him downstairs was the clink of sherry glasses.

And sure enough he now appeared: looking, May noticed, a trifle wary.

He had need to be wary. Earlier, May had said something about a tiger. But what? Ought he to have reacted to the news more strongly? He didn't know. He would, he decided, play it very carefully while he poured himself a sherry, keep his ears open and be ready to give an impression of having the whole situation under control.

May said, "That tiger," and sipped her sherry, watching

him closely.

"Oh. Ah, yes," said Jocelyn. Somehow he didn't feel or sound as masterful as he'd hoped.

May said, "They've got him. It's just been on the radio." She looked at him with her loving, but undoubtedly mocking, smile. "So you can relax, boyo."

"Oh good," he said. "Stop worrying, eh?"

"A fat lot of worrying you did," she said. "Why, I don't think you ever knew what it was all about."

And before Jocelyn could get a protesting look on to his face, his father was weighing in. "May's right, Jocelyn. You hide yourself away upstairs with no idea of what's going on. Why, if May hadn't dragged me forcibly indoors I might have been devoured in my own orchard." He turned to his daughter-in-law. "And I want you to know I appreciate it, my dear."

"Oh, you don't have to tell me how grateful you were, Father-in-law," May said sweetly.

"Momma," said a voice from the French windows. "Can I have some palm fronds?"

"I'm afraid I am out of palm fronds at the moment, dear. And what do you want palm fronds for? And what are you doing outside when I distinctly said you were not to stir from the dining room?" Her voice was rising ominously.

Gaylord was affronted. "Momma, only while I ate my tea. You said 'Now sit there and eat you tea. And don't stir from this room!' And I did, Momma, just like you said."

"*As* you said," Jocelyn corrected.

"Oh shut up, Jocelyn," said May. "I will not have wilful disobedience."

"And I," said Jocelyn stoutly, "will not have sloppy English."

Faced with attack from two quarters, Gaylord concentrated

on the real enemy. Poppa, he knew of old, could never bother to keep on about things. Whereas Momma could go on all day and all night. He said, "But Momma, you didn't say I'd got to sit there *always*. You only said while I ate my tea."

"I did nothing of the sort. I said 'don't stir from this room'."

"Only while I ate my tea, Momma."

"Pure semantics," murmured Jocelyn.

A kingfisher diving on a fish in a stream was nothing to Gaylord pouncing on a red herring in a crisis. He turned on his father a face eager and hungry for knowledge. "Poppa, what are semantics?"

"Well," said Jocelyn, "they're to do with the meaning of words. For instance – "

May said, "Jocelyn, stop maundering. This is important. If they hadn't caught that tiger Gaylord would have been outside with *him* at large. And if he'd got eaten he'd have had no-one to blame but himself."

That was disappointing news. "Have they caught him, Momma?"

"Yes they have, thank goodness. But next time when I tell you to stay in you stay in, remember. I don't – "

Gaylord witched off. He knew Momma well enough to know that if reprisals were going to be taken she'd have announced it before now. It was time, he decided, for reconciliation. He said, rather wistfully, "Poor old tiger. I bet he didn't half enjoy being free."

Surprisingly it was Grandpa who rose to this bait "You're right there, boy," he said. "Magnificent creatures like him shouldn't be behind bars."

Gaylord followed up his advantage. "I hope he managed to eat somebody before they got him. Something to remember, poor old thing. Can I go out and play now, Momma?"

"Oh, yes, off you go," said May. She had a feeling she'd been out-manoeuvred. If only Jocelyn would keep out of things! When dealing with Gaylord you had to keep strictly to the point, never giving him an inch. Why couldn't Jocelyn get that into his woolly head?

Gaylord too felt he'd handled Momma rather well. So much so that he said, "Thank you, Momma," and gave her a wet, smacking kiss. He even wondered whether to bring up the subject of palm fronds again, but decided against. Once Momma had said, "off you go," the thing was to go, like a streak of lightning.

On the way back to the tiger trap he found some palm fronds. They were lying under a willow tree Momma had been pruning.

He advanced behind a great swathe of branches like an over-enthusiastic soldier on the way to Dunsinane. Henry Bartlett said, "We don't want a trap any more, Gaylord. They've got him."

This negative and short-sighted attitude rather shocked Gaylord. But he was always very patient with his friend. So he said, "Lots of tigers escape from circuses, Henry. Tiger traps are always useful. Let's dig deeper. Then we'll cover it with palm fronds."

So they dug deeper and wider and Gaylord's mind was as active as his hands. And more and more his eyes kept straying to his plump, pink friend. Until at last he said, "What are we going to use for bait, Henry?"

Henry knew only of one kind of bait. "Me dad's got some maggots," he said.

Gaylord didn't think tigers liked maggots. Not as much as they liked kids anyway. In India they always used kids.

He wished he knew someone who kept goats. But he

didn't.

Yet he could not get out of his mind something Constable Harris had said (actually Gaylord had rearranged the truth a little when had told Momma the police had let him help them search. But he remembered what Harris had *really* said: "Oh, Lord, it's the Pentecost kid again." "Go home, sonny," he'd said, "and don't talk to any strange tigers. Hang around," he'd said, "and we'll use you for bait.")

Two key words! kid and bait.

Well, he knew quite well the difference between two kinds of kid. But the idea had been planted. He said, "Would you like to be the bait, Henry?"

"Not much," said Henry. Then feeling churlish, he said, "What do you have to do if you're the bait, Gaylord?"

"Just sit at the bottom of the hole," said Gaylord reassuringly.

Henry mulled this over. He didn't feel particularly reassured. "What do I do when the tiger comes?"

"You don't have to *do* anything," said Gaylord. "Just be bait."

There was a silence. Then: "I don't think I will, Gaylord, thank you all the same," said Henry politely.

Pity. So far as Gaylord could see, to a tiger Henry as bait would be almost indistinguishable from the kid as bait: same size, made of roughly the same material. But he was never one to persuade, still less to coerce. He said kindly, "That's all right, Henry. We'll just leave it unbaited then. Oh, hello Poppa."

"What are doing?" said Jocelyn, trying ineffectually to wrench his mind away from his novel.

"It's a tiger trap," said Gaylord. "Only it wants covering with palm fronds and they won't stay on top. They keep falling into the hole."

It was seldom Jocelyn abandoned his fictional characters long enough to come up with a practical solution to anything. When he did it gave him more satisfaction than a rave review in *The Observer*. He said, "Look, if I lay this branch across the middle of the hole, then it will support the willow branches nicely."

Gaylord and Henry were terribly impressed. It had never occurred to either of them that Poppa could be *useful*.

So Jocelyn laid a bare branch across the hole and helped put the palm fronds in position and then continued his walk with a lighter step, feeling that Capability Pentecost would not be a bad sobriquet for such a practical person as himself.

But his euphoria did not last long. He met his neighbour, Reuben Briggs, who had a very short way with other people's ego trips. Especially Jocelyn's.

And Henry and Gaylord went home. Henry feeling he had behaved very selfishly and had let his dear friend down, and Gaylord nobly refusing to let himself think that if they *didn't* catch a tiger it wouldn't be *his* fault, it would be because of Henry's lack of co-operation.

Jocelyn's heart did not jump for joy when he saw Reuben Briggs standing apparently deep in meditation at the end of Polly Larkin's Pad.

Reuben had a glittering eye. His few remaining teeth were black and gnarled. He wore, winter and summer, a mud-coloured raincoat, a cloth cap and wellies.

Two things about Reuben made Jocelyn fear him: that glittering eye always seemed intensely amused when it fell on Jocelyn; and the successful author sensed that this homespun philosopher was steeped in the world's greatest literature (which Jocelyn, frankly, wasn't). Flaubert, Goethe,

Dostoievsky, Dickens tripped off his tongue.

He stood, waiting, staring thoughtfully down at the toes of his wellies. Only when Jocelyn had almost passed did he say, "Just been re-reading that old Dusty-ever-so. My, he don't half show up some of these modern writers."

"Yes, indeed," said Jocelyn, who'd always meant to read 'The Idiot' but had never quite got round to it.

Reuben looked amused. Jocelyn felt uncomfortable. In an effort to boost his morale he pulled out his pipe and began to fill it. Mr Briggs gave signs of even greater amusement. Jocelyn felt ever more uncomfortable. Reuben said, "Been soiling your lily-white hands, I see, Mr Pentecost."

Jocelyn looked. Yes. Soil on his hands. Trust Reuben to notice that. Being Jocelyn he had to explain. "Yes. My little boy dug a tiger trap." He gave a nervous laugh. I – er – helped him with the camouflage."

Mr Briggs did not seem amused for once. "Lots of tigers hereabouts are there, Mr Pentecost?"

"Not a lot," said Jocelyn. "But you know what children are."

"Aye. I do that, Mr Pentecost." Reuben fell silent. It was, Jocelyn felt, a pregnant silence. He waited, anxiously, with a distinct sense of being weighed in the balance and found wanting.

Reuben repeated: "Aye. I do that. I know for instance some kids, brought up all their lives in the country, don't know better than to leave a five-barred gate open on a field of sheep and lambs."

It was Jocelyn's turn for a pregnant pause. His mouth was dry. "You don't," he asked, "– you *don't* mean Gaylord?"

"I do damn well mean Gaylord." Reuben was shouting now. "S'afternoon. He sat there supping my STS, pleasant as you like. Then, suddenly, off. 'Goodbye and thank you, Mr

Briggs.' And ten minutes later my old ladies squawking and panicking over an area from intake to ten acre." His voice sank almost to a growl. "And how the devil, Mr Pentecost, do you imagine a lone man in his seventies rounds up fifty demented sheep?"

Jocelyn liked to get things straight; especially when he had been faced with a phrase he did not know. "What do you mean – supping STS? What's STS?"

"Oh, never mind," said Reuben wearily.

"But – but why were the sheep so agitated?"

"Because that lad o' yours had agitated 'em, that's why. I seen him, running across the field like a mad thing. Wonder he didn't break a few legs, including his own."

"I'm – very sorry," said Jocelyn. "If it really was Gaylord."

"Of course it really was," said Reuben. "I'm not daft, Mr Pentecost. Nor are my old ladies. Not as daft as humans, anyway. Aye. And one of 'em's still missing so far. Let me tell you that, Mr Pentecost."

Suddenly he was moving away, amusement now flitting about his mouth and eyes as he stared at Jocelyn. "Aye, they're daft creatures. But they're not as daft as humans, any day."

Jocelyn said lamely, "I can see you must be getting very attached to them."

Mr Briggs said, "Books and sheep for me. You can keep the rest." And suddenly he was plodding away to his ramshackle cottage among the trees.

Chapter 2

Golden afternoon faded into lovely evening. Shadows stole into the orchard where the old man's deckchair lay abandoned, flimsy memorial to contented hours. And the old man strolled by the chuckling river and watched the shadows deepen into the pools, and the birds wing homeward across the tracts of sky and the gnats dance away their single, sunlit day. Poor ephemera, he thought: to spend but one day in the loveliness of this strange world; and then – the dark. He himself had had many days, and he certainly wasn't ready yet. Oh, life had been good, still *was* good. To make your mark in the world; and then, still to set your feet firmly on the earth you loved, going forward with the sun on your cheek and the wind on your face. But, to be a gnat, everything finished in one summer's day! John Pentecost seldom smiled, never laughed. But now his mouth twisted under his fierce white moustache, and a rumbling came from his deep chest. John was amused: me, feeling sorry for a cloud of gnats; even stranger, me thinking about death, the inescapable, the unthinkable. But, though he might think about it, he didn't damn well fear it. It could come when it liked. He just hoped it would give him a few more days like this perfect gem. He opened his mouth and took in a great draught of air, as though he would swallow the whole bright evening.

Jocelyn Pentecost walked glumly in an upland meadow, seeking as always the last sweet rays of the sun. He caught

Gaylord up on his way home. "Gaylord, you seem to have upset Mr Briggs and I'm very concerned about it. Tell me what happened."

Oh dear. Gaylord hastily wondered about the decision not to tell Momma about having seen the tiger. Perhaps it would be better to tell her after all. But he didn't know yet how he *had* upset Mr Briggs. He just knew that grown-ups were always upset about something. To give him time to find out he started with the cup of tea. "Well, Poppa, I went to see Mr Briggs to make sure the tiger hadn't called and eaten him, and he said, 'Come in, Gaylord, and have some STS', so I – "

"What is this STS?" If Jocelyn didn't find out much else from his son (and he didn't suppose he would) at least he'd find out what STS was.

"It's super," said Gaylord. "Strong, thick, stupefying."

"Browning," cried Jocelyn, astonished.

Gaylord began to feel a little easier. If he could shunt Poppa into a conversational siding – ? He looked up; eager, heart-breakingly innocent. "What's Browning, Poppa?"

"Who, you mean. He was a famous poet. The Victorians thought very highly of him." He pondered. "You know, Gaylord, Mr Briggs is a very well-read man. Not many people would have known that quotation."

"You did, Poppa." Gaylord didn't often descend to flattery. Only when he was feeling his way.

"My job," his father said, realising he hadn't got far. "But – Mr Briggs said you left the gate open and the sheep got out. It – it doesn't sound like you, Gaylord."

Only one thing to do: "I was frightened, Poppa. The tiger was coming."

"Now, Gaylord, you don't expect me to believe that. But it was very wrong of you. So promise it won't happen again.

I very much dislike inconveniencing a neighbour, Gaylord."

Poppa was starting to go on, an almost unheard of occurrence. So Gaylord skilfully brought the subject back to the meaning of the word 'stupefying', where Poppa was happy to remain for the rest of the walk home.

Half an hour later May was smiling enigmatically at her son, sitting up in bed to eat his supper.

Still a bit bouncy she thought. But she didn't hold it against him. She was ready to be friends again. "And what have you been up to?" she asked.

This was a question Gaylord never answered lightly. An unconsidered answer could lead to endless questions and prohibitions. But today he felt on safe ground; even felt a little smug. He also decided he could ignore his sighting of the tiger.

He grinned. "Making a tiger trap, Momma. It's ever so deep, and all covered with palm fronds."

"Good. But haven't you rather missed your tiger?"

"Oh, it's not for that one, Momma."

"No?"

"No. It's in case one escapes when the circus comes next summer."

"That's what I call intelligent anticipation," said Momma.

"Is that good?"

"A most desirable quality."

He looked pleased. She rose, kissed him. "Night, night, my darling."

"Night, night. Do you know anyone who keeps goats?"

"No, night, night. Goats?" She couldn't see the connection. But conversation with Gaylord was always strewn with non-sequiturs. She went downstairs. It was nearly time for the old man's supper.

At the circus the big cats prowled to and fro, sniffing at their bars, roaring, growling in a sunless, tawdry prison. One was more restive than the others. Today he had smelt a forgotten smell: freedom. Already the smell was fading from his memory. But royal anger remained: that he, superb, magnificent, ruthless, was again at the mercy of the little creatures any one of whom he could kill with a single blow from a single paw.

The sun had gone now. But May and Jocelyn sat by the open french window, watching the afterglow. May said, "Gaylord's been very enterprising. He's built a tiger trap."

"I know."

She looked surprised. "How do you know?"

He had to think for a minute. Then he remembered his brief excursion out of his fictional world, an incident that had already almost faded from his consciousness. "I saw him digging it." He remembered something else. "I thought they'd recaptured the poor brute."

"They have. This is for next year's circus. Oh, and he wants to know someone who keeps goats. Can't think why."

"Bait of course," Jocelyn said quickly. It wasn't often he beat May to anything. He glowed with simple pride.

"Clever clogs." She looked at him admiringly. "Your father's late," she said.

"We don't get many summer evenings like this. Dare say he's making the most of it." He pondered. "Strange. He's so down to earth. Yet he's a bit of a poet in his way."

"I'd like to be here when you try telling him that."

"I wouldn't dare." Then he said wistfully, "Fathers and sons don't really know each other. There's a gulf. I often wish –

we could talk."

From far away, on the still evening, came a sound as outlandish and chilling to this rustic scene as the roar of an Indian tiger: the undulating wail of an ambulance. It faded, its urgent commanding notes slipping down the scale like an old gramophone that need winding. May shivered. "I hate that noise. Disaster for someone: maybe the end of things for someone."

But Jocelyn's mind was still on his father. "Once he did talk. When Aunt Marigold died. He needed help and I believe I was able to help him. Been pleased about that. But then – he's not a man who either needs or asks for help."

"A proud man," she said. "A proud and solitary man."

"Let's drink to that," he said, suddenly moved. They clinked glasses. "To father," he said.

"To Father-in-law," she said. They looked at each other and grinned rather sheepishly. Such emotional behaviour, they both realised, had been verging on_

"Turning chilly," said Jocelyn. He got up and closed the french window, switched on a standard lamp. "Not often he's as late as this," he said.

He had turned the evening into sudden night. Now the windows had become mirrors reflecting the lighted room. There was no outdoors, only the blackness behind a mirror.

"Perhaps he's met someone," she said.

"Yes." He must be all right, they told themselves. An elderly English gentleman, treading his own acres on a June evening: the safest thing in creation, surely?

The door opened. They both spun round. But it was only Gaylord, drugged with sleep and vulnerable, drifting his way across the room to flop his head onto his mother's lap and throw his arms about her thighs. "Momma I had a nasty dream."

She stirred the dark hair. "What was it darling? Lions and tigers?"

The head shook without lifting from her lap. He clung.

She held him tighter. "What was it, love?"

"I don't know."

She yearned to bring him comfort, but could not. She lifted him from the floor, sat him on her knee, cradled his head on her shoulder. His cheeks glistened wet in the lamplight. Where is your swagger, now? She thought fondly. All gone, in the dark torment of an uncomprehended dream.

But already he was recovering. He murmured something. "What did you say?" she whispered.

"Does Poppa know anyone who keeps goats?"

"No darling. I asked him."

His soft little fingers began to tickle the inside of her palm: something he had always done when he wanted to ask a favour. "Momma?"

"Yes?"

"Could I use Amanda?"

"I shouldn't think so dear. Use her for what?"

"Bait, Momma. She wouldn't have to *do* anything," he explained. After all, much as he loved his little sister, he had no illusions about her ability to do anything except dribble. He noticed something. "Where's Grandpa?"

"He's gone for a walk."

"But it's dark. He's never out in the dark. Henry Bartlett's Uncle Fred went out in the dark and didn't come back. Henry says the next thing they heard he was in Australia with the lady out of the betting shop."

"An unlikely outcome in your grandfather's case," said May. "Now then. Bed. Poppa will come up with us." They all went up. She dropped him on his bed. He grinned up, kissed them both, and was immediately asleep. They came back to the drawing room. Jocelyn crossed to the window and peered out into the night. "Quite dark now," he said. He came back into the room. "I wonder what that dream was about."

"Some echo from the primeval dark," she said. "Something form the rag-bag of human memory."

"I wish I knew where the old man is," he said.

At ten o'clock Jocelyn said, "It's quite pointless. But I'm going out to look for him."

He had expected protests. But she said, "I'll stay here in case the telephone – "

He went and got the electric torch from his car and wasn't surprised to find it glimmered like an anaemic glow-worm. Batteries always died on Jocelyn. He found the torch in his father's Rover. By the brilliant light he examined the car. It offered no clues, except a cold engine. Wherever Father had gone, he'd gone on foot.

The old man's favourite evening walk was by the river. Jocelyn set off in the immensity of night, his only light the darting torch and a cold westering moon.

There was always a chance that his father might have called in at Reuben Briggs' house. He groped his way to the cottage among the trees: but, after the episode of the sheep, very unsure of his welcome.

Yes. There was a light. At least Reuben was still up. Through the uncurtained window he could see a naked electric light bulb. He knocked on the door. He heard feet shuffling across the stone-flagged floor. The door opened. Mr Briggs stood before him, a book closed on a finger, his cap still on his head, his glasses perched loosely on his nose. "Why, it's Mr Pentecost. I was just having a dip into Tolstoy's Resurrection."

"Have you found your sheep?" Reuben shook his head.

"I suppose – you haven't seen anything of my father?" said Jocelyn.

Reuben shook his head. "Neither sight nor sound, Mr P. Is he lost, too?"

"Yes. He went for a walk and – "

"I'll help you look." Reuben was already reaching for his wellies.

"No. Please, Reuben. You stay here with Tolstoy. There's nothing you can do."

Reuben gave him a long look. "There isn't really, Mr Pentecost. I just thought – moral support."

"It was very kind of you," said Jocelyn. It was too, he thought, setting off again.

"Father," he called. "Father," then listened intently.

He heard the scurry of the night creatures, the stir of the living water at his side. Once or twice he froze and his scalp tingled, misinterpreting the cry of a night bird as a cry of human pain. "Father," he called. The old man was as sturdy as an oak. Impossible to think he might be reduced to lying there in darkness and torment like a wounded rabbit!

Far away, far on the other side of the river, a clock was striking. He counted the heavy strokes: eleven. He turned for home. He would walk into the bright house. And his father would be sitting there, whisky glass in hand, scowling up at him. "Where the devil have you been, Jocelyn? Thought I'd fallen in the river, did you? I'm not senile yet, you know." Oh, let it be so!

But it wasn't so. Only May, looking as anxious as he'd ever seen that_

"I'll try the Police," he said.

The Police took it calmly. Had Mr Pentecost made sure the old gentleman wasn't in his room? It did often happen. Did the old gentleman – forgive the question – know where he was most of the time? Had there been any family quarrels? Was the missing person the sort who might take an overdose? Or take a bit of time getting home from the pub? After all, it wasn't much after eleven.

He came away from the telephone. "I don't think we live in quite the same world," he said. "They seem to assume that Father's either ga-ga or suicidal or drunk. They'll do their best. But they can't do much before daylight."

"So?" she said.

"You go to bed. I couldn't. I feel I need to be dressed in a crisis."

She came and kissed him tenderly. "I won't say don't worry, love. That would be foolish. But – there may be a quite simple answer. There usually is."

"I can't see one in this case," he said.

"I'm staying with you," she said.

"No."

"Yes. Look. We've always faced any crisis together. You're not sending me off to bed till this one's over."

"Thanks, May," he said. He switched on the electric fire. "What are we going to do? Open the gin bottle? Play Scrabble?"

They didn't do either. They sat and worried and heard the clock strike twelve, and one. They dozed. They made cups of tea. And then, the morning, hostile and grey, infiltrated the countryside like an occupying army. Jocelyn rose stiffly, switched off the light, couldn't stand the greyness and put the light on again. "Now what do we do?" he said.

Upstairs Amanda began to cry. "I'll go," said May, in some way relieved by this everyday occurrence. Without quite realising it she slipped into her comfortable routine. Unbelievably it was almost a normal day, after all: except that one inexplicable, threatening, frightening question mark hung over everything.

Then, at last: the telephone, insistent, demanding. It was Jocelyn who grabbed the receiver. "Pentecost here."

Constable Harris. "What was the name of the missing gentleman, sir?"

"Pentecost. John Pentecost."

"Of the Cypresses Farm, Shepherd's Warning?"

"Yes, for heaven's sake. What's happened?"

"There's been a bit of administrative confusion, sir. But we've traced him now. He's in the Ingerby Royal Infirmary, Ward 5."

"Thank you," said Jocelyn. He swallowed. "What," he asked calmly, "is the trouble?"

"I'm afraid it's some sort of heart attack, sir."

"Oh, dear," said Jocelyn. "I'll get over there at once."

One of the boons of an author's life is that he seldom has to drive in the morning rush hour. But today Jocelyn discovered how the other half lived. He joined a slow-moving stream of drivers converging like termites on a grey Midlands town where each of them would spend this summer's day, penned in office or factory, doing things he didn't particularly like doing, only to escape at six o'clock and face the weary jaunt home again. Jocelyn was appalled. How *did* they stand it?

Yet as he thought thus, and manoeuvred skilfully with wheel and clutch and brake, there was one over-riding thought in his mind and being: his sturdy, hitherto indestructible father, stood at the gates of Heaven or Hell. The old man, who had gone through life without a day's real illness, had been struck down with devastating suddenness. And, knowing him, he was going to take it as a personal insult. "Poor Father," muttered Jocelyn as he turned into the hospital grounds, "He just won't know what's hit him."

He entered the grim portals.

The Ingerby Royal Infirmary had been built massively in the days of Queen Victoria and Florence Nightingale. Nothing succeeding ages could do would ever banish the ambience of those earliest days.

The dark brown and green paint, the vast flights of marble steps, the echoing corridors, how could these things ever be camouflaged by a child's few drawings pinned around the wards, or by abolishing Matron, or by young nurses calling elderly patients by their Christian names? Such carryings-on simply made visitors aware of the awful brooding and abiding presence of the Queen Empress and the Lady of the Lamp.

Jocelyn hated hospitals and feared all who worked in them. They were people who knew the mysteries of death and pain, who walked daily with those mysteries. Now he said nervously to one of these creatures in Reception, "I would like to visit my father, John Pentecost, who was admitted overnight. I imagine he will be in Intensive Care."

The young lady flipped through a few lists. "No. No-one of that name in Intensive Care."

"I – I think Ward 5 was mentioned."

"Ah, now you're talking. Yes. Pentecost John. That him? Up those steps and right and keep on for half a mile or so."

"Thank you," said Jocelyn, deeply grateful. "Thank you." He set off. The place was crowded: little groups discussing earnestly and anxiously. Patients in wheelchairs waiting for examinations, for ambulances, for plaster – like so many mail bags on a platform at St Pancras; little ladies scurrying, sadly alone, down the vast corridors; each one, Jocelyn was convinced, hurrying to the bedside of a dying husband; doctors, nonchalant, their white coats flapping in the windless air; nurses, as young and lovely in this atmosphere of suffering as wild roses in a railway siding.

He stood in the door of Ward 5, and consciously braced himself for what he was going to find. He was in a deeply emotional state: his own loved father, fallen at last into what looked to the sensitive Jocelyn like an ante-room in hell!

Not a nurse in sight. Just eight beds, containing eight old men in various stages of consciousness, but otherwise quite indistinguishable one from the other. And not one of them remotely resembling his father!

He must have been given the wrong ward. He was just, greatly daring, about to tap on the door of an office marked "Ward Sister" when an unfriendly voice said, "And where the hell have you been? Got my pyjamas?"

Jocelyn leapt like a startled fawn. He looked at the bed nearest to him. "Over twelve hours it's taken you to get here. And look what they've put me in," said the occupant. He tugged disgustedly at the collar of what looked like a Victorian nightshirt.

"Father," cried Jocelyn, though this elderly gentleman seemed to bear little resemblance to his father. Again, Jocelyn had always imagined that people in hospital with heart attacks were wired up like 1920s wireless sets. And this gentleman was singularly free of such encumbrances. "Father!" he said again, and now at last he recognised the bristling white moustache, the baleful eye. "How is your heart?"

"Heart? Nothing wrong with *my* heart. Have you brought *The Times*?"

"I'm afraid – you mean – you haven't had a heart attack?"

"You mean – you haven't got my *Times*? Of course I haven't had a heart attack. What on earth gave you that idea?"

"The Police. But – then why *are* you here?"

"Because I've broken both my blasted ankles, of course. You mean you really haven't brought *The Times*?" He looked hopefully at Jocelyn as though he might see it sticking out of his pocket. Very absent-minded chap, Jocelyn.

"I'm afraid – not," said Jocelyn. "But May's got together a few things." He handed over a small suitcase.

The old man riffled through the case. Sensible, capable woman, May. But even her mind hadn't gone beyond toothpaste and soap and pyjamas apparently. But Jocelyn was still floundering. "So your heart's really all right, Father?"

"Of course it's all right. Sound as a bell. Just my goddamn ankles."

"When – where did it happen?"

"On my walk last night. One minute I was presumably strolling home from the river. The next I was perched up in this bed. Can't remember a damn thing. *And* it took you twelve hours to get here."

"Constable Harris said there had been an administrative slip-up."

"Administrative slip-up! Ah well, I suppose I'm lucky I've not got somebody else's heart ticking away in here by now. Don't trust 'em an inch. And do you know who the specialist chap is on my ankles? Peters. Member of my golf club. Plays off twenty-four. Absolute duffer. Ah, here he comes now."

A procession had entered the ward, redolent, in its solemnity, of ancient Rome or the Doge's Palace. "That's him," said John Pentecost, indicating the leader, who was followed by minions shoving a sort of tea trolley full of X-ray photographs. The procession stopped at John's bed just as John, with one of his rumbling chortles, was saying to Jocelyn, "Hope he handles a scalpel better that he does a niblick."

"Father be quiet," Jocelyn said nervously.

"Oh, he won't hear that," John said confidently. Then he put out a hand and drew Jocelyn closer. "There one thing you might do, dear boy. One of these young women – " he pointed at the procession – "that one in the navy blue – she keeps calling me John. Can't think why. Don't imagine I've ever met her socially. Just have word with her. Tell her it's Mr Pentecost. Come to that I'd settle for Pentecost. But not John, dammit."

Jocelyn said, "But that's Sister. And they always use Christian names nowadays."

"Not to me they don't," his father said, suddenly grim.

Jocelyn's heart was in his boots. What a beginning. His father already insulting the dictator of his little world and, far far worse, instructing him, Jocelyn, to seek an audience of the Queen. He said weakly, "Right. I'll have a word with her before I go, Father."

But something else was niggling at Jocelyn's plodding brain. Surely some element was missing in this little scene. Yes. It was. "Aren't you in a lot pain, Father?"

He was subjected to a stare of unparalleled ferocity. "Good God, Jocelyn, simply because I'm not yelling my head off doesn't mean I'm not suffering. I'm in agony, man. But – just a question of self-control." He gave a rare grin. "We Pentecosts – "

Jocelyn was suddenly very moved. He grinned back. He stooped down and kissed his father very tenderly, something he hadn't done since he was twelve. Then they both looked extremely embarrassed. Jocelyn said, "I'll be going now; let you get some sleep."

"Sleep? You don't think I can sleep with this pain, do you?" But he was already looking drowsy. "Don't forget to have a word with that young woman. 'John', indeed."

"I think," said Jocelyn hopefully, "she's still on her rounds." But at that moment she appeared and went into her office. "Damn," muttered Jocelyn. He went and tapped nervously on her door.

Gaylord came down to breakfast. "Where's Poppa?"

May said, "Darling, poor Grandpa's in hospital. Poppa's gone to see him."

"Why is Grandpa in hospital?"

"He's very poorly. He didn't come home last night."

"How do you know he's poorly then?"

"The Police telephoned early this morning."

"Really?" Gaylord's eyes showed a gleam of excitement. He didn't like illness very much. Not the sort that meant going to bed and taking nasty medicine. But illness in grand style – taken ill in the dark and the police finding you and ambulances and blue lights flashing and hospitals – May, watching him, realised his imagination was having a riotous time. She said, "Poor Grandpa. I'm afraid he may be very ill."

Gaylord was a kindly child. He told his imagination to sober up. He became practical. "Henry Bartlett's Great Aunt Ethel has something called an Elixir that cures *everything*. I bet Henry could get some for Grandpa."

May said, "I'm afraid Grandpa may be too ill for that, Gaylord."

"You mean he might die?"

"He might, dear. We all hope not."

Gaylord was appalled. If Grandpa was beyond the reach of Henry Bartlett's Great Aunt Ethel's Elixir he was ill indeed. But Grandpa couldn't *die. Could he?* God couldn't die and Grandpa was very similar to God, surely, except that you saw a bit more of him. He wept a little, May was touched to see. But life must go on. He pulled his schoolbag about his shoulders, kissed Momma more fondly than usual, and went and called for his friend Henry Bartlett. "My Grandpa's ill," he said. "He went for a walk last night and the Police found him ill and an ambulance came screaming up with its blue light flashing and rushed him to hospital."

Henry looked impressed. "I reckon he wants some of me Auntie's Elixir," he said. "I reckon she'd let the hospital have some."

"It's too late for that, Henry," said Gaylord sighing deeply. They walked on in silence. Life had suddenly taken a frightening and totally unexpected turn; and they didn't like it.

Sister was at her desk. She stared unsmiling at this tall, anxious-looking man edging his way nervously round her door. She maintained silence, giving the impression that she hoped he might go away. Then at last she said, "Yes?" Now giving the impression that she'd decided he wouldn't and she'd have to do something about it.

Jocelyn, by now thoroughly demoralised, said, "I wondered – my name's Pentecost – I wonder – "

She didn't wait to find out what he wondered. "Ah. We've been trying to get in touch with you all night. You the next of kin?"

"Yes."

"Well thank goodness you've turned up at last. Given us no end of trouble."

"The Police didn't ring until this morning. They said something about an administrative slip-up."

"Well now you are here we'd better have some particulars." She produced a form. "Name?"

She guided him through the form-filling like an irritable teacher helping an idiot child.

Jocelyn, knowing himself in honour bound to raise the Christian name question grew more and more flustered. And after a few questions about his father's condition, he said, "Oh, there is one point, Sister."

"Yes?" she glanced at her watch.

"My father is one of the old school. He does not like people of a younger generation calling him by his Christian name."

"Well, I'm afraid he'll have to get used to it, then. Standard practice, nowadays. Gives the patient a sense of belonging."

"I can assure you it doesn't give my father a sense of belonging."

Jocelyn, caught between the upper millstone of his father and the nether millstone of this bloodless dragon, was hating every minute of the conversation. But something was stirring. Suddenly, to his own and to Sister's amazement he banged on the desk and said, "My father is immobile and in great pain. He will have to suffer many indignities for many weeks and he will hate them all. But I don't see why he should suffer the indignity of being addressed as John by girls young enough to be his granddaughters."

Jocelyn stared at the pale bespectacled face. Lord, now I've done it, he was thinking, telling himself that the first rule for all hospital visitors was to fawn on Sister. Yet at the same time he was aware of a surging sense of triumph; especially when Sister went out into the ward, took a chart from the foot of his father's bed, came back and wrote on it in large capitals "ALWAYS ADDRESS AS MR PENTECOST." "That better?" she asked, with a sudden, friendly grin that pleased but completely bewildered him.

Gaylord and Henry Bartlett stared unbelieving.

The palm fronds, that had so cunningly hidden the foot-deep tiger pit, lay trampled and scattered, many of them at the bottom of the trap. The soil was trodden. There was every sign of a tremendous struggle having taken place.

And there was but one possible explanation. They had caught a tiger which, after a long fight for freedom, had got away!

"I reckon it was a big one," said Gaylord.

"Do you really, Gaylord?" Henry looked at his friend admiringly; nay, with a sort of worship. He said, "What should we have done if he'd still been here?" He experienced a frisson of fear that sent a whole cascade of water running down his back.

Gaylord said airily, "Oh, you just throw a big net over him and drag him away. It's easy."

Henry would never have admitted it to Gaylord but he felt rather glad the tiger *had* got away. It seemed to him it saved rather a lot of trouble and excitement. Henry decided he didn't really like excitement very much. "Where should we have got a net from?" he asked.

"Oh, there'd be one in our big barn," said Gaylord. "There's everything in our big barn." When it came to universality, Henry's Great Aunt's Elixir had nothing on the big barn.

"Two broken ankles!" cried May. "But he'll be laid up for weeks, months. Oh, poor old Father-in-law."

"Poor old you," said Jocelyn. "He won't be an easy patient."

"I can manage him," she said quietly. "But – oh Jocelyn, he'll miss the summer, his walks. He'll go mad."

"But he'll live." Jocelyn sighed. "When the Police said a

heart attack, I – " He fell silent.

May said, "Darling, I don't want to add to your worries. But – how did it happen? He must have gone down pretty heavily."

"He doesn't know. Says one minute he was walking home. The next he was in hospital. He can't remember a thing."

"That's what I meant. I hope it wasn't a black-out. In that case – we shall never dare to let him drive his car again, even when his ankles are better."

Jocelyn said, "We should have an awful job stopping him."

"I know. And he'd hate it – and *us*. So – see whether he can remember anything now, love. It would be a tremendous relief."

Gaylord came in from school. "Is Grandpa dead yet?" he asked anxiously.

May said, "Of course not, dear."

Gaylord said, "I don't see why 'of course'."

Jocelyn said, "I've been to see him, Gaylord. And – it's not as bad as we thought. He's broken two ankles, which is bad enough. But – "

"Oh, good," Gaylord said, without too much enthusiasm. He was pleased about Grandpa, of course; but he always found an anti-climax rather lowering.

Still it meant he could move on to the other subject that was filling his little mind. "Momma, you know that tiger trap?"

"Yes?"

"Well, it caught a tiger. Only he got away."

"Oh, what a pity. Never mind dear. Some other time."

Jocelyn had a very high regard for the creative imagination. After all, it was his bread and butter. But he did sometimes

feel that Gaylord's was inclined to run somewhat amok.
Now he said, "You know, Gaylord, there aren't an awful lot
of tigers roaming the Trent valley. You don't think it might
have been a – cat, say, that escaped from your trap?"

Gaylord was affronted. "But it was a tiger trap, Poppa."

Jocelyn said patiently, "But a tiger trap doesn't only catch
tigers."

"It does, Poppa." Oh, dear, Poppa did get some odd bees in
his bonnet. Probably came with being so old. "After all a mouse
trap only catches mice. And a rabbit snare only snares rabbits.
And a hippopotamus trap only catches hippopotamuses," he
finished triumphantly.

Jocelyn wished he had never started. "You don't know
that," he said tetchily.

"I do. You never find a rhinoceros in a hippopotamus trap.
Never."

May grinned at her husband. "Get yourself out of that
one, boy," she said cheerfully.

Jocelyn sighed. Once they got on to African fauna this
could go on all night. He said, " Sorry. I'd better be going."

"Coward," said May.

Jocelyn looked hurt. "If I'm not on the doorstep with
Father's *Times* the moment they open the flood gates, I shall
be in the doghouse. I must get ready."

An hour later he stood again outside those dread portals,
hating the prospect of going in, convinced that a consultant
would say quietly, "Ah, Mr Pentecost," take him by the arm,
lead him to a quiet corner and impart some terrible news
about his father, or that Sister would inflict on him some
planned and dreadful humiliation.

But no such things happened. Sister earned his gratitude
by giving him a thin smile. His father was drifting amiably
on a cloud of drugs. Jocelyn had never realised the old man

could be so relaxed or so co-operative. He obviously racked his drug-laden brain to remember how he had come to fall: a patch of mud, a loose stone, a trailing briar?

But he couldn't remember a thing.

Nevertheless, Jocelyn did not come away completely empty-handed. When he was leaving his father suddenly gripped his hand and said, "Funny thing, Jocelyn, one of the nurses here has read some of your books. Wants to meet you for some reason. Damn pretty girl."

"Really?" Jocelyn was agog. He looked eagerly round the ward. "Of course I'll have a word with her. Which one was it, Father?"

"Which one was what?" John's voice was suddenly slurred.

"The one who'd read my books?"

"What books?" said John, drifting into sleep.

"Oh, damn," said Jocelyn. An author living in the Trent valley didn't often get a chance to be fawned upon. Especially by a damn pretty girl.

But John was well away in drugged sleep. Jocelyn, as he left, looked surreptitiously round the ward to see what was on offer. But none of the nurses showed the slightest interest in him.

Jocelyn came home, weary. Life had changed. Yesterday, and all his yesterdays, it seemed, he had flitted happily between a very pleasant real world and an equally pleasant fictional one. Today, and all his tomorrows, he was caught up in a real world – a world that was suddenly harsh, demanding, endlessly worrying.

He remembered another burden that awaited him: ringing up the family with the bad news.

To delay the evil moment he made a list: his Aunt Bea, his Aunt Dorothea, his sisters Rose and Becky.

He hated telephoning. Slow brains like his needed the smiles, the gestures, to disguise the long silences while he sought for le mot juste. Telephone conversations for Jocelyn had something of the tension of the centre court at Wimbledon. In particular he disliked telephoning in front of May, since he always forgot something while she never forgot anything, and either interrupted him while he was speaking, which sent his carefully prepared sentences flying, or reminded him after he'd replaced the receiver. So he said, "I shall go and telephone from the study."

She smiled and nodded. "Give 'em my love."

Basically, mankind is divided into two classes: those of strong moral fibre who, on finding one last cramped space in the car park, insist on manoeuvring into it backwards despite all difficulties and hazards, and those of weak will who think "what the hell?" and go forwards, regardless of the miseries they are storing up for themselves later.

The same division covers mankind on the telephone: those who, with several calls to make, get the difficult ones out of the way first; and those who put off the Great Aunt Beas of this world until the last possible moment.

Jocelyn was definitely in the second class. He rang his lovely young sister Becky first and got exactly what he knew he would get: cheerful offers of help and sympathy and a personal sadness and understanding; next he rang his elder sister Rose and again got what he expected: dismay, sympathy: but this time he was left with an acute feeling of depression.

Rose, the nicest of women, had a knack of making you feel that all was lost, and it was no good going on fighting. ("Both ankles, dear? Goodness, you can't expect much of a recovery at his age. I'm afraid you and May aren't going to have things very easy for a long time to come, Jocelyn.")

He rang the next aunt. But he put the receiver down eventually on his Great Aunt Dorothea with the feeling that she hadn't quite cottoned on to who her brother John was, or who Jocelyn was, or why he had rung her up. But duty had been done. And now he was faced with telephoning Great Aunt Bea.

As a Nursing Officer in the Voluntary Aid Detachment, the young Bea had struck as much terror into the hearts of junior subalterns on the Western Front, and even into the hearts of majors and colonels, as had a strong and ruthless enemy. And by now, half a century later, age had given up trying to wither her. Striding down the fairway, niblick in hand; calling six trumps in ringing tones; chairing a cowed meeting of the local Conservative Association: there was only one word to describe her: formidable. Little wonder Jocelyn, dialling her number, hoped weakly that it would be engaged.

It wasn't. "Who's that?"

"Jocelyn here, Aunt."

"Who?"

"Jocelyn. Your nephew. Jocelyn Pentecost."

"Jocelyn, dear boy. How are you?" she chortled hugely. "And how's that young pickle, Gaylord?"

"He's fine. But – "

"Good. Give him a big kiss from his old aunt."

"Thanks. But – it's about my father."

"Who – ? John? What's he been up to?

"He's broken both his ankles."

"Good God." She was silent. "How on earth did he manage that?"

"He – just fell, apparently."

"He was always falling as a child. Bet he's swearing, isn't he?"

"Actually, he's taken it rather quietly, for him."

"H'm. Bad sign. Right. I'll be over one of these days. Tell May I'll be no trouble." Down went the receiver.

"Well?" asked May.

"They're all coming. Except Dorothea. I don't think she quite knew who I was. But Bea's certainly coming. She says she'll be no trouble."

May turned a little pale. Husband and wife looked at each other thoughtfully. There was no doubt about it. Life had taken a sudden and fearful turn.

Chapter 3

So the weary business of hospital visiting began in earnest.

Before long, both Jocelyn and May began to imagine that the hospital was the real world, while the people outside, getting on and off buses, going into shops and cinemas, driving motors (and showing no particular signs of revelling in their wonderful freedom) had no more substance than the drifting clouds.

And John Pentecost?

John Pentecost withdrew into a shell of silence. He never complained. He accepted the indignity of bedpans without a murmur, even though it came as a deep shock to his sensibilities. He was unfailingly courteous to doctors, nurses, and auxiliaries (and especially the auxiliaries). He welcomed visitors and was thankful when they left. He was, incredibly, a model patient.

But inside, he raged. Inside, he was a banked-up fire of anger. A quick-tempered, outspoken man who always "got things off his chest," he had never before known the slow corrosion of resentment.

Yet now he was filled with a bitter and simmering resentment. And the person for whom he felt this was himself, and his own body, his robust body that had brought him to the age of seventy, almost without a twinge, without a murmur; and then, suddenly, in the twinkling of an eye, robbed him of his health, his freedom, turned him into a prostrate and shackled prisoner. And he who had been in charge of this splendid mechanism of bone and muscle and sinew, he had allowed it in one moment of carelessness to betray him to a cruel enemy.

Not only that: he had pulled Jocelyn and May down with him. Their lives were disrupted while was in hospital: would be even more so when he was an invalid at home.

From his window he could see a single tree, a segment of sky, clouds and the flight of birds. This was all. A tiny segment of the great sky that should have been his, at seventy, for another ten years, but for his body's treason.

Well, it would pass. They would cobble him up and he would walk again. But at seventy, every month, every day, should have its own sweetness. And the days, and the precious months, were passing; on a rationed piece of sky, and a single tree and a winging bird.

One visit gave him great pleasure. He awoke to find a forlorn figure in mud-coloured raincoat, wellies and a cloth cap standing, watchful and silent beside his bed like the Angel of Death. "Reuben!" he cried. "Have you come to see me?"

" 'Course. Here." He dumped a wrinkled paper bag on the bed. "Brought you summat."

John eyed the bag warily. "What −?"

"Half a dozen eggs. Now you get one of these lasses to boil you one, every day for your tea and get it down you. Do you the world of good. Anyway, how are you feeling?"

"Between ourselves, bored. Frustrated, Resentful."

"Aye. Well just do what Hamlet told Horatio to do."

"What did Hamlet tell Horatio to do?"

" 'Absent thee from felicity awhile'," Reuben said. "Good advice, Mr Pentecost. Good advice in a situation like this. Nice bit of wool, that," he said, picking up a protective elbow cap. "Could have come off one of my old ladies," he said dreamily; he wandered into the corridor.

After one of his visits Jocelyn said, "My father surprised me today. He quoted Hamlet to me."

"No!"

"Yes. Apparently when he found himself in hospital, and knew what was in store for him, he thought: now I've got to adapt consciously to an entirely new way of life, and accept it. And he told me today that he remembered Hamlet's 'absent thee from felicity awhile', and he knew that was just what *he* must do." He looked at May with a stricken smile, and his voice trembled. "My father has – absented himself from felicity awhile."

They were both silent; then she said, "He's a brave old man. And a surprising one."

"Yes. Oh, that reminds me. He'd like a visit from his grandchildren."

"Good. Gaylord was asking when he could see him. Let's all go tomorrow."

Jocelyn said nervously, "They only allow two visitors at a time."

"Children don't count do they?"

"They do, you know. They abominate children."

"Well, you can just have a word with Sister. It'll be all right."

Jocelyn looked glum. But not only was it all right. Sister made quite a fuss of May and Amanda. And she not only smiled at Jocelyn. She sent a nurse to the children's ward for some books for Gaylord to read.

But Gaylord looked around him with mounting disapproval. When he'd been in hospital the ward had been filled with toy trains and rocking horses. Here, nothing. Even

Grandpa himself was something of a disappointment. The Grandpa he knew was a gruff, knowledgeable companion and guide to the fields and lanes; a big, comforting paw to get hold of on the rare occasions when Gaylord felt a little moral support would be welcome; broad shoulders for a piggy-back when there was a stream to cross or a sea of mud to avoid; a man as old, as powerful, as omniscient as God.

But this Grandpa was a different creature: a stranger; and, Gaylord sensed, a man whose authority had been drained away. Gaylord felt shy of him.

But now the nurse came back with a pile of books. "Here you are," she said to Gaylord, sliding the books on to his lap.

"Oh, thank you," said Gaylord. "What super books."

But nurse had eyes for no one but Jocelyn. "You're the author aren't you?"

"Yes." Jocelyn beamed.

"I've read some of your books."

"So I gather," said Jocelyn, preening himself. She was, he noticed (and May noticed) a pretty but rather brusque little thing.

"You're as I imagined you," she said. "Tall, tweedy and untidy."

What a damned rude woman, thought May. But Jocelyn kept to the matter in hand. "Which – books have you read?"

"Oh, I can't remember titles: one of 'em the girl married the wrong man. Matter of fact, I've written a book myself."

As Jocelyn knew, these dreaded words spelt the end of any discussion of *his* books. "Really?" he said.

"Yes. You'll have to read it and tell me where I've gone wrong."

"I'm afraid I can't do that," said Jocelyn mildly. But May

said, "Working authors can't do that sort of thing, Nurse. They'd never get anything written themselves."

The nurse gave her a cool look and turned back to Jocelyn. "Dear me," she said. "So that's that." And she flounced away.

Despite his books, Gaylord was not one to neglect social conversation. "Grandpa, do you know anyone who keeps goats?"

"You are not having a goat."

"I don't want a goat, Grandpa. Only a kid."

"Kids become goats. Anyway, what do you want a kid for?"

"To bait a tiger trap. Grandpa, Henry and I built a tiger trap, and we caught a tiger in it but it got away."

"Wouldn't be a tiger," said Grandpa. "Cat, maybe"

"But it was a tiger trap, Grandpa."

"Oh Lord, don't start that again," murmured Jocelyn.

"So it must have been a tiger?" said Grandpa.

Gaylord didn't spot the question mark. "Of course," he said. He gave his parents a triumphant look. You could always rely on a bit of common sense from Grandpa.

"And where did you dig the trap?" asked Grandpa. Not that he cared. But when you are in a hospital bed, tiger traps are as good a subject of conversation as any.

"In Polly Larkin's Pad," Gaylord said enthusiastically. Thank goodness someone was showing a bit of interest.

"Oh, yes," said Grandpa, disappointingly, and began to ask Poppa what he thought about something dull in the paper. Clearly he had forgotten all about tiger traps. Well, Gaylord wasn't surprised. The butterfly nature of the adult mind never ceased to amaze him.

Suddenly on the stroke of four, a loud bell rang down the

corridors. Jocelyn said nervously, "Time we were going, May." Sister had graciously allowed them to break the rules once this afternoon. He wasn't going to risk breaking them twice.

But now John Pentecost was clawing at his son's arm and saying, "Jocelyn, what Gaylord said has reminded me. I can remember gong into Polly Larkin's Pad, and then – nothing. Oh Lord, so I must have blacked out." He said pathetically, "Will they stop me from driving the Rover?"

"Polly Larkin's Pad?" said May in a stricken voice. Then, with her usual quick thinking she said, "It's more likely you tripped over something and banged your head when you fell. I believe concussion can blot out recent memory."

She was subjected to one of the old man's basilisk stares. "My dear May, I've been traversing that path for twenty years. Know it like the back of my hand. Nothing to trip over."

There was a silence. Jocelyn said, "Sister's looking. We really ought to be going."

They went. What on earth do we do now? thought May. Our child has done this awful thing to an old man, yet it's not his fault, you can't blame a child. She just had to discuss it with Jocelyn. Yet how could she? Gaylord was clinging like a leech to her hand as they traipsed down the long corridors. There'd be no chance of talking in the car. She probably wouldn't get a chance to talk until Gaylord was in bed. She said, out of the corner of her mouth, "Jocelyn, isn't this *awful*!"

"What's awful?" said Jocelyn.

"What's awful, Momma?" asked Gaylord, intrigued.

"Oh, nothing," said May crossly. Then suddenly she stopped in her tracks. "Gaylord what on earth are you doing with that great pile of books?"

"The lady gave them to me, Momma."

"She did *not*. They belong to the poor sick children in this hospital."

"Well, can I take them home and bring them back tomorrow?"

"Of course not. Oh, give them to me." She dumped Amanda in her father's arms and took the books. "Jocelyn, don't you ever notice *anything*? Except pretty nurses who read your books," she added cruelly. "Now you carry on and get in the car. I won't be long."

"I'll take them," said Jocelyn. But she'd gone. Amanda began to cry. Gaylord said, "Why is Momma cross, Poppa?"

"I really don't know," said Jocelyn miserably.

Gaylord didn't like Momma to be cross. And he particularly disliked it when she was cross with Poppa as well. Poppa seemed so vulnerable, somehow. Gaylord longed to cheer him up. He groped in his pocket, but all he could find was a toffee that had lost its wrapping and gathered rather a lot of fluff. "I don't suppose you'd like this, would you, Poppa?" he asked, holding it out.

"Not much, thank you, Gaylord," Jocelyn said politely.

Gaylord popped it in. It was nice. He spent the next few minutes pulling bits of sticky stuff out of his mouth and concealing them about his person. Then, seeing the forlorn look on Poppa's face, he slipped his hand into his father's.

It was a kindly gesture; but, like so many of Gaylord's kindly gestures, not altogether appreciated. Poppa quietly removed his hand and began wiping it on his handkerchief. "Was I sticky?" asked Gaylord.

"You were a bit," said Jocelyn.

"Sorry, Poppa," said Gaylord. He was always very understanding of adult foibles even when he found most of them pretty potty.

It would have been hard to say which ground the more slowly; the Mills of God or the mind of Jocelyn Pentecost. But they both got there in the end. Jocelyn suddenly said, "Gaylord! Where did Grandpa say he could remember being?" the looseness of his grammatical construction showed his agitation.

"Polly Larkin's Pad," said Gaylord.

Jocelyn was silent. He had a quite physical feeling of having been hit on the side of the head by a realisation as heavy as concrete. He, a mature man, had helped his son to inflict this terrible injury on his father. Thoughtless, *wicked* fool that he was!

Momma returned, pushed a book into Gaylord's hand. "Here you are, you spoilt brat. Sister sent it to you. Says you can take it back when you've read it."

"Oh, thank you, Momma." He was delighted. He began reading it as they went down the endless corridors, chortling happily to himself.

Jocelyn walked stiffly, staring blindly ahead. At last he could contain his anguish no longer. "May! I've had an awful thought."

"Ah," said May, who had been waiting for him to get there.

He looked at Gaylord, still deep in his book. "It's about – you know – father's accident," he whispered.

"I know," she said. "Leave it."

"Yes," he said. They found the car, drove home. Gaylord, who would normally have been straining on the leash to go out, settled down with his book. "This *is* a good book, Momma," he said.

"Is it, dear?" said May. "But don't you want to go out to play?"

Gaylord was alert immediately. Momma wanted him out

of the way. That meant she wanted one of those urgent conversations with Poppa: conversations that were sometimes disappointingly dull but at other times concerned Gaylord deeply. "I'd rather read my book, Momma," he said.

"Very well, dear," Momma said sweetly. "You read your book. Poppa and I are just going for a little walk." And they set off immediately. He ran to the window and watched them go. But it wasn't very interesting. They were obviously making for Polly Larkin's Pad and the path by the river. Just as he would have expected. Grown ups, often so utterly unpredictable, could be depressingly predictable at times.

They walked in silence. Jocelyn, who needed so urgently to confess everything, now could find no words to admit his fearful guilt. They came to a gloomy entrance to the overgrown path. May took a deep breath. "Now," she said. "The moment of truth."

John Pentecost looked out at the blue evening sky, and at his single tree.

He imagined them driving home, throwing off eventually the town's traffic, the town's noise, coming to the lanes, and the snaking river road, and the quiet house, his home from which he was as cruelly banished as a medieval exile. Would he, at his age, ever return, he wondered.

"Yes, of course you will," he said aloud, startling the ward. "Good God, man, stop feeling so damned sorry for yourself." But it didn't help. He was seventy and the days he so loved were inevitably few. Must he spend them shut away from sunlight and the summer wind? A heavy punishment, surely, for an old man's moment of carelessness?

But was it carelessness? No. He knew it now. He'd never have tripped in Polly Larkin's Pad. For a short time his brain had switched off. And the whole, infinitely complex, structure of his being had collapsed. And he'd gone down – crash! – like a felled tree.

And at any moment it could happen again, now it had happened once: on the stairs, in a crowded shop, doing seventy on the M1. Someone had got a gun trained on him. And the finger was on the trigger.

Polly Larkin's Pad held the heat of the summer's day. The air was heavy, still, for a low canvas of cloud sagged over the earth. And they walked, scarcely breathing, each knowing and dreading what they must find.

And they found it: a shallow trench across the path, littered with willow branches and its soil scattered.

"This must be it," said May.

"It *is*," said Jocelyn heavily.

"Poor Gaylord," said May. "He dug a trap for a tiger. And caught his own grandfather." She laughed unsteadily.

Jocelyn was a good and decent man. Inordinately sensitive, perhaps? But looking down at the evidence that he had helped to cause pain and suffering to a fellow human being was an unbearable strain. He tried to speak. But only croaking noises came out.

He felt faint. Was it the enclosed air of this overhung and scented path? Or was it the weight of guilt he bore on his shoulders?

"It wasn't," he began. But normal speech was impossible. His mouth was too dry. He was reduced to whispering (or perhaps subconsciously he felt his crime too shameful to be spoken aloud). "It wasn't only Gaylord," he whispered.

She looked at him in bewilderment. "What do you mean?" Then, urgently, "Darling, are you all right?"

He said, " It wasn't just Gaylord. I – helped him finish the job."

She stared at him, unbelieving. "Jocelyn, I don't understand. Are you feeling ill?"

He said, "I helped Gaylord to arrange the willow branches over the hole." He gazed down into the pit. "Look. There's the support I used."

She said, "What's that branch got to do with it?"

Jocelyn never shouted at anyone. But he shouted now, and at his wife. "I laid it across the hole, woman, and then arranged the willow branches over it so that the pit was camouflaged and hidden. So my father would fall into it and destroy the last of his days."

May stared at her husband in bewilderment and fear. She had never seen him like this before. She knew him as a deeply sensitive, anxious man, always over-ready to cry *mea culpa*. But she also knew him as a controlled man, a man in the high Roman fashion, who would die rather than give way to his feelings. And here he was, desperate, his voice drowning in tears.

She grabbed him, held him tight, gazed into his face. "Jocelyn, what are you telling me?"

"It wasn't just Gaylord. It was me. I helped him. I thought I was being rather clever. Fool! I never once thought – someone might –" He looked at her beseechingly.

"Come home," she said. "Come home, my love."

"And what do I do when I get home?" he cried. "What comfort is there in home? What comfort is there anywhere?"

None, she thought bleakly. None. But she was steering him away from the place. She was silent. What could she say? What was there to say? Nothing.

He was speaking quietly now. "My father's always thought me a bit of a fool. What – ?"

"Now that's not true," she said sharply. "I know he can't

understand anyone making a living by writing. But he's got a very high regard for you." But she was thinking desperately, choosing her words as carefully as a man seeks footholds on a cliff face. At last she said, "Darling, this was an accident: suppose your father had tripped over the cable of my vacuum cleaner when I was working, and been taken to hospital. I should have felt bad about it. But I shouldn't have felt as personally responsible as you're doing over this."

"It's not the same," he said quickly.

"It is, Jocelyn." Oh God, make him believe me. "I don't see that you need even mention it to your father."

He looked at her in amazement. "May! That doesn't sound like you. Of course, I must tell him. 'See how your fool of a son has crippled you, Father!'"

"Jocelyn," she pleaded. "Don't talk like that. You're not a fool. You're a wise and good man and I love you."

He ignored this. "Can't you see, I've got to tell him. He's blaming himself bitterly for carelessness. And another thing," he remembered. "He's convinced he had a black-out and that Dr Pemberton will stop him from driving his precious old Rover. He's worried to death about that."

But before May could think of an answer to that a cheerful voice cried, "Hello, Poppa. Don't fall into my tiger trap." Gaylord knew there was no need to warn Momma. As well as having eyes in the back of her head, Momma had them in the soles of her feet. But Poppa was different. Poppa needed protecting.

"Hello, Gaylord," Poppa said sadly. He thought of the small square of sunlight that, on bright evenings, travelled across the wall of the hospital ward. On this dull ending of the day even that wouldn't be there.

They turned for home, silent because Gaylord was once more sticking like a limpet, and Jocelyn, lurching forward grim-faced, tight-wrapped in misery, was wrestling with the problem of that absurd tiger trap: to hush everything up, as May surprisingly suggested? Or to open wounds that, once opened, might be a very long time healing.

In the ward they were bedding down for the night: the dreary ritual of teeth and tablets and bedpans and a lick and a promise from the face flannel, and a carefree "Have a good night" from the Administrative Sister just as you'd dropped off. "How long, O Lord, how long" muttered John Pentecost. He, a man of vaunting independence of mind and body, reduced to humiliation, unable even to get his hands on a cup or a newspaper a centimetre out of reach!

And, a dark louring shadow over all these minor frustrations and humiliations, the black-out fear: having to call on Jocelyn every time he wanted to go anywhere by car. No. He was damned if he would.

Jocelyn would do it willingly, too willingly. But he wasn't having that. Jocelyn had his own life. It would be taxis from now on: everywhere he went listening to Taylor's complaints about a world that Taylor could run much more satisfactorily than the Almighty.

John Pentecost would have found it both difficult and embarrassing to say what he believed in. Yet every night of his life, as he laid himself down to sleep, he murmured, "Lord, into thy hands I commend my spirit," and crossed himself. And, since he had been in hospital, he had taken to adding, "And get me out of this place as quick as you can, dear Lord."

They came home.

As soon as Gaylord was in bed Jocelyn went out into the dusk with a spade and carefully filled in that damned hole.

He smoothed the soil, found a few clods of turf, slapped them down over the earth. At least, he thought bitterly, I've got the sense to stop others hurting themselves, even though I couldn't save my own father.

He came back into the house. "I've filled it in," he said.

"Good," she said.

She looked at her husband anxiously. Now they would be back to the questions of guilt, and remorse, and confession. And the questions were many.

Was she right? Or had Jocelyn a moral duty to tell his father that he, by negligence or thoughtlessness, had robbed him of part of his remaining store of days. How would the old man react to the knowledge? He was a large-hearted man. Surely he would be big enough to forgive? And could Jocelyn, always so eager to cry mea culpa, live with himself without confession?

But what about Gaylord? If Jocelyn implicated himself, Gaylord must inevitably be implicated.

One of the happiest things in May's happy life was the warmth of friendship between the rugged old man and the boy. He learns more from his grandfather than he does from either his school or Jocelyn or me, she thought: a love of, and respect for, life: and a deep and ancient wisdom. And I will not, she thought, risk destroying or souring that relationship. A tragic accident happened. But how and why it happened was of no moment. The scar was mending. Let it mend. Don't tear the bandages from a healing wound.

She brought in the Ovaltine. And this was the time-honoured moment when they discussed their problems. She waited... She said brusquely, "I want you to tell me why your father's accident has suddenly stricken you like this."

He looked at her pitifully. His wife was forcing him to

peer down once again into that litter of soil and willow branches. And into the dark depths of his soul. He said, "Gaylord dug a trap. As usual, the wrong thing from the highest motives. Then I happened along. And instead of ensuring that it wasn't a danger to anyone I – showed him how to camouflage it." She was silent. There was nothing to say.

He swallowed. "If it hadn't been for my – help, Father would have seen it a mile off."

Still she was silent. She reached across and took his hand, "I feel such a fool," he said. "Apart from everything else."

"What is – everything else?" she asked.

"Guilt, remorse, even fear."

"Fear of *what*? Telling your father?"

"Even that. I'm like a small boy, really. Never grown up."

"Nonsense." She spoke sharply. "So you think I would have married a weakling?"

"I should have been in a bad way if you hadn't," he said bitterly.

They sat on in silence. They had finished their Ovaltine. He thought: she despises me. She must do.

So deep was he in his thoughts that it was some time before he realised that she was tugging at his hand. "Come here," she said. "Look at me."

He went and sat beside her. She said, " I still think you should say nothing."

"I can't," he said. It's not – honourable."

"Darling," she said. "I'm a woman. An honourable woman. But when honour is set against my family, honour can go hang."

It was his turn to be silent. Was this the strength of women, he wondered: that they were prepared, when it came to their families, to discard in a moment all the bright flags and banners from which men drew their strength: honour, loyalty, truth? He said, "I think you denigrate your sex, May. But you may be right." For the first time for a long time, a smile flitted across his lips.

"Of course I'm right. We're basic creatures, we women."

"But I couldn't," he said. "I – couldn't look my father in the face."

She said, "Think it through man. What will you say? That you dug a pit and covered it with branches to catch a tiger? He's no fool. He'd never believe that."

Jocelyn said, "No. I realise I should have to involve Gaylord. But – he wouldn't blame a child."

"You don't know. If he did, it would destroy a wonderful relationship. And how's Gaylord going to feel? The knowledge that he's crippled his grandfather? No-one can say how a child would react to that."

"But I should be living a lie," he cried desperately.

"That can be done," she said grimly, "if only you had a woman's strength."

Twenty minutes later he was sleeping like a child. May, awake beside him, thought: how difficult good and sensitive men make life for themselves; and, she thought ruefully, for their nearest and dearest. Yet would I have him any other way? No, she thought. He's my husband, with his own muddled collection of loyalties and beliefs. He'd hurt himself rather that risk hurting anyone else. He goes through life tormented by a conscience other men would have sent packing years ago. And though he's sleeping now he'll wake before dawn bracing himself against another day. Poor Jocelyn! Dear Jocelyn! She bent over, and kissed him on the lips. He stirred, but did not wake.

Chapter 4

As though the trials and pains of hospital life were not enough, John Pentecost had other crosses to bear.

Visits from relations, for instance. One sultry afternoon he awoke from a sweet dream of peace to hideous reality: who should be sitting on his bedside chair but his elder sister Beatrice. It was a dreadful shock for anyone in his weak state. "Good God," he cried. "What the devil are you doing her?"

"Just come to see how they were looking after you, John," she said with the amiability of the tiger who has just dislodged the young lady of Riga. "And from what I've seen while you were asleep it's high time I did."

He looked at her in baleful disbelief. "You don't mean to say you took your life in your hands – everybody's life in your hands – to drive fifty miles to see me? How many things did you biff?"

"Only a milk float. But I should like to biff the Matron of this so-called hospital."

"There isn't a Matron."

"Why ever not?"

He shrugged. "All anyone knows is they went extinct. Like the dinosaurs."

"Then I'll have a word with Sister. When I think – how we did things in the VAD. Who – ?"

John paled. "You can't. You mustn't," he cried. "Don't upset her, Bea, for God's sake."

Bea looked at him thoughtfully. "John, I always thought I was the only person you were afraid of. And now I find you're terrified of that chit of a girl. I'm surprised at you." She tut-tutted vigorously.

"Me? Afraid of you?" He had never heard such nonsense in his life. He glared. She scowled. Aunt Beatrice and John Pentecost were two of a kind: quirky, cantankerous, opinionated Britons. He stoutly maintained over seventy years of life that she used to augment her pocket money by cheating at Happy Families. She accused him of shifting a surreptitious pawn at the age of seven. Battle was in their eyes whenever they met. But, today, she smelt victory. Could this demoralised creature really be her bouncy younger brother? Could the first illness of his life have reduced him to this?

Yes. It obviously had. And she could afford to be magnanimous. For once she could lower her guard. She could even afford the luxury of pity for this broken creature. She said, "Now. John, you and I haven't always seen eye to eye."

"And whose fault is that?" he demanded truculently.

She was determined to be magnanimous. "Perhaps it hasn't been entirely your fault," she admitted. "Be that as it may, John, I just want to say – " her voice became almost tender. "– I don't want you to worry about who's going to nurse you when you come out – " now her voice broke with emotion. "I am, John." She gave him the smile she usually bestowed on the runner-up when she won the Captain's Cup.

There was a stunned silence; followed by a strangled "You?"

"I, John. With my Voluntary Aid Detachment training I consider myself the ideal person. In fact – " she lowered her voice " – I could certainly teach some of these young creatures a thing or two about nursing." Her voice rose again." Especially that Sister."

"Sssh!" John looked round anxiously. He was horrified, For once in his life he found himself in a situation he wasn't strong enough to cope with. Frankly, he felt like climbing under the bedclothes.

He found a little strength. "My dear Bea, things have changed since you were in Crimea."

"It wasn't the Crimea, you fool. It was the 1914 war."

"Same thing."

"Nonsense. Now you tell May and Jocelyn not to worry about a thing. I've no ties, you know. So the moment you get a date for discharge I'll be over. I can do it in an hour."

John groaned. These weeks in hospital had been bearable only because of the light at the end of the tunnel: a life of convalescent peace in his own house. And now suddenly, the light at the end of the tunnel had become a glare of a rampaging express: Bea! She'd watch his every mouthful, she might even put him on a diet! Good Lord, he wouldn't put it past her to hide his whisky! If, with God's mercy, he ever walked again, she'd walk beside him. There'd be no escape, no hiding place. Talk about "raise the stone, and there thou shalt find me, cleave the wood and there am I", that was his sister Beatrice to a T.

She rose and kissed him, began getting her things together. "Drinking plenty of water, are you?"

"Gallons," said John, who never touched the stuff.

"Good. Show me your tongue."

"I'm damned if I will."

"Suit yourself. John, I've had an idea. I'll call tonight and see May and Jocelyn. Set their minds at rest about your convalescence. May will put me up for the night."

"God help us all," said John. Great Aunt Bea's Mini tootled happily along the lanes.

Great Aunt Bea was just as happy as her motor. She was nearly there now. She was bringing a message of happiness and comfort to May and Jocelyn. And if there was one thing Aunt Bea loved it was to bring a message of happiness and comfort.

Passing what she thought of as an ancient rustic leaning on his cottage gate, she waved cheerily.

There was a horrified squawk from somewhere underneath her car, followed by an outraged ball of feathers projecting itself towards the cottage. "Dammit, Missus, you've winged Ophelia," shouted Reuben Briggs, neatly fielding the hen in its passage. "Why can't you look where you're going?"

"Why do you let your blasted hens wander all over the road?" countered Aunt Bea. She climbed out of her car, went and ruffled Ophelia's feathers. "*She's* not hurt. Just livid."

Reuben looked at her scornfully. "What do you know about hens?"

"A great deal." She glanced towards the fields. "I know even more about sheep."

"You do?"

"I do. I know they're a fine lot."

"Best lot this part Derbyshire. You'd best come in and have a cup of tea, Missus."

"That's very kind of you. But – "

Reuben ignored the 'but'. "I can tell you like the daft creatures." He seemed to forget about tea and led her into the fields. Where he soon found that she really did know something about sheep. "Lost one of my old ewes recently," he said.

"Bad luck," said Bea. She saw tears in the old man's eyes. "What was it? Scrapie?"

"No. Some kid left the gate open. One ewe never came back. Found her at last. Poor old girl. Dead as a doornail."

"Ought to be locked up."

"Aye. Like mums?"

"I beg your pardon?"

"Chrysanthemums?" But he was already in his garden, gathering a few flowers from among the brussels and the cabbages. He went into the house, brought them back (to her great surprise) wrapped in a crumpled *Times Literary Supplement*. "I can get on wi' your sort," he said.

"Thank you. You probably know my brother, John Pentecost? And my nephew?"

"Aye. I do that."

She drove on. She felt she had had a very great compliment bestowed upon her.

No sooner had Bea left the hospital than John Pentecost surprised everyone by demanding a telephone. He, who had been willing to wait interminably for his tea was now thumping his pillow and threatening to sue the Area Health Authority and the Sister personally, if he wasn't given a telephone immediately.

An auxiliary said she didn't think they had telephones for patients, love, and brought the Staff Nurse to deal with this alarming old codger. Staff Nurse said she'd see what they could do tomorrow, dear. The old man said he didn't want it tomorrow, dammit, he wanted it now. They fetched Sister, who explained the difficulties, nay, the virtual impossibility, of rigging up a telephone at this time of night even if a telephone could be found.

John Pentecost listened, unmoved. And then said that either they got him a telephone tonight or he discharged himself tonight. The choice was theirs.

They got him a telephone.

Only Momma, thought Gaylord, would put anyone to bed on June evenings. It was against nature. Sunlight filtered through the drawn curtains and peered boldly round the swaying edges. Through the open windows came the sounds of summer: the clatter of a lawnmower, the snap of shears, laughter and birdsong. Gaylord wished he were a bird. Birds could stay up just as long as they liked. And mother birds didn't fuss all the time asking their offspring whether they'd washed their claws or cleaned their beaks. Flying must be fun, too. One of these days he's invent a pair of wings and fly out of the bedroom window. That'd give Momma something to think about.

The telephone began ringing.

It went on ringing.

Well, the telephone wasn't his department. A lot of thanks he'd get if he went downstairs to answer it! That would rank as "just another excuse to go wandering about like a dog at a fair when you should be in bed." Gaylord had no illusions about adult gratitude.

But why didn't someone answer it?

Because, obviously, Momma and Poppa were in the garden, and couldn't hear it for the noise of the lawnmower. In which case he had a clear duty.

He padded downstairs, looked at the telephone somewhat nervously. He always had the feeling that an unanswered telephone was about to get red hot or explode.

Or both.

To avoid these alarming eventualities, he gingerly picked up the receiver. "Hello," he said warily. "Who's that?'

A voice said, "Gaylord? Look. Get you mother. Tell her it's urgent."

Gaylord was intrigued. It was Grandpa! But Grandpa was in hospital. How could he possibly be on the telephone? "Are you in a call box?" he asked.

"Of course I'm not. I'm in a blasted hospital bed. Get your mother. Or your father, for heaven's sake."

"Are your ankles better, Grandpa?

"Will you get your parents to the 'phone!"

"Which one do you prefer?" asked Gaylord, who always went to great lengths to give satisfaction.

"Just get one of them. Tell them my very survival depends on it."

This was exciting. Gaylord shot into the garden. "Momma! Poppa! Grandpa's on the telephone and he says his very survival depends on it."

His parents looked alarmed. But it was May who made a bee line for the house. "What's survival?" asked Gaylord.

"Going on living," said Jocelyn, that walking dictionary; then wondered whether he had given a full enough answer. But Gaylord appeared satisfied. So Jocelyn ran towards the house. May came out. "Jocelyn, your father's terribly upset. Aunt Bea's visited him and she's threatening to come and nurse him back to health. He vows it will kill him."

"It'll kill *me*," said Jocelyn.

Gaylord was appalled. "Would she stay here?'

"Of course, she would," said May.

Gaylord felt his imagination boggle. Great Aunt Bea always came for Christmas and Easter which meant that during those sweet Christian Festivals he became a hunted animal, skulking in corners to avoid that inveterate nephew-kisser, that bossy-boots who knew everything. Why, it was like having two Mommas about the place.

But Christmas and Easter were both over in a couple of days. Get Aunt Bea permanently installed in the household and life would be unbearable. He decided the only thing would be to emigrate, like Henry Bartlett's Uncle Fred.

Jocelyn said, "What did my father say?"

"He said, 'Stop her, May. Stop her, whatever you do. I will not have my latter days ruined by that female Barbarossa!' Gaylord, go back to bed."

Gaylord was outraged. "Momma, I got up to answer the telephone. It was ringing and ringing and you and Poppa couldn't hear it. I bet if I hadn't answered it, it would have blown up."

Or your grandfather would, May thought to herself. Aloud, she said, "Yes. Well, thank you, Gaylord. But it isn't ringing now, is it?"

Gaylord stuck out his lower lip. Talk about ingratitude! "How do you emigrate?" he asked.

"Gaylord, don't be cheeky."

He glared. He was, if possible, even more outraged. "Momma, I was only asking, really. I only meant – if Great Aunt Bea came – I might emigrate. I wasn't being cheeky, really."

"All right, dear. But go to bed. Poppa and I want to talk."

As usual! Just when there was something interesting afoot: get Gaylord out of the way before you say a word about it. "Will Great Aunty Bea really come?" he asked plaintively.

But he did not need an answer from his mother. There was the sound of rending wood. Great Aunt Bea's Mini advanced into the drive, bearing part of the gatepost on its left wing. "Why, there's my little pickle," trumpeted Great Aunt Bea from the driving seat. A few seconds later May was astonished to see her son's face peering furtively from his bedroom window. Good for him, she thought. He must have sliced a good four seconds from his previous record. There was no doubt about it. Aunt Bea concentrated Gaylord's mind wonderfully.

Aunt Bea, sipping a large gin and tonic, beamed fondly on May and Jocelyn. She settled herself more comfortably in her brother's vast armchair. "I don't wonder John gets lumbago in a chair like this. No support. We'll have this out when he comes home. Ah yes." It was time for her good news. Her beam became brighter, warmer, as when the rising sun floats free from the horizon. "My dears. I have an announcement."

They tried to look suitably agog. "Really, Aunt?" cried Jocelyn looking, despite all his efforts, like the accused watching His Lordship adjust the Black Cap.

Aunt Bea savoured the moment. She watched their eager faces, and made a mental note that Jocelyn was looking a little peaky; probably he's been wondering how on earth he was going to pay for a Bupa Home Nurse.

Then "Yes," she said. "And I thought I'd let you know as soon as possible to save you worrying. I'm going to come and nurse John for just as long as it takes."

For a time they were both speechless with astonishment and gratitude. Then May said, "But Aunt Bea. We couldn't possibly let you do such a thing. We can't expect you to sacrifice yourself in this way."

"Certainly not," said Jocelyn, trying to sound masterful, but feeling as masterful as a Victorian Miss with the vapours.

Bea said, "My dears, since your Uncle Ben died my life has lost its purpose. I have no-one to guide, to succour, to protect. Now" – her eyes shone – "now I shall once again have a Purpose."

Since it was widely accepted that poor Uncle Ben was much

better off where he was, this remark brought comfort to no-one. May thought, I must find some reason to put her off. But what? Given a seven-bedroom house, accommodation's no problem. And we couldn't afford a Home Nurse. In a way she's an answer to prayer. And she remembered what someone had once said: that prayer *was* answered. But you sometimes got more that you bargained for.

Jocelyn thought, we must stop her somehow. We owe it to both Father and Gaylord, as well as to ourselves. But May's obviously stumped. And if *she* can't find an answer there's not much hope of my coming up with anything.

Aunt Bea said, "Now, I've been thinking. You'll need to get a bed downstairs of course, Jocelyn. Oh, and where's the downstairs loo?"

"Next to the cowshed," said Jocelyn.

He got a look that reminded him of his father. "You mean – *outside?*"

May said, "This is an old farmhouse, Aunt. Not a desirable town house with all mod. cons."

"Well, John certainly will need something different from that. What sort of hand are you at plumbing, Jocelyn?"

Before Jocelyn, who was already deeply depressed at the thought of getting a bed downstairs, could think of an answer, May said, "Jocelyn has always believed that he should write, which he does well, and pay others with the proceeds to plumb and paint, at both of which, frankly, he's dreadful."

"Oh, I've no time for that airy-fairy twaddle," said Aunt Bea robustly. "Ben couldn't do a thing when we were first married. But he was soon the handiest of men. Do you know, he installed our central heating single-handed."

Well, bully for Uncle Ben, thought May. But then she thought: Bea's right, of course. And neither Jocelyn nor I have given it a thought. Had she, she wondered, assumed smugly that she had everything – husband, children, life itself – under control? If so, life was taking a sudden lurch, had done so on the day the old man fell; and things were out of kilter, the car of life was bumping along on the grass verge, anything could happen and, without a firm hand on the wheel, probably would. She looked across at her dear Jocelyn, so loving and thoughtful and well-meaning – yet so, let's face it, ineffectual. And her heart failed her, and she was afraid.

But not for long. When Aunt Bea had taken herself off to bed with a plate of biscuits and a glass for her teeth and a book in case she couldn't sleep ("anything will do dears. I know, give me one of Jocelyn's. Can't imagine why I shall like it, but you never know.") – When Aunt Bea had taken herself off May said seriously, "You know, darling, Bea's right. We haven't thought this through. We *shall* need some plumbing. And a decent downstairs bedroom for your father. And we'd jolly well better think what else we need before your aunt starts rearranging the whole house."

Jocelyn gave her a hunted look. To his unpractical brain the turning of an old junk room into a shining modern bathroom seemed in the same class as turning a frog into a Fairy Prince. He understood there were men who could effect such translations. But they weren't the sort of men he knew, and he certainly wasn't one of them. He said, without conviction, "I'll try to get hold of an architect. Must be one in Ingerby."

She said, "We don't want an architect, dear. We want a plumber and someone to do a bit of decorating. That's all." Architect, indeed! "And," she added beginning to feel herself again, "we must redecorate the blue room for Aunt Bea, and we'd better get any steps built up into ramps for a wheelchair, and you father will need somewhere downstairs for his clothes, do you think you could get his big wardrobe down or shall we buy some fitted furniture? Oh, and we'll have to find a suitable chair for him to sit on if Bea turfs out his armchair. And if we're having the inside loo, that outside loo would make a very nice potting shed if we tear out the seat and put a few shelves in." She took a deep breath. She felt a lot better. Now she'd been jolted into getting her teeth in, by George she'd got her teeth in. No-one was going to tell her what was needed in her own house.

Gaylord said morosely, "You got any Great-Aunts, Henry?"

"Lots," said Henry.

"Are they all potty?"

"They are a bit," said Henry.

They walked on. Henry said, "You got any Great-Aunts, Gaylord?"

Gaylord nodded. "One of 'em's coming to stay. She's *awful*."

Henry exuded silent sympathy. At last he said, "I reckon you want a priest's hole."

"What's that?"

"It's a little room that no-one knows about except you, where you can hide a priest."

"Why do people want to hide a priest?"

"Because of the Roundheads."

Gaylord felt as though he were doing a jig-saw with several pieces missing. He cogitated. Great Aunt Bea, priests, Roundheads? They didn't connect. The only thing that made sense was a little room that no-one knew about, or anyway had forgotten about. He said, "A little room? Like our outside loo?"

It was Henry's turn to cogitate. He didn't think he'd ever

read about Royalists hiding priests in the outside loos. At last: "Not really," he said. "More like something behind the wainscot, or in the chimney."

Anti-Great Aunts Gaylord might be. But even he drew the line at putting Aunt Bea in a room in the chimney. But Henry, feeling that perhaps he hadn't quite been as clear as he might have been, said, "The room's for *you* to hide in, Gaylord."

A great light dawned. Gaylord said, "No-one ever uses our outside loo. I could store food there – Mars Bars and that – and disappear for ages and ages."

"What if your mother noticed you were missing?"

Henry had put his finger on the nub. You left Momma out of your calculations at your peril. But Gaylord thought he could cope. He already had a very developed ploy for suggesting his presence without actually being present for more that thirty seconds: in at the front door, singing loudly; a rapid tour of the house with a certain amount of banging and clattering; a few moments in his room tootling on his recorder; then a stealthy exit from the back door and into the bushes, leaving Momma happy with the subliminal impression that Gaylord was around.

Henry said, rather accusingly, "John the Baptist didn't have Mars Bars. He lived on locusts and wild honey."

Gaylord didn't fancy living on locusts. They looked more fiddly even than shrimps. "I reckon Mars Bars'd be more nourishing," he said. And in Momma's book, thought Gaylord, nourishingness was what mattered, however horrible the taste.

Henry said stubbornly, "I reckon John the Baptist managed all right." He pondered. "I wonder if he dipped the locust in wild honey, or ate all the locusts first and then had the honey, like us with the roast beef and then the apple pie."

But Gaylord failed to share his friend's interest in the Baptist's diet. He was already apportioning his pocket money into Biscuits, Crisps, and tins of Coca-Cola. He reckoned he could sustain life for the whole of Bea's visitation. Until his friend shattered his cosy illusions by saying, "I reckon your Ma will notice if you don't turn up for meals."

Gaylord's heart sank. It was true. His vision of himself leading the comfortable life of a recluse, safe from Auntie Bea's embraces, living deliciously on Mars Bars and crisps, faded. And all because Momma had to stick her oar into everything he did. If only, he thought wistfully, God hadn't invented mothers. How pleasant life would be. Poppa would never notice whether Gaylord was at the table or not. But Momma!

Nevertheless, he didn't alter his plans. Slowly he built up a stock of nourishing crisps and chocolate bars. Whatever happened, he was *not* going to be prey to Great Aunt Beatrice.

And one day, as he was sitting there, happily working his way down a packet of biscuits, something beautiful happened. He became aware of a distant, urgent twittering noise. He was intrigued. He began to search. And there, in a dark corner, he fond a palpitating, pulsating, heap of very naked little bodies. "Aaah," breathed Gaylord, deeply moved by these tiny, helpless creatures. With infinite gentleness, he picked one up. It struggled nervously. Gaylord got the impression it wasn't very happy. He put it back with its brothers and sisters. It wriggled gratefully into the heap. "Aaaah," Gaylord breathed again. It had been such an emotional experience, seeing such helpless innocence, feeling such love for a fellow creature. He wondered vaguely what the animals were. It would be nice if they grew up into squirrels, he thought. But he didn't ask Momma for her views, on the general principle that the less Momma knew about *anything*, the better.

The outside loo was a lovesome thing, God wot. It was one of those blessed places where Jocelyn put anything he couldn't find a home for: dying cyclamens, ostensibly to await an autumn rebirth, but with the sure knowledge in his heart he would forget them and that they would be there for all eternity. Pieces of timber he intended chopping up for firewood one day; garden chairs awaiting repair, while generations of spiders lived, and spun their webs, and died among_

Its original purpose had long been abandoned and it smelt of geraniums and warm brick and potting compost and long ago summers. It was a super place, thought Gaylord, as he watched the newborn creatures. The door was shut, the sun-warmed window was overgrown inside and out, by a Russian Vine. Gaylord had found a refuge where even Momma would never think of looking for him, and where Aunt Bea could simply be locked out.

Plump and bland Henry Bartlett might be. But he was a staunch and loyal friend. And when he discovered that some vandal had destroyed Gaylord's tiger trap he was incensed – nay, outraged.

But his loyalty did not stop at mere moral support. Gaylord was very occupied with stocking up his priest's hole, wasn't he. So Henry simply got on with things. He fetched his little trowel. He collected the scattered palm fronds. He dug. He tore off clods of grass. He went on digging. In a few days he had restored the trap to its original state of usefulness. The vandal's work had been destroyed. Henry really did feel very pleased with himself. And he hugged the thought that one day, when Gaylord wasn't so busy, he would tell his friend how nobly he had helped to carry on his selfless work for humanity.

Chapter 5

The first time Jocelyn saw his father supporting himself with a pair of elbow crutches it cut him to the heart. There was something of a crucifixion in the twisted posture, in the helplessly striving legs, the straining arms.

But there was more, much more, than compassion here. There was remorse, guilt, regret. *If only I had thought for a moment when Gaylord showed me that ridiculous trap. If only I hadn't tried to impress two little boys with my cleverness, then – my father would not be dragging himself, like a broken-backed spider, across a hospital ward. He would be marching stoutly across his own acres, his face to the sun.*

I shall have to tell him, he thought. Sometime. I can't carry this burden of remorse forever on my shoulders.

His father, that independent Englishman, would not have taken kindly to being compared with a broken-backed spider. He simply set his formidable jaw, did a great deal of quiet swearing, and set himself to learn to walk again with the minimum of fuss, self-pity, and wasted time, and with the maximum of determination and grit. And when the physiotherapist said, "Of course, Mr Pentecost, we must expect it to take longer at your age," he was subjected to a stare of such savagery, and a growling, grumbled, "don't you believe it, young man," that he almost expected the patient to fling away his crutches there and then, and walk back unaided across the ward.

Jocelyn, seated beside his father's empty bed, watching and pitying his father's exertions, was startled by a voice saying, "Can I give you a copy of my novel, Mr Pentecost? I think you'll like it."

He rose, slowly. That pretty, pert nurse (with, he now noticed, hair or the finest spun silk) was shoving a bulging, obese folder at him. He backed away. "No," he cried, "No. I simply haven't the time, Nurse."

"Oh, do take it," she said. "I promised to let your father read it, and it's sure to get forgotten when he's discharged."

"Oh, very well," he said. "But I really can't read it myself."

"You won't be able to put it down once you start," she said, grinning. She pushed it into his arms and disappeared.

And before he could recover he was suddenly aware that Sister was bearing down on him. He leapt to his feet. "Good evening, Sister," he said, fawning.

"Hello, Mr Pentecost. Your father's doing well. I think we may let him come home late next week."

"Really?"

"Yes. We feel he may do better in his own surroundings than he will here. I take it you have all the necessary facilities?"

"Yes."

"I thought so. We do usually take patients down to the kitchen for a spot of rehabilitation before they leave, make sure they can make a cup of tea and so on. But I'm sure that won't be necessary in your father's case."

"God forbid that you should suggest such a thing to him," said Jocelyn devoutly.

"Yes. Well." She gave him a funny look. Jocelyn wished he hadn't spoken.

But his father came back. The physiotherapist helped him

into bed. Jocelyn said, "Father, you're coming home." They were joyful words.

They were not joyfully received. "Right. Now for God's sake keep it from Bea."

"Father, I can't. She'd never forgive any of us."

"What's the matter?"

Jocelyn said, "She's your *sister*, dash it."

"So?"

They stared at each other in exasperation. At last John said, "Oh, get May to see to it. She'll find a way to choke her off."

"But she won't. She can't. After all, Aunt Bea means well."

"So did Hitler, by his lights. Damn dangerous business, meaning well."

Jocelyn went home thoroughly miserable. Confrontations were looming: with Aunt Bea, with his father, perhaps even with May. And, as if that wasn't enough, he carried his crushing burden of guilt wherever he went.

"He's coming home," he said flatly.

May looked at him in surprise. "I thought you'd sound more pleased," she said.

"Bea," he said.

"Ah."

He looked at her like a man desperately seeking a cause for hope. And found none. "I'm afraid – " she began.

The telephone rang. "Probably Bea," she said wryly.

He picked up the receiver. It *was* Bea. "Jocelyn. When's John coming home?"

"End of next week," he said.

"Splendid. I'll be with you on Tuesday. It'll give me time to check your commissariat and so on. Oh. Tell May I shall be accompanied. Messalina. She'll be no trouble."

Jocelyn looked at his wife. She returned his look impassively. He said, "Who's Messalina?"

He saw May prick up her ears. Bea said, "A beautiful Persian."

"Human or feline?"

There were great peals of laughter from the other end of the line. "Sorry to disappoint you, Joss, old man. Feline."

"She's bringing a cat," he mouthed to his wife.

"Just what your father needs, rubbing against his legs when he's learning to walk again," she muttered.

Jocelyn said desperately, "Look, aunt, It's terribly good of you, but we really can't put you to all this trouble."

"Nonsense, Joss. See you Tuesday, then." She put down the receiver.

They looked at each other. He said, "She called me Joss. Twice."

She gave him a look he could not fathom. But he didn't think it was a friendly look. "What did you say?" she asked slowly.

"I said, 'She called me Joss. Twice.' Is that what you mean?"

"That's what I mean. And that's all that matters, I suppose. She called you Joss. Your father's coming home, an invalid. Your aunt – a capable woman, a good woman, but an infuriating one – is coming to stay for months. She's bringing a blasted cat. But none of that matters. All that matters is that she called by a name you don't approve of. Twice!"

He stared in amazement. Ever since his father's accident he had had a sense of coming disintegration. A cosy, ordered world was beginning to crack.

Yet though disintegration might be almost upon them, he had always assumed that he and May, together, could weather any storm. But May – strong, cool, cheerful May – was surely changing under the stress. Her serenity could no longer be taken for granted. Her gentle mockery was developing a very sharp edge. And if the strain could affect *her*, how long could he, poor fool, hope to survive the daily blows to his nervous system?

He jumped up and put his arm around her. "May, my dear, listen. We've both been under a lot of strain while he's been in hospital. And we both know it'll be a lot worse after he comes out, even if we hadn't got Aunt Bea to stir things up."

She gazed at him, silent. It was a long time since he had seen her wet-eyed and – yes – hostile. He held her close. And then – welcome as a sunrise after a night of sorrow – she smiled. "Sorry, Jocelyn, sorry." The April storm had passed, almost before it began. They were together again.

But for how long, Jocelyn wondered. The screw was being tightened. And he'd had his first warning. He must keep her – and his marriage – as the apple of an eye. Poor Jocelyn! The prospect that he might have to be the strong one was chilling indeed.

But, being Jocelyn, he soon had other things to worry about. May, far from weakening, really got her teeth in. It was no house for a writer anymore. From morn to eve it was filled with banging and hammering, the slosh of paintbrushes, the savage, snarling bite of electric drills, the mindless chatter of the workmen's pocket radio. And when finally the cacophony ceases, thought Jocelyn, it will be succeeded by another kind of uproar: the endless ding dong battles between my father and his sister; the conflict between May and Bea, as courteous and deadly as an eighteenth century duel; a conflict that will probably engulf us all, he thought, remembering May's tension of the other evening.

But now, at last, the jobs were done. Silence fell. May came into his study, fairly bursting with satisfaction, and said, "Darling, want to come and look? It's all finished."

"Of course," he said. (Farewell the tranquil mind; farewell content!) He put down his pen, closed his notebook, followed her through the door. They toured the house. He was amazed. The downstairs junk room had turned into an elegant, comfortable bedroom into which his father's bed and wardrobes and dressing table had miraculously moved. The blue room gleamed and shone with new paint, new carpets. A small pantry had changed, apparently overnight, into a shower room and lavatory. He slipped an arm around her supple waist. "May! Thank you. You really can organise things."

She said, "Well, I knew you'd rather pay the bills than do it yourself. And – darling, I am a bit ashamed about the other night. I was edgy, wasn't I? So. It's a sort of peace offering."

"Oh, May." He pulled her close. "It wasn't necessary."

"Anyway it's done. Oh, there's one thing. Aunt Bea clobbered the gate post the other evening. I meant to get the men to do it before they left and I forgot. So if you'd just do that." Smiling, she put back her head. Tenderly he kissed her lips. Gaylord, who had been trailing them unheard and unseen, was interested and really quite affected. He thought it was nice. Henry Bartlett said *his* mum and dad never kissed each other. He went further. He said no married people ever kissed each other, it would be potty and they'd probably be sent to prison if anyone saw them. Gaylord had said that you couldn't be sent to prison for being potty, and Henry said yes you could if your pottiness consisted of kissing your wife, at which point Gaylord cunningly changed the subject. He liked his friend very dearly. But though he would argue with Momma till the cows came home, he found Henry's brand of stubborn argument quite wearisome.

But May had been saving one tit-bit to enjoy on her own. Life had been pretty humdrum lately. What she needed was a little treat. So she promised herself that when everything necessary had been done to the house (and not until then) she would turn the old outside loo into a potting shed worthy of Chatsworth, nay, of Sandringham itself. She would cast out with her own hands the old deck chairs and the rotting timber, and destroy them with fire. She would redesign. She would redecorate and repaint, she would build around herself a potting shed that would be for her a haven of refuge.

The tour of inspection over, she threw off Jocelyn (never difficult. "Now I'm sure you want to get back to your study" had much the same effect as "Walkies" on a wire-haired terrier.)

"Now!" she said to herself. She tripped across the stockyard. The homely little edifice stood before her, touched beautifully by the mellow rays of the sun. "Now," she said again. She flung open the door and marched in.

Jocelyn picked up his pen. And then he froze. From below came scream after scream. He dashed downstairs. What, who, could it be? He had never heard May scream in his life. He ran into the stockyard. May was standing outside one of the outhouses wringing her hands, gasping, and she was flanked by a distinctly uncomfortable looking Gaylord.

Jocelyn ran and threw his arms around her. "May, what is it? What's the matter?" She pointed at the old loo. "I went in," she said. "I was going to – to make it beautiful. But – there were – " She couldn't bring herself to say the word.

"What were there?" he coaxed.

She stared at him wide-eyed. "Rats," she hissed. "Rats! Everywhere. Running. Dozens of them. And – " she looked accusingly at Gaylord – "biscuit wrappers and crisp bags everywhere." She gave Gaylord another look that made his toes curl. "I'll talk to you later, my lad."

"I'll see Reuben," said Jocelyn hurriedly. Jocelyn's usual answer to the chances and changes of this mortal life (especially those concerned with natural disasters) was to see Reuben, who had a totally undeserved reputation for curing anything from warts to molehills to plagues of rats.

"It was a priest's hole," said Gaylord.

"What was?" demanded Jocelyn.

"The old loo," said Gaylord.

Jocelyn looked baffled. "What do you want a priest's hole for?" he asked with interest.

"Jocelyn," shouted May. "*Do* something! Go and get Reuben."

"Ah, yes. Reuben," said Jocelyn. He set off for the grove of trees that held Reuben's cottage like the hand of God. He knocked on Reuben's cottage door. "Come in," called Reuben, sprawled in his old basket chair. He went in.

Reuben said, "Did I see that nice Aunty of yours about the other day?"

"Yes. Why, do you know her?

"Yes. She damn near killed one of my hens. Nice, sensible woman."

Jocelyn couldn't quite understand the reasoning. But he hadn't come to discuss his Aunty.

"Reuben," he said. "We've got rats."

"Have you now, Mr Pentecost?" cried Reuben. "And what do you expect me to do about it?"

Jocelyn was appalled. It was part of his belief that if a

merciful God sent natural disasters it was only right and proper that He should send men like Reuben to deal with them. He said feebly, "I – thought – hoped – you might get rid of them for us."

"And what gave you that idea?" asked Reuben blandly.

Jocelyn said, "Look Reuben, have I said something to annoy you? You don't seem to like me much nowadays."

"Don't I, Mr Pentecost?"

Jocelyn was silent. Then he said, "Very well, Reuben. I'm sorry you feel like that. But I wish you'd tell me what I've done wrong."

"Aye. Well. Happen you do. Goodbye, Mr Pentecost."

Jocelyn hung about. "Was it – my son leaving that gate open?" he asked. But Reuben had gone back to his book.

Jocelyn came away. He had seldom been more depressed. He had never felt comfortable with Reuben, feeling that Reuben not only regarded him as a writer vastly inferior to old Dusty-ever-so (which he accepted) but also as a figure of fun, which hurt like the devil. But Reuben had always been willing to cope with disasters before. This was the first time he had shown hostility rather that contempt.

And it wasn't only hostility, painful though that was. It was rats! "Hamelin town's in Brunswick," he muttered. "And I wish I was." To be anywhere, away from this plague that had suddenly become his responsibility!

He telephoned the County Council, to beseech the Rodent Operator to come to his rescue. But it was a law of nature that Disasters always struck at five o'clock on Friday afternoon, when doctors, dentists, rodent operators, plumbers and electricians go to ground like rabbits at the sound of a gun. So the rats had a whole weekend to enjoy themselves feeding on the remains of Gaylord's biscuits, and increasing and multiplying.

And Reuben nursed his unaccountable hostility. And Jocelyn worried himself sick because his eccentric neighbour was no longer in love and charity with him and because the nearer his father came to being back at home the more sure he became that he, Jocelyn, could not keep his guilty secret to himself; and because May obviously thought he ought to be able to do a Pied Piper act over the week-end, instead of waiting supinely for Monday morning to bring the Rodent Operator.

He tried one final throw.

No sooner had Aunt Bea arrived than he took her surreptitiously on one side and said, "Oh, by the way, Aunt, we've got one or two rats in the outhouses. Do you think we might turn your cat loose in the outside lavatory?"

He was subjected to a stare that reminded him of his father's. "Jocelyn, you're not serious? Messalina doesn't *catch* things. She's *far* too high-born. Bless my soul, I never heard such a thing."

"Sorry, Aunt," he said. "I just thought – " He trailed off.

Chapter 6

John Pentecost, Esq., LL.B., was slumped in a wheelchair, wearing pyjamas and a dressing gown, and clutching a great plastic bag on which was printed in black letters PROPERTY OF INGERBY ROYAL INFIRMARY.

It contained the personal property of the said John Pentecost, Esq., LL.B.: toothbrush, towels, soap, slippers.

He was one of a dozen such forlorn figures in the hospital entrance hall.

Time passed. He had no idea how long he had been awaiting collection, couldn't be bothered to find out.

"Oedipus at Colonus," said Jocelyn bitterly, as he and May came through the doors.

May said, "No. Oedipus retained dignity. They have robbed your father of the last vestige."

Jocelyn said, "Not they. They've cured him, set him on the path to health, anyway. It's the sickness of the body that's the enemy. It's that takes the heart and the dignity out of a man."

They stood before him. He greeted them wanly. It looked impossible he should ever walk again. Jocelyn thought, I've brought him down to this. I can never bear to tell him. Yet I cannot live my life in silence. He said, "Hello, Father. It's good to be taking you home."

John sighed, "I'm sorry to be a burden to you both."

"You're not a burden," May said cheerfully, though her stout heart almost failed her. The old man had never been easy. But now, frustrated and immobile, he was going to be a handful.

Jocelyn seized the handles of the chair and began to propel it forward. He felt as a man feels who lifts a heavy burden on to his shoulders, knowing that the way ahead is long; yet on the other hand taking the burden gladly because it is to help a loved one.

They settled the old man into the car quite easily, much to Jocelyn's surprise. "Right," he said, flushed with triumph. "I'll just put the wheelchair in the boot; then we'll be off, Father."

He wheeled the chair round to the back of the car. May said, "Well, Father-in-law, is it nice to be outside the prison walls?"

"I suppose so," he said gloomily.

Oh dear, she thought. What's happened to him? She said brightly, "It must be wonderful to think you'll be sleeping in your own bed again tonight."

'Yes," he said.

He's changed, she thought. They've made him think he's an old man. Oh, damn. What's happened to all that stimulating abrasiveness? A short time ago she had been dreading that abrasiveness. Now she longed for it, fearing it had gone forever; realising that it was far preferable to this wan acceptance.

Jocelyn came and flopped into the driving seat. He was holding up one hand in an attitude of suffering. "Get me a bit of Elastoplast, May. That damn chair's bitten me."

She found him the Elastoplast. He looked at it helplessly. "You really need three hands," he said, "when it's your hand you're putting it on."

"Oh, give it to me," she said cheerfully, knowing that Jocelyn could make a smooth strip of healing tape look like a relief model of the Alps. But she wasn't feeling very cheerful: a father-in-law suddenly grown geriatric; three children: Jocelyn, Gaylord and Amanda; and Great Aunt Bea. She certainly was going to have her hands full. "How did you do it?" she asked.

"I tried to fold the chair and it wouldn't budge. Then suddenly it snapped together, like a blasted man trap. I was lucky it didn't get my leg," he said plaintively. He too stared into a future as depressing as May's but with the additional menace of grievous bodily harm from a hostile wheelchair.

John Pentecost appeared to doze – May and Jocelyn were busy with their thoughts. It was a sad and silent journey. They drew up at the front door. The old man opened his eyes, stared at the house without comment. May, longing for him to show some pleasure in his homecoming, said, "Here we are, Father-in-law. Aren't you glad to be home?

"Should I be?" he said listlessly.

Her spirits sank still further. His depression was like a great black cloud hanging over them all. She glanced at Jocelyn. He looked tense and worried. "I'll go and get the chair out," he said. "Better have the Elastoplast ready, May." But before he could move, the front door was flung open and a glad, ringing voice cried out, "Welcome home, John Pentecost," and Aunt Bea came running, flung open the passenger door and called "Come along, Joss, where's that wheelchair, sharp's the word." She began tugging at the patient.

John flapped at her irritably. "I might have realised you were here when I saw that gate post."

"Now don't pretend you're senile, John, you know perfectly well. I've come to nurse you back to health."

"To chivvy me into the grave, more likely." He looked round like, thought May, a trapped lion. "Where the hell's that wheelchair, Jocelyn?" he bellowed.

May looked at him almost joyously. He glared back. His

white moustache was bristling. "Stop pawing me, woman," he growled at Bea, who was trying to unfasten his safety belt. He turned back to May. "May, I thought you were the one person I could trust not to sell me down the river," he said reproachfully.

That's my boy, thought May. Bea's done it, brought him back to life. I don't think anyone else could have done. And when Jocelyn appeared with the wheelchair (sucking his thumb but apparently otherwise unharmed) and they got the old man into the house, there was no sign of the black cloud that had so recently enveloped him. He was in fine fettle. May said proudly, "Jocelyn's got your bed downstairs, Father-in-law."

"Then he can damn well take it up again," John cried, causing Jocelyn great mental anguish. "I'm not sleeping downstairs."

May flung open the door of the new indoor loo. "There! Isn't that nice. And look. We've managed to install a shower in the corner."

The old man stared. He said slowly, venomously, "I once took a shower, my dear May. Back in the thirties. The damn thing scalded my head, neck and shoulders. It then attacked me with jets of ice-cold water. I will never again, May, risk my life and well-being in a shower."

"Well, you can't have a bath in the foreseeable future," said Aunt Bea.

"Then I'll damn well go unwashed. Good God, what is this monstrosity?"

"That," said Aunt Bea coldly, "is my Pussykins."

"Also known as Messalina," murmured May.

John spoke to his sister quite affably for once. "You know, Bea, to hear a female Attila like you talk about your Pussykins is carrying the ridiculous too far. Do be your age, woman."

"Oh, stop addressing me as 'woman'," Bea said fondly.

Pussykins, who had been eyeing John with a nice blend of calculation and venom, now sprang onto his knee and peered closely and inquisitively into his face.

John stared back as though hypnotised. He had never been at all intimate with cats. He saw huge yellow eyes beautifully set in a pretty feminine face. But the prettiness and the femininity, and the great twin globes of eyes, were a mere mask, it seemed to him. The creature's expression was one of downright menace. John saw Messalina, not as her mistress saw her, but as a blackbird, chancing upon her in a shrubbery would see her: all evil and cruelty. He gave Pussykins a hearty shove. Pussykins, outraged, squawked and landed on the hearthrug.

Bea snatched her up. "I see you haven't changed, John. Once a bully, always a bully."

May thought: well this is splendid. I really think that if Bea hadn't been here, he'd have slipped into senility. As it is, ever since he set eyes on her he's been in cracking form. She said, "Now, Father-in-law, Jocelyn will put you in the drawing room and I'll bring in the tea."

John said, "Dammit, May, Jocelyn will put me nowhere. I'm not a bloody parcel. I shall propel myself. Oh, I shall knock bits off the furniture, and scrape all the doors, and hopefully run over that blasted cat. But I will not be treated, or spoken of, as an inanimate object, a *thing*. And he propelled himself forcefully into the drawing room; whence, a moment later, came a great bellow: "May! Where's my chair?"

May thought, I don't see why I should handle this one. She said sweetly, "Would you like to go and explain, Aunt?"

"I most certainly will," said Great Aunt Bea. She swept into the drawing room. "John, when did you last have lumbago?"

He scowled. "Last March. Why?"

"And before that?"

"Christmas. What is all this? I want to know what's happened to my armchair."

"I'm telling you, John. I've removed it. It's got no lumbar support. So when you can abandon your wheelchair, you'll use this one. Hard. Straight. Just what your back needs."

"Well, it's not what I need." He looked at her almost in awe. "Bea. Some of these tinpot African dictators aren't as high-handed as you."

"They don't have to deal with people as high-handed as your Brother."

May and Jocelyn came in with the tea.

Jocelyn looked at his father. It's still going to be a long job, he thought. He's back in his surroundings, his comfortable home, his loved farmlands. But he's not *of* them. Despite all his brave bluster, he's dependent on us for everything. He's demeaned, humiliated. In spite of all pretence, he relies wholly on our good nature.

And it's my fault. I've got to tell him. I wasn't sure when he was in hospital. But now he's back at home I know I can't live under the same roof and keep this awful thing to myself. I should feel a veritable traitor.

He'd do it this evening. When the children were in bed, May and Bea usually went gardening, or played bezique. He could do it then, in a quiet chat with his father. But he felt the old, nervous tension in his stomach at the very thought; and the old indecisions, asking him whether he really was being wise, and asking how many relationships he might destroy.

May said, "You're very quiet, darling. Anything the matter?"

He swallowed. He said, "Now Father's home, I realise I can't keep this thing to myself." He looked at her beseechingly.

"Oh, Jocelyn. I'd hoped you'd put all that from your mind. Though, knowing you – darling, it will serve no purpose to tell him. And it might – sour relations."

"I know. That's what's so awful. But I've *got* to, May."

She sat looking at him thoughtfully. "Yes," she sighed. "I suppose you have. And I respect you for it. But I still think you'd be better employed doing something about those horrible rats," she said, with a rather bleak smile.

Gaylord and Henry Bartlett leaned on a five-barred gate, heads down, deep in philosophical discussion.

The sun shone, the birds twittered in the hedgerows, the leaf-shadows dappled the dusty lane. But they neither saw nor heard. They were chewing over a moral problem: was murder justified when the prospective victim was as awful as Great Aunt Beatrice?

Henry thought it was. Though he was phrasing it rather differently from Caiaphas, he too thought it expedient that one man, or one great-aunt rather, should die for the people. "I reckon you and your Grandpa, and your Mam and Dad, would all be ever so much happier if she wasn't there."

"Aunt Bea wouldn't," said Gaylord doubtfully.

"She would if she goes to Heaven," said Henry.

"I don't think she will," said Gaylord.

Henry pondered this. "It's four to one, anyway," he said at last. "Think how grateful they'd all be. Think how glad you'd be."

Gaylord wrestled with his tender conscience. He remembered, almost with tears in his eyes, the happy days of yore when the only fly in his ointment had been Momma.

And, he thought, long experience had taught him ways of lessening Momma's impact.

But not Great Aunt Bea's. Having Aunt Bea around was like having a rollicking great hippo in the house. Henry was right. The world would be a happier place without her.

But – "thou shalt do no murder." Even to Gaylord's subtle brain, that looked pretty watertight. He didn't think he could do it, somehow.

Henry the Tempter said, "Me Uncle Arnold's got some stuff that kills *everything*: weeds, wasps, cockroaches, people –"

"Even Great Aunt Bea?"

"Sure to."

"What's it look like?"

"Bit like flour. In a cardboard box."

"She'd never take it."

"She would if you put it in her Ovaltine."

It was certainly true of Gaylord that his heart had its reasons that the reason knew not of. It all looked so easy. And the rewards would benefit everybody, except perhaps Aunt Bea. But he couldn't do it. "I'm sorry, Henry. But I don't think we ought to. I'm sorry."

Most boys would have jeered at this, accusing Gaylord of weakness and cowardice. Not Henry. "That's all right, then, Gaylord," he said magnanimously. "It was only a suggestion."

"Thanks, Henry," said Gaylord. He was very touched. He didn't think anyone had as nice a friend as Henry in the whole wide world.

He went into the house. "Here's my little pickle, then," cried Great Aunt Bea, holding out her arms. "And what have you learnt in school today?"

"Not much," he said, trying, really trying, to put a little

warmth into his kiss. He had a vague feeling that when you'd been plotting to kill someone you ought to be a bit extra nice to them, even though you'd decided not to do it.

"Now come and see who's here," cried Bea, and seizing his little paw she propelled him into the drawing room.

It was Grandpa: a smaller, shrunken, paler, older Grandpa, whose dressing gown accentuated his present frailty. "Hello, lad," said Grandpa.

"Hello, Grandpa," said Gaylord.

The two friends stared at each other. Gaylord felt wooden and ill-at-ease. Aunt Bea boomed, "Aren't you going to give your old Grandpa a nice kiss, then?"

Gaylord shuffled forward and kissed the remembered, bristly cheek. Aunt Bea hovered over them both like an overweight angel, filling the room with eager bonhomie.

"Isn't it nice to have Grandpa back from hospital, even though it'll be a long time before you can go for walks together again."

Gaylord, who felt completely enveloped by this boisterous female, and who had assumed that he and Grandpa would be going for a walk as soon as he'd had his tea, began to cry.

Aunt Bea was used to dealing with cowardice in the face of the enemy, even when, as in this case, she hadn't much idea who the enemy was. Jolly 'em along a bit, make 'em feel ashamed of themselves; that's how she'd dealt with the Tommies inexplicably reluctant to go back to the front from the Base Hospital. She stared at Gaylord in amazement and disbelief. "Gaylord! What's this? Big boys don't cry. What are you thinking about?"

Gaylord wept the more.

"A big boy like you!" persisted Bea. "What is the matter?"

Gaylord didn't know what the matter was. He just knew he felt miserable and overwhelmed and wanted to talk to his old friend Grandpa man to man without this woman drinking in every moment of it. But he couldn't explain this.

But Grandpa understood. Grandpa knew that there are women whose personalities are so strong and pervasive that they cow the gentler male simply by their presence in a room. And he knew that his sister was such a woman. He said, "Bea, shut up and get out. Can't you see you're distressing the boy?"

Bea said amiably, "Of course I'm not distressing him, John. But I never thought my little pickle would be a cry-baby." She gave Gaylord a reassuring, but reproachful, smile.

"Oh, stop rabbiting and go away," said John.

"Very well," she said, still cheerful. "Never let it be said Beatrice didn't know when she wasn't wanted." And she went, giving Gaylord a friendly pat on the cheek as she passed.

Gaylord and Grandpa looked at each other.

Grandpa said, "Your Aunt's not a bad sort, you know. Just far too big for her boots. That's her trouble."

Gaylord said, "Henry Bartlett thinks we ought to murder her. His Uncle Arnold's got some stuff we could put in her Ovaltine. It kills everything."

Grandpa, usually fairly inscrutable, looked startled. "And what do *you* think?" he asked.

"It'd be nice, " said Gaylord wistfully. "But I don't think we ought, not really, somehow."

Grandpa said, "On balance, lad, I think I'd agree with you." He pondered. He sighed. "But I admit it's very tempting."

"Yes," said Gaylord.

They were silent. Then suddenly Grandpa held out his arms, "Come on, boy. But, mind my blasted ankles."

Gaylord flung himself on top of the old man, kissed again the sandpaper cheek. "When can we go for a walk?"

"Not tonight, Josephine. But I promise you we'll go as soon as I can walk." He gripped the boy's shoulders. "Now where shall we go, that first evening?"

"The High Meadow," said Gaylord. It was his favourite spot. You could see most of the world from there. He'd never actually seen America, but it was only because it was never clear enough. And he had a theory that if you lay down there and began to roll you go on rolling right down and into the river: something he'd always meant to try but had never got round to. He said excitedly, "If we walk up there and you were too tired to walk back you could roll, couldn't you?"

"Do my ankles the world of good," said Grandpa. "But I've got a feeling your Aunt Bea's idea of my first walk will once around the stockyard."

Gaylord thought that sounded potty. "Why?"

"Because she'll expect me to fall all over the place. She'll probably insist on following me up closely with the wheelchair and have you walking in front with a red flag and your parents supporting me on either side."

This sounded fun. But now there was an interruption. Jocelyn came in. "Hello, you two. How are you feeling, Father? Sitting comfy?"

Gaylord said, "When Grandpa's better we're going to the High Meadow and we're going to roll all the way down."

"Good," said Jocelyn, whose mind wasn't on it. "Oh, Gaylord, your mother wants you. Your tea's ready. Father, can I have a word?"

"Of course, dear boy."

Jocelyn said, "Oh, first of all, that nurse asked me to give you the manuscript of her new novel." He put a large folder on his father's table.

"Oh, thanks. Any good?"

"I'm afraid I've only dipped."

"And that's enough?"

"Quite, I'm sorry to say."

"Pity! I say, there's no law against drinking whisky at four thirty in the afternoon, is there?" Jocelyn heard the internal rumbling that passed with the old man for a chuckle.

"Not that I'm aware of," said Jocelyn, trying to match his father's light mood. But he was amazed. The old man had come home as one returns home to die. Yet here he was, an hour later, full of jollity and roaring for whisky. And now he said, "Young Gaylord's got the right idea. He suggests putting some of Henry's Uncle Arnold's poison in Bea's Ovaltine." He chortled deeply.

Poor Jocelyn! Bracing himself for this interview had taken a lot out of him. Perhaps only the knowledge that his father appeared to be verging on senility had given him the courage to face the interview. And now Father was as bright as a button. He'd chosen the wrong moment.

But he'd got to get it off his chest. He sat down, clutching his glass, the fingers of the other hand nervously exploring nook and crannies in the crystal. His father gave him the nearest thing he ever got to a smile. "Well, Jocelyn, I can't thank you and May enough for all you've done, dammit. And I'm only sorry my old bones have taken to letting me down, and landed you with an incubus like me."

It was clearly a prepared speech.

Jocelyn said, "You think it *was* a blackout?"

"Sure of it, dear boy. No other explanation." He sipped his whisky. "Can't see old Pemberton letting me go on driving." He looked forlorn.

Jocelyn took a deep breath. He said, "Please don't worry about the car. It wasn't a blackout. You'll be driving till you're a hundred."

The old man looked at him with a heartbreaking gleam of hope that was like a watery sunset. Then the grey cloud closed over the sun once more. "Sorry, Jocelyn, but you're wrong. There I was, enjoying the evening in Polly Larkin's Pad. Then, the next thing I was strung up like a blasted turkey in a hospital bed. No recollection. My brain must have flickered out like a damn neon tube. Only blessing is, I suppose, the current was eventually restored."

Jocelyn said, "It wasn't like that, Father. Someone had dug a hole in Polly Larkin's Pad. You must have tripped into it and knocked yourself unconscious – and broken both ankles."

The old man stared. "Dug a hole in Polly Larkin's Pad? What bloody fool would do that?"

"Well, that's what I'm coming to. I'm afraid – "

"Fellow wants horsewhipping, whoever he is." But then another thought struck him and he took a swig of whisky so hurriedly that it went down the wrong way and he finished up coughing and wiping his eyes. Then: "Good God" he said. He went on staring at his son. "Could you make Dr Pemberton believe this, Jocelyn?"

"Of course. It's the truth. But – " he swallowed. "There's more to it than that."

The old man ignored this. "So perhaps I shan't have to get rid of the Rover after all," he said with dawning hope.

Jocelyn said, "I'm terribly sorry about this, Father. You see, the fact is – "

"Damn good car," said John. "Tremendous character, the old 3.5." He sighed. "Don't make them like that anymore." He handed Jocelyn his empty glass. "If only we can talk Pemberton into seeing it this way."

Jocelyn said, "Father, this is how it *was*. There's no

question of your not driving when your ankles are better. But – well, I mean it was well meant."

"What was well meant?"

"The tiger trap."

"Tiger trap? What are you talking about? Jocelyn, I've just remembered. The car's due for its MOT. Have to get that done."

Aunt Bea bustled in just as the old man was taking a sip from his refilled glass. "Jocelyn, dear boy. You'd left the reading lamp switched on in your study. It's all right, I've put it off for you. John! What's in that glass?"

"Cold tea," said John blandly.

"Nonsense." She turned to Jocelyn. "Jocelyn, has anyone ever told you you're spineless?"

"Practically everybody," Jocelyn said bitterly.

"I should think so. Letting your father bully you into feeding him whisky in the middle of the afternoon. Like giving a box of matches to a backward child."

John snapped, "I find that metaphor both insulting and offensive, Bea."

Jocelyn said, "It wasn't a metaphor. It was a simile."

"What?" The blow lamp of a glare that had been playing ineffectually on Aunt Bea swung round to play on Jocelyn, who said, "It was a simile, Father. Bea said it was 'like'. If she'd said it *was* giving matches to a backward child, that would have been a metaphor."

"And even more bloody insulting," said John, fuming nicely.

May marched in.

"Oh, no," cried Jocelyn. A man who has finally decided to confess all is like a kettle that has been brought to the boil. He's either got to let off steam or explode. And he couldn't let off steam. His father wouldn't let him. And Aunt Bea wouldn't let him, and now May was going to stop him. He cried urgently, "Father, *I'm* responsible for your accident. I've condemned you to this servitude. I, and *no* one else."

"Eh? What's that Jocelyn? Look, just ring up the garage and make an appointment for that MOT test. We don't want any slip-ups there."

Jocelyn, pained by this loose grammatical construction, baffled and frustrated by everyone's refusal to let him make his carefully prepared confession, decided he might as well go. "I'll ring upstairs," he said. But in the doorway he remembered something. "Father, did you say Henry's Uncle *Arnold?*

"That's right, dear boy."

"Thanks," said Jocelyn.

John Pentecost sighed. He looked at Bea, who was cheerfully vandalising the precious *Times*. He had been about to say, "Leave that damn paper alone, woman. You're not laying a fire with it." Instead he said, with great concern, "Bea, my dear, I don't like to think of your house being neglected like this. After all, we're getting into autumn. Don't you think you ought to put your own interest first for once, and go home?"

Aunt Bea took off her spectacles and gave her brother a long, level look. "John, this is the first time in seventy years I've known you to give a thought to anyone but yourself. What are you up to?"

John was shocked: deeply shocked and even more deeply hurt. "Up to? My dear Bea, I am thinking entirely of your well-being. You can't leave a house empty for long at this time of the year. Frost, snow, squatters – "

Most women would have blanched at this catalogue. Aunt Bea said, "I'd like to see any squatters still in the house after I've been back five minutes." She continued to stare at her brother. "No, John, as long as my younger brother needs my help, I shall not be found wanting, I do assure you." And she put an end to the conversation by chucking the ravaged newspaper on the floor and making a bee line for the kitchen. "Now, May, what can I do to help?"

"Nothing, thank you, Aunt. Everything's under control."

"Well, it will be even more under control if you let me help you. Come on. Give me an apron."

Oh who will free me from this turbulent aunt? thought May wistfully, then felt terribly unkind.

Great Aunt Bea was a good woman, an enormously good-natured woman. Women like her were the backbone of England. Her only faults were that she filled the house and got on everyone's nerves and knew everything. May told herself she ought to be jolly thankful to have her father-in-law off her hands.

But despite these charitable sentiments she was still edgy. Gaylord, barging in, sensed the atmosphere and tried immediately to barge out again. He was too late. "Here's my little pickle," cried Aunt Bea.

Gaylord unleashed a witty riposte that he had been stifling for days. "Chutney," he said rudely.

"Gaylord! What did you say?" cried Momma.

"I only said chutney, Momma. Aunt Bea said pickle, so I said chutney."

May was suddenly very angry: not so much because Gaylord had been rude: rather because she sympathised with him for wanting to be rude, didn't blame him for saying chutney, yet she knew she had to chastise him. She looked at Great Aunt Bea to see her reaction.

Aunt Bea, to her surprise, was looking helpless: presumably, May thought, for the first time in her life. She said to May, "Can I have a word with you, my dear?"

"Of course," said May. "Gaylord go up to your room."

"I only said – it can't be a swear word, Momma, really. Poppa says it."

"Go," said May. Gaylord went.

Bea said, "I'm sorry, May. I'm such a fool. How I must have irritated him to get that reaction. And he's such a grand lad."

May said, "I will not have rudeness."

Bea said, "Don't punish him. If you want to reproach anyone, reproach me." She looked at May almost piteously. "May, am I insufferable? John thinks I am."

May was silent. What could she say? "You're a very fine woman, Aunt. But you fill any room you happen to be in?" "To Gaylord you have the attributes of a playful grizzly?" "You are an intrusion on the serious business of childhood?" That was good, she thought. But she daren't damn well say it. She said, "No, you're not insufferable, Aunt. It's just – "

"Just what, my dear? Don't be afraid of hurting me. I've already hurt myself too much for that to be important."

May said, "Thank you for being so understanding, Aunt. It's just that – you have a very strong personality. Stronger than I think you realise. I think that if I were as little as Gaylord it would overwhelm me."

The room was suddenly filled with Aunt Bea's laughter. "Poor little scrap. I see your point. I was rather good at quelling colonels in my time. Now you're not to punish him, May."

"He's got to apologise," said May stoutly.

"No."

"Yes, Aunt." She went to the foot of the stairs. "Gaylord!"

Gaylord came down. You could have lodged a coin on his lower lip, warmed your hands against his burning cheeks.

May said, "You hurt your Great Aunt Bea. And she doesn't

deserve to be hurt. What are you going to do about it?"

Gaylord stared at the carpet. He shuffled his feet.

Aunt Bea stood as still and silent as a rock.

Gaylord, muttering at the floor, said, "I'm sorry if I hurt Aunt Bea. But I don't see why it hurts her if I call her chutney when it's not supposed to hurt me when she calls me pickle?"

May said, "But pickle's only a term of endearment, darling."

"So's chutney," said Gaylord.

"Not the way you said it," said May.

Bea said, "If I promise never to call you pickle again, will you promise never to call me chutney?"

"'Course," said Gaylord. He wondered whether he might get away with adding a rider about kissing, but decided it wasn't likely. Aunt Bea said, "Well, that's a storm in a teacup settled."

"Thank goodness," said May. Say what you like about Aunt Bea, she thought. She's a sensible woman. There are times when I quite like her. She felt almost euphoric. She glanced at the clock. "Bed, Gaylord."

Gaylord was outraged. "Momma! That clock's fast."

Bea said, "Give him another ten minutes tonight, May. Just to please me."

The two women smiled at each other. "Very well," said May.

"Whoopee," cried Gaylord. "Can I go and play outside, Momma?"

"I'm afraid not, dear. It's nearly dark."

"That reminds me," said Bea. "Who was last in the loo?"

"I don't know," said May. "Why?"

"Whoever it was has left the light on."

May said, "Jocelyn, probably. He always leaves lights on.

After all, he pays the bills."

"Well, if he likes burning money. But it's the principle. When I see those great power station chimneys belching out smoke, and think it's all to light up an empty loo in the Cypresses Farm."

May said coldly, "You exaggerate, Aunt."

"It's steam," said Gaylord.

"What?"

"It's steam. Not smoke. And they're cooling towers, not chimneys."

May said, "I don't care if they're gigantic tea urns." She was almost in tears.

Suddenly she wanted to switch on every light in the house, to cry, "You leave my husband alone. He writes books, he creates, I don't expect him to waste his precious time clipping pennies off the electricity bill." She didn't say it. She thought, Oh Lord, what's happening to you? Had you got into such a rut that the addition of one elderly aunt has made you neurotic? Pull yourself together, woman.

Great Aunt Bea was watching her closely. At last she spoke. "Gaylord, you've got eight minutes left. Care for a quick game of chess?"

"Oh yes, please," cried Gaylord. They played three hard-fought games in eight minutes and Gaylord won them all. He went to bed well-satisfied.

He began to have the feeling that Aunt Bea was not quite the ogre he had imagined. After all, he really had been a bit scared when he actually heard the word chutney leaving his lips.

Yet he'd got away with it. And anyone who could lose three games of chess in eight minutes couldn't really be quite as indomitable as she appeared, could she? It was with renewed hope that, having said his prayers, he curled up and gave his mind over to the pros and cons of disposing of Great Aunt Bea.

Chapter 7

Jocelyn, still yearning for confession (and, dare he hope, absolution?) came downstairs.

May and Bea were in the kitchen. That meant his father must be alone in the drawing room. He'd give it another try.

He went in. "Hello, Father," he said. "I've arranged the MOT."

"Thank you, my boy."

Jocelyn went on hurriedly, "Father, I want you to understand it was all my fault – "

"That's all right, my boy. Bit dilatory, but you got there in the end. They will fetch the car, won't they?"

"Yes. Tomorrow. But – are you all right?" He looked at his father in alarm. The voice had been shaky and tearful. And now he was distressed to see an actual tear running down the old cheek.

This was awful. What could have brought about so alarming a change? One of Jocelyn's greatest fears was that his father would give way to melancholy and abandon the struggle. In which case he, Jocelyn, would be helpless indeed. He was not by nature a cheerer-upper. He needed too much reassurance himself.

He said, "Father, you're not getting despondent, are you?"

The voice was a shade stronger. "Despondent? Who? Me? Don't be daft, Jocelyn."

That was encouraging, so far as it went. But there were still tears in those eyes. Jocelyn said, "I know it's slow, Father. Uphill all the way. But – "

"What the devil are you talking about, man?"

"This business of learning to walk again. And, Father, while we're on that subject, I do want you to know it was my fault – "

The old man cut in irritably. "But we're not on that subject, dammit."

"Aren't we? Jocelyn was looking bewildered. "But – you were upset. I naturally thought – "

"Well, don't naturally think. It's this damn book. Best thing I've read for years. Most moving. There's this girl, Mariana. Terribly tragic figure." He blew his nose loudly.

For the first time Jocelyn noticed the manuscript. "You mean – you like it?" he cried.

"Like it? Told you. Best thing since *Gone with the Wind*."

"But – it's impossible, Father."

His father was threshing about on his chair, always a bad sign. An alarming one too, since he was balanced precariously on a dining chair, thanks to Aunt Bea's edict about lumbago. "Impossible? Good Lord, when you think of some of the muck that gets published nowadays. That girl's going to be a millionaire with a little help from you. So stop being dog-in-the-manger about it." He glared. "Don't like professional jealousy."

"It is not professional jealousy. It's just – I'm sorry to say this, Father – it's just a very bad book."

"Skipped through it, I think you said," said John nastily.

Jocelyn said, "The first paragraph is sometimes enough."

"So," said John. "I've read three chapters. You've read one paragraph. Yet you're prepared to make a critical judgement that could rob the world of a masterpiece." He sat and simmered.

Jocelyn said, "I didn't e say I'd only read one paragraph." But it was no good. Argument got him nowhere. The only thing was to leave it and hope his father would forget about the whole thing. He said, "Actually, Father, I had come to speak to you about a quite different matter. Something rather dreadful. Your accident – "

"Oh, yes. Your theory about some fool digging holes. Would anyone do something so daft, Jocelyn?"

"I'm afraid they would, Father. In fact – "

"Then they should be prosecuted. It's my land. Have a word with Constable Harris, dear boy."

Jocelyn said, "I'm afraid that's no good, Father. You see – "

He had said the wrong thing. "Right. If that's how you feel. I'll speak to him myself. And now – if you'll excuse me. This girl Mariana's just said goodbye to her childhood sweetheart." He gathered up his book. "No, Father," cried Jocelyn. "You must listen to me."

Slowly, the book was closed. The old man glared. "Well?" The door opened. Dr Pemberton came in. "Oh, damn," said Jocelyn, and departed.

John Pentecost and Edward Pemberton were two of a kind. John said, "You're not prodding me about, Edward. Only one thing I want from you."

"What's that?"

"Permission to drive my car."

"I don't turn people who have blackouts loose on our roads, John."

"I didn't have a blackout, dammit. Ask Jocelyn."

"What's he know about it?"

"Everything. Apparently some clown dug a hole in Polly Larkin's Pad and I fell into it and knocked myself out."

PIG IN THE MIDDLE

"Prove it."

"How can I prove it?" His voice was becoming softer. "Look, Edward, I'm a model patient. You know me. I wouldn't – "

"I know every tablet I've ever given you has gone straight down the loo. I know you drink too much whisky – "

"Now talking of whisky," said John, " what about a dram, my dear fellow?"

"I'll pour," said Dr Pemberton. "And you're not having more than a finger."

"As if I ever do," said John. "Now then. Have quick look at my ankles and my liver and my lights. And tell me I'm fit to drive."

Time passed. At last Dr Pemberton snapped his case shut. "I wouldn't trust you with an ox-cart," he said.

"Give me a good reason."

"I could give you half a dozen. But one's enough. Too much strain on your ankles. Give 'em another three months." In the doorway he turned. "Sorry John. I know what it means to you. But we've got to be sensible."

"Sensible! You were always an old woman, Edward. But – thanks for coming, all the same."

May was asleep when Jocelyn finally came to bed. He undressed quietly, slid into bed beside her. She didn't wake. He had something to tell her; something of which he was rather proud. He, Jocelyn, had shown initiative. He felt ready for a little quiet boasting.

But it would have to wait till morning. And he was tired. Goodness, he was tired. Life nowadays had taken on so many strains. He found he needed his eight hours a night.

But May stirred. "Where've you been?"

Well, he wasn't going to spoil his story just because he was sleepy. He began at the beginning. He said, "I went and got some poison from Henry's Uncle Arnold. And I've spread it all over the outside loo." He couldn't resist adding, "So I think you can sleep soundly now, darling. I don't think you'll see another rat."

"Mm. Oh Jocelyn, thank you. The thought of those rats was making me feel quite ill." Her voice trailed off into sleep.

For a few moments Jocelyn lay in bed and basked in his wife's approval. Then thoughts and images began to blur and mingle. He switched off his bedside light. Sleep wrapped him like a mother's arms...

The night passed. The stars wheeled, the earth turned towards the sun, the cock crew.

Something rattled against Gaylord's bedroom window.

Silence.

It came again.

Gaylord (together with his unfailing imagination) was immediately awake, assessing the situation. It was light, but not very. Something (hail, small-shot, gravel?) was rattling against his window. It was a secret, furtive sound. And if there was one thing Gaylord loved more than another it was sounds that were both secret and furtive. He strained his ears for the longed-for sound of someone down below saying, "Psst!"

And that is exactly what he did hear!

It was not an easy word to say. But Henry Bartlett, sounding like a punctured bicycle tyre, didn't do badly. "Henry," cried Gaylord, leaning dangerously out of the window. "What's the matter?"

It was dawn. The sun, casting loose from the horizon, illuminated a spruce world. In particular, it lit the smooth, pink cleanness of Henry Bartlett's face, and struck fire from his round spectacles.

Henry swallowed. He had prepared his announcement to produce maximum dramatic impact. And now he was about to drop his bombshell.

He swallowed again, "Gaylord. You know your dad?"

"Yes?" said Gaylord eagerly.

"Well – " Long pause for effect. "I reckon he's going to poison your Auntie." Another pause. "If he hasn't already, that is."

Eager though Gaylord was to hear more, he would not hurry this delicious moment. "What makes you think that, Henry?"

"He's asked me Uncle Arnold for some of his stuff," Henry said with unconcealed relish.

Gaylord was shaken. He'd never seen Poppa in quite that light. But he knew Poppa didn't enjoy Aunt Bea's presence. He said, "You'd better come in, Henry. If I knotted my sheets together do you think you could climb up?"

"I'd rather come in through the front door, if you don't mind, Gaylord."

"'Course," said Gaylord, feeling vaguely that perhaps his friend lacked style. With exaggerated stealth he crept downstairs and let Henry in. They went into the kitchen.

"I reckon we ought to warn your Auntie," said Henry anxiously.

"If it's not too late," said Gaylord lugubriously. He was worried. He didn't trust Poppa not to make some silly mistake, like leaving his fingerprints on the 5 ml spoon. And he didn't want Poppa going to prison. It would be worse than having Grandpa in hospital. Strange. It had all looked so easy when he'd thought of doing it himself. But he felt so responsible for Poppa. He sighed. Poppa seemed to need protecting from himself, somehow.

"That's it," Henry said suddenly.

A small cardboard box stood in the middle of the kitchen table. It was half full of white powder. "I wonder if he's used it yet," said Henry.

There seemed no way of telling, short of finding out whether Aunt Bea was still breathing. Gaylord said, "You'd better take it back to your Uncle Arnold." No point in leaving incriminating evidence on the kitchen table.

"Yes," said Henry. He crammed the box into his trouser pocket. He departed as silently as he came. "Be exciting if he has given her some," he whispered.

"Yes," said Gaylord doubtfully. But much as he loved drama he wasn't happy. He had a feeling it might be a bit *too* exciting.

Suddenly Jocelyn was wide awake. It was daylight and the clock was striking seven. And May was perched up in bed like the sheeted dead on Resurrection Morn. "Messalina," she was crying.

"What – ?"

"Messalina! Where did you leave the empty carton?"

The short, honest answer was "on the kitchen table. But it was not an empty carton. It's still half full."

But short, honest answers are not in great supply. Jocelyn said, "Er – Oh, Lord, I'd forgotten that blasted cat."

May didn't waste words. "Come on," she said. They leapt out of bed, ran downstairs to the kitchen.

May's eyes focused on one point: Messalina's basket. It was empty. Jocelyn's eyes focused on the kitchen table. That too was empty. Jocelyn licked his dry lips. "The poison's gone." But it was only a stricken whisper. He needed to do some desperate thinking before he passed this information on to his wife.

May said, "We've got find the cat, make sure she's all right. She must be in the house somewhere. She's never allowed out."

They went into the drawing room. "Messalina," they called in seductive whispers. "Nice Pussykins." And, less seductively, "Messy, you little beast. Where are you?"

No Messalina. Jocelyn said anxiously, "They creep away into a dark corner to die, don't they?" "Yes," said May unfeelingly. Jocelyn began to creep about in dark corners.

They tried the hall. No Messalina. Jocelyn, in his dark corners, was wondering desperately how to tell his wife the dire fact that he'd left the poison on the kitchen table, and the even more dire fact that it wasn't there anymore. Until he had decided that he could only string along with the Messalina hunt. "She must all right," he muttered.

May said, "But we've got to prove it. I couldn't face Aunt Bea otherwise."

They went into Aunt Bea's room. Darkness, silence.

"Aunt Bea," said May quietly. And switched on the light.

"Hello, my dears," said Aunt Bea, smiling.

Then: "Gaylord," cried Momma. "Gaylord," cried Poppa. "Gaylord," cried Aunt Bea.

The light had revealed a distinctly uncomfortable Gaylord standing beside Aunt Bea's bed. "What are you up to?" demanded May.

"I only wanted to see if Great Aunt Bea was still alive," said Gaylord.

"Had you any reason for thinking I might not be, child?" asked Aunt Bea, enjoying herself. "And come to that," she added, "to what do I attribute this early morning visit from your parents?"

May said, "We were looking for Messalina, Aunt. Gaylord,

what are you talking about?"

Gaylord said, "I thought Poppa might have poisoned her."

"Can you really imagine your father poisoning an animal, child?" May asked angrily.

"No, Momma. Poisoning Great Aunt Bea."

Aunt Bea guffawed. May said, "Aunt, I really do apologise. He gets the oddest ideas."

"Oh, I don't call that an odd idea at all. Lots of people would like to see me out of the way."

Jocelyn said, "Honestly, I can't think what – "

Gaylord said, "Henry Bartlett said Poppa had borrowed some of his Uncle Arnold's stuff. He says it kills everything: people, cockroaches, wireworms – "

"And Great Aunts," said Bea, still enjoying herself hugely. "Jocelyn, I'm surprised at you. I really am."

Jocelyn could bear the strain no longer. He said, "Seriously, Aunt, there's no sign of Messalina anywhere and – as a matter of fact I did put some poison down, but only in the outhouses, and – "

"Right. We'll have a look later," said Aunt Bea calmly. "And now perhaps you will allow me to rise," she said, beaming all round. They departed, hurriedly. Bea reached down into the bed, pulled out a tousled and sleepy Messalina, held her up facing her. "Still breathing, old girl?" she said. "More than you deserve, then. You know Auntie May doesn't like you sleeping under the bedclothes." She shoved the cat out on to the landing.

Five minutes later Jocelyn pulled a live Messalina out of a dark corner. One of his worries was over. But what on earth had happened to the guilty secret he had not yet shared with anyone: the box of poison?

Gaylord was surprised when Poppa followed him into his

room. (Momma, yes, for periodic checks on the back of his neck and behind his ears. Though why anyone, even Momma, should be so anxious about those particular areas…? No one could see them when he was dressed, anyway. But Poppa?)

And Poppa was behaving very strangely, even for Poppa. Going and staring out of the window, hands in pockets. Coughing nervously. Calling him 'old man.' "Gaylord, old man" (and Gaylord was immediately on the alert). Another anxious cough. "Gaylord, old man. You haven't moved a little cardboard box I left on the kitchen table, have you?"

"No, Poppa." Well, he hadn't had he? Henry had. No point in getting implicated, even with Poppa.

"I just thought," said Poppa miserably, "you might have – moved it." He added, with a faint ray of hope, "Perhaps you remember seeing it?"

Gaylord racked his brains. "Sorry Poppa," he said after a thorough examination of his memory, his conscience, and his own self-interest (rule no. 1: other things being equal, deny everything).

"Thanks, old man," Jocelyn said. He went to have his bath, something he usually enjoyed. But not today. He was, he realised, on a course of action that would be very unpleasant indeed.

Before breakfast he did a surreptitious search of the house. To no avail. Where could that wretched box be? Oh, what a fool he'd been to leave it lying about. Probably enough there to wipe out the entire population of Derbyshire!

He went into breakfast. Everyone was already there. His father was filling the interval between finishing his porridge and starting his eggs, bacon and sausage by reading the headlines. "Sorry to be last," said Jocelyn. "You usually are," said his father, lowering his paper and glowering.

Oh Lord, thought Jocelyn. That's a good start. I was hoping he might be in a good mood. "I'll just have toast and marmalade, thank you, May," he said. And even that'll choke me, he thought.

"You couldn't have told me earlier, I suppose?" said May.

"Oh, never expect a man to look ahead," said Aunt Bea. "Then you won't be disappointed." She grinned cheerfully at Jocelyn.

Jocelyn swallowed and took the plunge. "I'm afraid something rather serious has happened," he said.

May looked at him in alarm. His father lowered his paper again. This time his glower was mixed with interest.

Jocelyn braced himself. "Last night," he said, "I put down some poison in the outhouses. But – I'm afraid I left the half-empty box on the kitchen table when I went to bed. Very remiss of me, of course."

"Very," said John drily.

"Oh, Jocelyn," said May, with deep reproach.

He gave her a beseeching look, and plodded on. "The awful thing is, that this morning the poison has disappeared. I've searched everywhere."

May flung down her napkin. "Why on earth didn't you ask me to look? You know you can never find things."

"Why, do you know where it might be?" he asked with a glimmer of hope.

"Of course I don't. If I did it wouldn't be there. I just mean you can never find a thing unless it jumps out and bites you." She gave him a friendly, but exasperated, smile.

"Poison," said John. "And you leave it on the kitchen table!"

Jocelyn said, "I'm sure it was there. But this morning, gone. Clean as a whistle."

Suddenly everyone was looking at Gaylord. He wondered

116

why. "Why are whistle's clean?" he asked, partly because he wanted to know and partly because he felt a change of subject might be desirable.

"I've always wondered that myself," said Jocelyn. "I feel clear as a whistle might be more apposite."

May said coldly, "What do you know about this, Gaylord?"

"Me, Momma?" Surprise, hurt, disbelief.

"Yes. You!"

Gaylord needed time to think. And there wasn't time. With a puzzled brow he asked, "What is it Poppa's lost?"

"Only a few ounces of poison," said his grandfather bitterly. "Nothing to worry about."

"Oh, good," said Gaylord.

Momma went on looking at him in a nasty, suspicious way. But it was Poppa Gaylord was feeling sorry for. Everyone seemed to be getting on to him. He said stoutly, "I don't see why you all think its Poppa's fault." Suddenly, his brow cleared. "Poppa! I've just remembered something. Henry Bartlett put something in his pocket in the kitchen. I bet it was the poison."

"When was this?" snapped May.

Here we go, thought Gaylord. Do you wonder he never told Momma anything he needn't. "About five," he said.

"This morning?"

"Yes."

"And what was Henry Bartlett doing in my kitchen at five o'clock this morning?"

The interrogation lasted all through breakfast and washing up. And long before it was over Jocelyn had escaped and had rushed off to see Henry Bartlett's Uncle Arnold.

Henry's Uncle Arnold had taken one look at Jocelyn and said, "Lord, Mr Pentecost. You shouldn't rush about like that.

Do yourself an injury."

"That poison," panted Jocelyn. "Did Henry give it back to you?"

"'Course, he did, Mr Pentecost. Anyway, no need to get steamed up like that! Worse for you than the poison would be."

"Really?"

"Really. Doesn't do rats much good. But it don't hurt humans."

"Oh, thank God for that," breathed Jocelyn. He hurried off.

Arnold watched him go. He sighed. "Don't take much to put *his* mind at rest," he muttered scornfully. "Thank the Lord he didn't try eating the stuff."

So Jocelyn breathed a great sigh of relief. And Gaylord was overjoyed, surprised and amply rewarded when, later in the day, his father ruffled his hair fondly and slipped him a half-pound bag of Nuttall's Mintoes.

Chapter 8

So, as the summer waned, John Pentecost faced the slow climb back to mobility.

A wearisome and difficult climb: the way littered with disappointments and little successes and the rages of frustration: across the drawing-room on a walking frame, the length of the hall on elbow crutches; every such effort, for a proud man like him, a humiliation and a degradation. He loathed every moment of it, it put him in the vilest of tempers. But by God he did it. Nothing was going to stop him walking again, neither angels not devils, neither pain nor weariness, neither grating bones or rebellious muscles or aching limbs. Nothing. He slogged away from morning till night, cursing, swearing, bellowing.

Nobody understood, of course. They nearly drove him mad. "Now be careful, Father-in-law." "John, you've been far enough. You'll tire yourself out." "Father, what on earth are you doing on those stairs?" ("What the hell do you think I'm doing? Climbing up them, of course. If I were falling down 'em I'd let you know.")

He was impossible. He flatly refused to be seen outside the house in a wheelchair. ("I'm not a blasted invalid.") But he got there in the end. And one late autumn morning was so unbelievably lovely, so beckoning, that the old man saw in his mind's eye the river, trailing scarves of mist, dancing with delight in the sun. He saw the coloured cattle, strewn over the higgledy-piggledy English fields. He saw the deep, immensely satisfying blue of the heavens. He knew a craving, sweeter, more urgent than the cravings of youth; for youth has eternity to play with, which old men have not. True, he might have many more days. But how many days would have the glory of this one. He must see that river, before the clouds come marching up from the west to quench the sun.

He felt strong again, purposeful. He barged himself and his wheelchair into his room, struggled into his shoes, stood up, grasped his walking stick. Moving slowly but firmly he went into the kitchen.

Gaylord was sitting at the table, totally absorbed in drawing a Monster. The Monster was so horrible that even Gaylord was beginning to feel pleasantly scared by it.

May was drying the breakfast dishes. Her face lit up. "Father-in-law, you are walking well. Oh, this is lovely."

Great Aunt Bea was bending over the sink, washing up. Now she spun round. "John!" she ran across the kitchen and grabbed his free arm. "You mustn't take these risks. It's not fair to any of us. You know who'll have to pick you up and dust you down if you fall."

"I'm not going to fall, woman." He was enjoying himself. He was beginning to feel his own man again. Dormant muscles had been bullied back into life, the good red blood was once more coursing through veins and arteries, carrying life to the sturdy limbs. "I'm going out," he said.

May said, "Just let me get rid of this apron, Father-in-law, and I'll be with you."

"Thank you, May," he said courteously. "But I don't want you. I have to be alone."

With an author for a husband May could accept that. But she was uneasy. If he did fall again it would be ghastly. On the other hand, if you stopped a patient taking any risks he would never recover. She said, "Very well, Father-in-law. But you will be careful?"

Aunt Bea was made of sterner stuff. "John, if you take one step outside that door, I go with you, whether you want me or not."

"No, you don't," said John.

"Yes, I do. Good Lord, he was just the same in the nursery, May. Wilful, obstinate, determined to get his own way."

"If I hadn't been, you'd have made my life a misery even more than you did."

Bea had spreadeagled herself against the back door. "John, if you go out there on your own, I leave."

John had been moving steadily towards the door. At these words he checked so suddenly that he nearly fell. He stared at his sister in disbelief. "Do you mean that?"

"I most certainly do."

"Right." He moved on towards the door. He held on to the sink while he brandished his stick. "Stand aside, woman."

Bea stared at him hard and angrily. Then: "Very well," she said. "I'll go and pack." She groped behind her for the door knob, pulled the door open. "Goodbye, John." Then, more softly, "You really are being extremely foolish, you know."

May was silent. If Bea left and the old man came back from his walk on a hurdle, she was going to have her hands full. But who was she to try to interfere in this battle of giants?

John said, "Don't think I don't appreciate you coming, Bea. Good of you, very. Just a pity you're so bloody impossible." And he went carefully down the steps, pulling the door to behind him.

May looked at Great Aunt Bea questioningly. Bea said, "I always mean what I say, May."

"I know you do, Aunt. But – in this case – I wish you'd give him another chance. Don't go, Aunt."

Bea looked at her searchingly. "You mean that?"

The slightest of pauses. Then, "Yes," said May.

Gaylord couldn't believe his ears. At the words, "I leave," he had totally abandoned his Monster and had sat, staring at the adults, drinking in every word, and hugging himself. This was it, the moment he had longed and, yes, prayed for.

He had continued to hug himself until Grandpa had closed the door behind him. But it was then he stopped both hugging himself and believing his ears. His own mother, instead of seizing this glorious opportunity with both hands and rushing upstairs to help Aunt Bea pack, his own mother had begged Aunt Bea to stay; and, what was worse, appeared to have succeeded!

Had succeeded, in fact. For Aunt Bea threw her arms round May and said, "Then I'll stay. Oh, May, you are a brick."

He said reproachfully, "Momma, I don't think you ought to persuade Aunt Bea to stay if she doesn't want to."

May said lightly, "Oh, I shouldn't persuade Aunt Bea if she didn't want to be persuaded. Should I, Aunt?"

The two ladies smiled at each other and began discussing supper. Women! thought Gaylord disgustedly.

John Pentecost sniffed the air like a horse released from his stable. He would have liked to run wild, kick up his heels in rejoicing. Well, that would never be again. But he was free. And alone. And he knew that only if he were alone would the sweetness of the countryside seep into him. Only if he went alone would he become one with the aura of this sunlit day. He wanted to run to embrace it, as a woman runs to meet her lover. But he would be content with hobbling like a shackled prisoner.

It wasn't easy. Cobbles here in the stockyard, and sticky patches of mud and wrinkled asphalt. But he soldiered on. And his friend the sun was touching his cheek, and the old remembered things were giving him their quiet welcome. He paused, took a deep breath. "I might have been a gonner," he muttered. "Thought I was, several times. But I'm not – yet. I'm back. Don't know how long for; but I'm back. And it's even lovelier than I remembered it."

Ahead of him was the shade of Polly Larkin's Pad. And at the other end of that lay all the glory of the sunlight, all the extravagant welcome of an autumn day.

He could smell the river now: the ancient, uncompromising smell of dankness and decay; yet a smell that for him had always heralded quiet delights.

But now, he came to where someone, as Jocelyn said, had been digging in the narrow lane. There was quite a trench across the path. He was incensed. How many years had he been traversing this quiet way? Twenty, thirty? But it was only now, in this graceless age, that anyone would have dared to interfere with this ancient byway.

Still, he'd come so far. It would take a more formidable obstacle than this to stop him reaching his goal. He came nearer the trench to plan his crossing, peered down.

And saw, strangely, a scatter of willow branches.

And suddenly everything snapped into place: his memory of walking home in the dusk, of falling; the sudden blotting out of consciousness. He saw it all. So here must have been the start of his long travail, all those lost and wasted summer days ago!

And some – some unspeakable oaf, some loutish vandal had caused all his suffering. "Hell and damnation," growled John Pentecost. He'd find the fellow somehow. And when he did –

But the fellow wasn't going to spoil today's pleasure for him, anyway. This trifling obstacle wouldn't stop him. One stride and he'd be over.

But he wasn't. He soon realised that if he tired to cross in his present condition this hated trench might land him in hospital a second time.

The box hedges and the elders crowded him in on either side. The trench lay at his feet like a mantrap. At the end of this tunnel of vegetation was a sunlit vignette of grass and trees and sparkling river, just as he had imagined it. And he was forbidden it by the action of some mindless oaf. In a fury he turned and stumped off home. Good God! An elderly gentleman who had little left to him in life now had his last innocent pastime taken from him by a generation that had nothing better to do than dig up other people's land.

But that walk home was a nightmare. His damned legs wouldn't go where he wanted them to. However firmly he gripped his stick it waved about like a reed in the wind. His limbs, his head seemed to belong to someone else. Being a man who had seldom felt ill in his life, he took it for granted he was on the point of death.

No. He was not a man to give up. But when he came to Reuben Briggs' smallholding he knew he had no choice. Reuben would help – give him a cup of tea while he recovered, or run him home in his banger. Reuben was an oddity. (Who wouldn't be, living alone and addling his brain with all those books?) But he was a good neighbour. John struggled with the latch on the wicket gate, staggered up the garden path, oblivious of the chrysanths and kidney beans and roses and cauliflowers.

And now the cottage door was in front of him. He lunged at the knocker, caught it, and hammered. "Oh God, let him be in," he was praying.

His prayer was answered. He heard footsteps shuffling along the stone flags inside. He heard the drawing of bolts, the grinding turn of the great key. The door opened. Reuben, still in cloth cap and wellies, stared at him.

John gasped, "Reuben, I'm all in. Would you – ring my son, ask him to come and pick me up. I – hate to trouble you, but – "

Reuben stared at him in silence. Then he said, "Mr Pentecost, he that begetteth a fool doeth it to his sorrow; and the father of a fool hath no joy. Good day to you, Mr Pentecost." And he shut the door in John's face.

John's knees were buckling. He wasted no time knocking again at the door, still less on wondering at Reuben's behaviour. He staggered back down the wild garden, lurched through the gate, and somehow got himself home.

He wrestled with the back door, elbowed it savagely to one side, ignored May's and Bea's anxious questionings, barged into his room, fell into a chair. But the room was heaving like a ship. This, he supposed, was Death. And, suddenly, dying appeared a very lonely business. Even the presence of Bea would be better than nothing. He dragged himself out of his chair, and stumped into the kitchen.

Bea took one glance at the drained face and said, "John, you're a fool."

She got a sour look. "I thought you were packing."

"I'm not leaving May saddled with an old man who's no more sense than a child. Now you'd better go and lie down and I'll bring you a warm drink."

"I'm damned if I'll lie down." He pushed aside thoughts of soft sheets embracing weak limbs, of pillows cosseting a head that had somehow lost control of his body.

May said, "Aunt Bea's right, Father-in-law. You look

awful."

The world gave a lurch. It could, thought John, have been a small earthquake. He looked at the others anxiously. No one else seemed to have noticed it, he was disappointed to see. He said, "I shall now go to my room for a bit of peace and quiet. Perhaps there I shall not be incessantly badgered."

"How strange to hear you make a sensible suggestion, John," said Aunt Bea. She got another sour look. With great concentration he went to his room. He was about to sit in his chair when he looked at his bed.

Even his strong will couldn't fight the lure of that bed. He partly undressed, slid between the sheets.

It was one of the most wonderful sensations of his life. The sheets embraced him like a summer pool. The pillows gently cushioned his head until the world regained its equilibrium. He floated into sleep like a battered and rudderless ship drifting into harbour.

When he awoke the light had changed. It was no longer bright day. His room had filled with shadows. Gingerly he lifted his head – and his world was steady! Yet to lie here, in the gloaming, and the hush of evening, lapped in comfort in a settled world once more, was very heaven. He hoped they wouldn't disturb him just yet. He needed to calm his mind on the matter of this outrageous attack on his person, and on Reuben's extraordinary unneighbourliness.

But he couldn't calm his mind, dammit. He sighed, switched on his bedside light and tried to immerse himself in the nurse's manuscript. Even that compelling work, however, failed to banish thoughts of human wickedness. In the end he was quite relieved when a hesitant knock came on the door and Jocelyn entered. "Hello, Father. May and Aunt Bea sent me in to make sure you were all right.

Apparently you've been asleep for ages."

"Nonsense. I've been reading this splendid book. Anyway, leave that. Something – I hardly know how to tell you. I'm so angry – how does apoplexy make you feel?"

"I don't know, Father. Physically stricken, I imagine. Why? You're not feeling – like that, are you?"

"I don't know how I'm feeling. Murderous, I know that. God, there are some fools about."

"Father, I think I'd better call Dr Pemberton."

"Too late, I imagine." A sudden, devastating glare. "Well, don't you want to know what's happened?

"Yes. Of course. But there's no harm in calling – "

"I went for a walk. First bloody walk for months. Going to look at the river." He stared up at Jocelyn pathetically. "Now you'd think a man who'd spent weeks in hospital, and who hadn't much left to live for anyway, might be allowed to walk by the river."

Jocelyn's mouth was very dry. Yet he'd filled the hole in? Oh Lord, he thought, I suppose I didn't do the job properly. Typical! The moment of truth was upon him. He said, "I think I know what you're going to say, Father."

"Don't be a damn fool. How could you? No. I found that some – some mindless oaf really had been amusing himself digging up Polly Larkin's Pad." He paused to let this enormity sink in.

"I – " began Jocelyn.

"But that's not all," said his father. "This same feeble-minded lout has destroyed what should have been for me an unclouded Indian Summer. Because, Jocelyn – " he took a deep breath to give his next words the maximum of emphasis, "it must have been that trench that brought me down and put an end to my summer days."

Jocelyn said, "Look, Father, I know you can't believe it

now, but there will be other summer days. You're making excellent progress even if it is slow." But his lips were still dry. He knew he ought to have given priority to confessing that *he* was the mindless oaf.

Mindless oaf. Unspeakable lout. They were hard words. Yet deserved, surely. Jocelyn said miserably, "I could have told you who the mindless oaf was, Father."

"You could? Then why in hell's name didn't you?"

"It was me," said Jocelyn, a little troubled even in this crisis that he had not said, "It was I."

The silence seemed to stretch into eternity. Then: "It was – *what?*"

"Me." It came out in a dry whisper.

The old man propped himself up on an elbow, the better to stare at his son. "You?"

"Gaylord dug a tiger trap. But you wouldn't have fallen into it if I hadn't camouflaged it with willow branches."

Another devastating silence. Then, gropingly, "A – tiger trap, did you say?"

"Yes. I know it sounds silly. But – "

"A tiger trap? In the Midlands?"

Jocelyn sighed. "I'm afraid so."

John said, "Tell me it isn't true. My son and grandson, building a trap for tigers in the Trent Valley?"

Jocelyn said, "You can't blame Gaylord, of course. He did it from the highest of motives. But in my case – "

Sadly the old man cut in. "Believe me, Jocelyn. The more trouble that lad causes, the higher his motives." He stared like some visionary at the wall. Then he said, "I can see his obituary now: 'Inadvertently, he started World War 3. But his motives were impeccable.'"

Jocelyn said, "Father! Gaylord's an innocent and highly imaginative child. But I – I feel terribly to blame."

John was silent, looking hard at his son. At last he said helplessly, "I don't know what to say. I just don't know, Jocelyn."

"No," said Jocelyn.

"All those weeks in hospital," said the old man, almost in a whisper.

"Yes," said Jocelyn.

John propped himself on an elbow. "Anyway, there's another thing. Coming back from my walk; felt a bit tired. Called at Reuben's for a little rest." He looked hard at Jocelyn. "Got the door slammed in my face."

Jocelyn stared in amazement. "You? Reuben?"

John nodded. "Yet not long ago he was bringing me eggs in hospital. What have you done to him, Jocelyn?"

"Me? Nothing that I'm aware of. Unless it's something to do with Gaylord leaving a gate open. But – " He began to feel hard done by. "I don't see why you should think it's anything to do with me, Father."

"Something he said about the father of a fool having no joy. Sounded like the Book of Proverbs to me."

Most men would have muttered something dismissive about religious mania. Not Jocelyn. He took things on the chin. He felt physically sick. The discovery that not only his father, but now his neighbour, thought him a fool, was unbearable. He said, "I'll have to see him, find out what he's got against me."

"Aye. If he'll tell you." But now John was beginning to thrash about the bed in an alarming manner. "But never mind that. This other business: kept it pretty quiet, didn't you? Until I was able to do a bit of detective work for myself."

"I tried to tell you, Father, on several occasions."

"But never quite managed it, eh? Did May know about

this?" he suddenly barked.

"Yes." Jocelyn's mouth was very dry. "But her advice was not to tell you. She said it could do no good and might do a lot of harm."

"Did she, by George? And she was quite right. A lot of harm. But I still think it needed saying." He pondered. "Bit surprised at young May, over that."

Jocelyn had been prepared to bow his head to any tirade. He deserved reviling and censure. But he was taken aback to hear the old man criticising Gaylord and May. Especially May. To John Pentecost his daughter-in-law was the rose without a thorn. He was beginning to realise how much his father must have suffered to be in this unforgiving mood; and how bitter it must have been for him to find out that his own loved ones had not only brought about his downfall but had joined in a conspiracy of silence about it. He said (and his voice was thin and tired like an old man's), "Father, this is your house. You must feel we have done you irreparable harm, and also deceived you. You must long to be rid of us. If you want us to go – ?"

Before he could answer May marched in with a tray of tea. She looked at their faces in amazement. "Goodness, what's the matter with you both?"

Jocelyn said, "I'm just offering to go and live somewhere else."

"What do you mean?"

"Father knows now who caused his accident. And he feels we have conspired against him, that we should have told him when we first realised."

John said, "It's out of character, May. I've always looked upon you as such an honest, and honourable, person."

May said, "I thought it was best for all of us." She walked across and put her hand on her husband's shoulder. "However,

Jocelyn was braver (though I still think more foolish) than I and told you."

"Whereas you would have gone on living in my house, in the full knowledge that you all knew something I didn't. And finally you would have buried me and buried with me the nagging fear that I might somehow have found out. And you would have uttered a great sigh of relief that I, and your guilty secret, were off your hands for ever." His voice trembled. He had moved himself very deeply.

May sat down on the bedside chair. "Now listen to me, Father-in-law. First of all Gaylord still knows nothing of this and I want it to stay that way. And whatever you say I still regard myself as an honest and honourable person, and I should like to black your eye for suggesting otherwise. And lastly when we do bury you there'll be no sighs of relief, and no guilty secrets; only a great sadness that we're saying goodbye to a man we loved because he was as prickly as a thorn hedge and as harmless as a babe in arms. Now. What's all this about wanting us to leave?"

John said, "I shall take it very unkindly if Gaylord breaks any more of my ageing bones, whether in tiger traps, man traps or any other barmy traps he may wish to put down. He's a grand lad and I'm very fond of him. But – Good Lord, he could have killed me, May. With the help of his father, of course."

Jocelyn looked at May and realised storm cones were being hoisted. He said urgently, "Father's tired, May. Don't you think we should leave this till we've all slept on it?"

May looked at him fiercely. Then she seemed to deflate with a great sigh. "Perhaps you're right," she said, rising.

They crossed to the door. Jocelyn stared hungrily at his father's face. "Good night, Father," he said.

"Good night, both." The voice was impersonal. John

might have been wishing good night to a couple of strangers, passing in the dark.

Chapter 9

No-one, not even Gaylord, could claim that Henry Bartlett was an unqualified success as a trapeze artist. He was too portly, too out of condition, and too jolly scared.

In fairness to Henry, however, it must be admitted that the trapeze itself did not inspire confidence. One of grandpa's elbow crutches, connected by a rope at each end to the branch of a tree, was not ideal. Perhaps that was why Henry invariably launched himself into space with what seemed to Gaylord a noticeable lack of panache.

Eventually Henry said, "I don't reckon I shall ever do it as well as that Circus lady, Gaylord."

Gaylord was inclined to agree. "Perhaps she's had more practice than you, Henry," he pointed out kindly.

"Yes." They abandoned the trapeze and wandered off towards the house, Gaylord keeping a sharp lookout for Momma. He had a feeling it was nearly bedtime and he didn't want the sight of him to put ideas into her head.

Then he heard Momma's voice coming from an open window. And Grandpa's. Well, it was always important to listen to grown-up conversations. They were almost always of an unbelievable dullness; yet just occasionally something useful turned up.

Today's conversation, however, was interesting from the word go. Momma was threatening to black Grandpa's eye. Then, as if that were not enough, she was talking about burying Grandpa, presumably when he was dead.

Gaylord and Henry crouched under the window, agog. Or rather Gaylord was agog. Henry was uncomfortable. He was less personally involved than Gaylord, and therefore more liable to be influenced by the fact that listening to other people's conversations is not very nice.

Now Grandpa was speaking – and actually talking about them leaving. And a lot of talk about tiger traps and if Gaylord broke any more of his ageing bones he'd take it unkindly and Gaylord might have killed him. What was it all about?

Gaylord's cheeks were burning; his mouth was dry. Grandpa was his friend who strolled with him through the woods and by the river and found birds' nests. Yet now it sounded as though Grandpa thought he, Gaylord, had tried to kill him. It even sounded as though Grandpa thought they all ought to go and live somewhere else because of something Gaylord had done!

He'd heard enough. He was sick at heart. Grandpa had talked about him as though he were some stranger. The two boys continued their walk. "What you reckon, Henry?" asked Gaylord miserably.

Henry, with great acumen, said, "I reckon it wasn't a tiger we caught in your tiger trap, Gaylord."

Gaylord greeted this revolutionary suggestion coldly. "What you reckon it was, then, Henry?"

"I reckon it was your Grandpa," said Henry.

Gaylord was silent. Henry was presenting him with the unthinkable. If his stoutly-held belief that tiger traps caught only tigers could be proved wrong, then – ? He said, "You mean, perhaps Grandpa fell into the tiger trap and – and that's why the ambulance came and took him to hospital and that's why he had to stay there for a bit?"

"I reckon it was more than a bit," said Henry, a true but outspoken friend. "I reckon it was about six weeks."

Gaylord was silent. Henry said, "Broken ankles, too." He pondered. "Me Gran says it's enough to finish him."

Gaylord rather wished his dear friend Henry in Hanover. He wanted to be alone to meditate on his guilt and wickedness. So he was very relieved when Henry suddenly turned into Concorde and took off noisily for home, leaving his friend to consider this position.

And a very nasty position it was. Left alone, Gaylord felt an outcast, friendless and forlorn.

If Henry was right (and Gaylord thought he probably was) then Gaylord had caused Grandpa untold suffering, and Grandpa hated him, and he and Momma and Poppa might have to go and live somewhere else because he had done this dreadful thing, in which case Momma and Poppa would hate him too because they didn't want to go and live anywhere else, and Henry's Gran reckoned broken ankles might finish Grandpa, in which case he, Gaylord, would probably be hanged for murder.

He was alone, utterly alone and comfortless. Gaylord, who normally rode troubles as bouncily as his rubber duck rode the waves in his bath, did not cry easily. But now he cried miserably, wretchedly, in the still and lonely evening: not so much because he faced imprisonment and hanging; but because, it seemed to him, he had destroyed what he had always assumed was indestructible: the world of Momma, Poppa, Grandpa, Amanda (and himself) preserved for ever in the Cypresses Farm beside the eternal river.

Hands deep in pockets, sniffing and snuffling, he mooched through the fields wrapped in misery, when suddenly he was plunged into even deeper despair by cries of, "Gaylord, yoo-hoo, Gaylord," from somewhere behind him.

He froze, turned. Great Aunt Bea was bearing down on him at a rate of knots!

The last person he wanted to meet at this crisis in his life! Not only would her cheerfulness be unbearable. But the only other time she'd seen him crying she'd called him a cry-baby.

Yet escape was impossible. He went on mooching, kicking out first one leg then the other, hands even deeper in his pockets, and waited for the inevitable to catch up with him.

It did. But the ringing cries of cheerfulness were absent. Aunt Bea was staring down at him thoughtfully. "What's the matter, Gaylord?" she asked quietly.

"Nothing," he said.

"Don't be ridiculous, child. Here." She threw a coat on to the grass. "Now. Let's sit down and you can tell me all about it."

Gaylord flopped on to the coat. Aunt Bea lowered herself gingerly like a hippo becoming waterborne, and looked at her nephew with some distaste. "I say, would you mind if I cleaned you up a bit first?"

Gaylord shook his head listlessly. Aunt Bea went to work with a not-too-delicately moistened handkerchief. "That's better," she declared after a final inspection. "You look almost human again."

"Oh, good," said Gaylord, who didn't care tuppence whether he looked human or not.

Aunt Bea settled herself more comfortably. "Now then. Tell," she ordered.

"It's nothing, really," said her maddening nephew.

"I'm waiting."

Gaylord said, "There was a Circus in town and one of the

tigers escaped so Henry and I dug a tiger trap and we caught a tiger but it got away and Henry thinks it wasn't a tiger anyway."

"Really? So what does Henry think it was?"

"Grandpa," said Gaylord wretchedly.

Aunt Bea gave a sudden hoot of laughter, quickly stifled. "And why does Henry think it was your grandfather?"

"Because he fell and broke both his ankles and Henry's Gran says she reckons it'll finish him. Aunt Bea?" he asked anxiously.

"Yes, dear?"

"Will they hang me if Grandpa dies?"

Aunt Bea shook her head. "No dear," she said gravely. "There's no chance whatever of that." She became cheerful suddenly. "So you can forget all your worries, can't you."

"Not really," said Gaylord, still lugubrious.

Aunt Bea looked at him sharply. "Why? Is there something else on your mind?"

There was a long silence. Then he said, "Grandpa's ever so cross and I don't blame him, he says I could have killed him, and I think he doesn't want Momma and Poppa and me to live here any longer in case I break some more of his ageing bones."

It was Bea's turn to be silent. At last she said, "There's some mistake here, boy. You've got it wrong."

"I haven't, Aunt Bea. He said 'If you do stay and Gaylord breaks any more of my ageing bones I shall take it very unkindly, he might have killed me.'"

Bea put out a hand and pulled the dark head down on to her shoulder. "Now I want you to leave this to me, Gaylord. You've misunderstood something. Your grandfather talks a lot of nonsense sometimes, and says things he doesn't mean. I'll tackle him and get the truth out of him, but in the meantime I want you to stop worrying. At your age, and on a day like this, it's a crime against nature."

Gaylord swallowed. "You can't, somehow."

"I know," she said quietly. "But you've got to try. Come on, now. A bright smile."

Gaylord tried. But it didn't even feel like a bright smile. "That was hideous," said Aunt Bea. "But keep trying. And now I'm going to tackle that grandfather of yours." She squeezed his shoulder, didn't even try to kiss him, and bustled off. Gaylord watched her go reverently. He thought she was a super person.

John Pentecost was just hovering in that delightful state between waking and sleep when his sister Bea burst into his room. "John! What the devil have you been saying to that lad?"

Dream images had been drifting like wisps of cloud about John's brain. Now suddenly they cleared, leaving the craggy hills of waking life clear and stark. The dream image of a dancing elephant in his room became suddenly the awful reality of his sister Bea carrying on about something. He groaned. "I preferred the elephant," he muttered.

"What elephant?"

John didn't quite know. "You turned into an elephant," he said. "No. An elephant turned into you."

"Thanks. Now about Gaylord. He thinks you're going to die of broken ankles, and he'll be hanged for your murder."

"Bea! Only you would be daft enough to believe I told him that."

"I didn't. Of course not. But he believes it. And at his age it's a terrifying thought."

John raised himself on one elbow, glared. "Stop rampaging, woman, and sit down. Gaylord? I haven't even spoken to the boy."

"That's not his story. He says he dug a trap and you blundered into it and that's how you broke your ankles and now you want that nice family to give up their home here in case he catches you in any more traps." She returned his glare with considerable force. "I'm surprised at you, John, upsetting a child!"

John began threshing about in his bed. "Dammit, woman, he and his father did amuse themselves digging a trap, just where they know I walk. And it naturally tripped me and landed me in hospital. And I suffered, and am still suffering, and am likely to go on suffering grief and pain to my life's end. But have I ever uttered a word of blame or censure to Gaylord? No." He brushed his white moustache, looking rather saintly. "Such would not be in my nature, as you should well know, Beatrice."

"Rubbish." But she was shaken. John wasn't one to lie to defend himself from anyone, let alone her.

John lay back in the bed. "Right. Now if you'll simmer down and stop imagining things and making wild accusations I'll tell you what happened." He repeated the conversation between himself, Jocelyn and May. "It was the fact that they'd both known about it for months and hadn't said a word that really hurt," he finished up.

"Yes," she admitted. "I can see that. But it's the boy I'm concerned about. He really is in quite a state, John. You'll have to have a friendly word with him. He thinks you hate him."

"Good Lord." He looked a bit sheepish. "No, you're wrong somewhere, Bea. Gaylord could never think that."

"He could and does. Look John, I'll find the lad and bring him in here, and you can reassure him."

There was a tap on the door. May came in. "Oh, sorry to

disturb. Just wondered whether Gaylord was here."

"No." Beatrice said, "I left him down by the river, May. Actually he was a bit upset."

"Upset?" May looked startled.

Bea smiled. "He thinks he's going to be hanged. But I've reassured him, May."

"Thanks. But he's very naughty," said May. "I'm cross. He must know it's long past bedtime."

The countryside was settling down for the night. Owls were taking up their patient stations, bats careered madly where half an hour ago swallows had carved the air, cattle accepted the slow descent of dark as they accepted most other things, with a swish of the tail, uninterrupted chewing, and a total lack of interest, the embers of the western sky flared for a last minute of glory and then died, the evening star pierced the fading azure.

May telephoned Henry Bartlett's mother. That was where he would be.

But he wasn't. Mrs Bartlett, a woman of few words, handed the telephone to Henry, who was not reassuring. He'd come home ages and ages ago, and couldn't think where Gaylord could possibly be, but he reckoned there'd be no harm in dragging the river since he reckoned Gaylord was upset about something.

May said, "He's not there. Henry thinks we ought to drag the river."

"Henry would. Aren't they little ghouls."

"I'll give him ghouls," said May, grimly.

They went round the outhouses, calling, without result. And Gaylord, in the now ratless outside loo, was, as Aunt Bea had said, in quite a state. Suddenly his world had turned topsy-turvy. His friends (and now, he discovered, he longed to think of even Momma as a friend), his friends hated him.

Even the faithful Henry had held up a mirror to show him his faults. Yet Aunt Bea, from whom he had so often run to hide, now appeared his only friend.

He heard the calling voices grow nearer. He heard someone try the latch, and longed for them to open the door and find him. But they didn't and he couldn't bring himself to take the step that would set him face to face with these people who hated him.

The voices passed, and faded into the distance, and he sat there immobile, unable to step back into the world that had rejected him. The shadows gathered in the little, flower-sweet room. What would happen to him, he wondered. He supposed they'd find his sad little corpse one day, far in the future, and no one would have any idea who he was. Or perhaps an ancient, grey-bearded Henry Bartlett might look at the pathetic heap of bones and say, "I reckon that was my friend Gaylord. He killed his grandfather, but they never hanged him for it because they never found his body, till now, that is, and now it's too late." Gaylord shuddered deliciously. He suddenly remembered that some murderers had been hanged long after they were dead. That would be something to tell Henry about if it happened to him. Except that he didn't quite see how he could, being twice dead by then, as it were.

Bea seemed the most worried. "Jocelyn, I remember the stretch of river where I left him. Let's go and see if we can find any clues."

"Certainly," said Jocelyn.

"I'll stay," said May. "And if he turns up I'll call."

They strode off. Aunt Bea always walked as though she was just following a two-hundred-yard drive down the fairway and Jocelyn's long legs were only too pleased to keep up with this spanking pace.

It was almost dark. The river chuckled evilly, the trees mopped and mowed over them. "This is the spot," Bea said suddenly. "We sat on my coat. If it's not too dark we can probably see where the grass is still flattened. Got a torch, have you?"

"Sorry, Aunt."

Aunt Bea tut-tutted. "Always carried a torch behind the lines on the Western Front. Saved my life a hundred times." She went down on her knees, peered at the grass. "No. Too dark. Got a match?"

"Afraid not," said Jocelyn, who always assumed that the Aunt Beas of this world must think him effete.

He said, "I really don't think we shall do much here. Gaylord's a sensible boy. He'll turn up." He loved the river. But in this situation he found it dank, damp and dismal. He wanted to go home.

"Only hope you're right," said Bea doubtfully. "Well, you're the Brownie Leader. Which way for home? This, isn't it?"

"No. There's a short cut if we go this way."

And there, stumping towards the river, was Reuben Briggs. "Reuben," called Jocelyn. "Reuben, have you seen Gaylord anywhere?"

Reuben changed direction, came across. "Neither sight nor sound, Mr Pentecost." But he was regarding Aunt Bea with interest, even agitating his cloth cap in some sort of greeting. Jocelyn said, "Aunt, this is our neighbour, Mr Briggs. Reuben, this is my Aunt Beatrice, Mrs Browne-Forsyth."

Reuben smiled, drawing rather too much attention to his teeth. "How de do?" said Aunt Bea, sticking out a friendly hand. She said, "No need for introductions, eh, Reuben." She turned to Jocelyn. "Reuben and I are old friends."

"Yes, indeed, Mr Pentecost. Very knowledgeable about sheep, is your Aunty."

"Ah. Then you've found the way to Reuben's heart," said Jocelyn.

Aunt Bea smiled at Reuben. "And how are the old ladies?" she asked. "Has Emma Bovary got over that bit of whatever-it-was?" She turned to Jocelyn. "Did you know that every one of Reuben's flock is named after a heroine in world literature?"

"No I didn't."

"Typical." Back to Reuben. Teasing now. "Really, you'd think a novelist would know if everyone from Elektra to Mrs Malaprop lived next door." She stuck out a powerful hand again. "So long, Reuben. I'll be round for a mug of STS again one of these days."

"Goodbye, Reuben," said Jocelyn. "Send young Gaylord home if you see him."

"I will that, Mr Pentecost. Goodbye, Mrs – er." He shook hands warmly, loped off. Jocelyn said, "I didn't know you knew our Reuben."

"Course I know your Reuben. Great pal of Gaylord's. He and I take tea there sometimes."

"Aunt. You don't – *drink* anything in that cottage?"

"Don't know what else you can do with a mug of tea, Jocelyn."

"And – it's not made you ill?"

"'Course it damn well hasn't."

Jocelyn said, " I didn't even realise Gaylord knew him until recently."

Aunt Bea said, "Don't know a lot, you writer chaps, do you?" She strode on. Then she suddenly said, "Poor old Reuben. He thinks I'm the cat's whiskers. Only one thing I've go to watch."

"What's that?"

"Stop him proposing."

"Oh my God," said Jocelyn.

They set off at the same rattling pace. It really was exhilarating, thought Jocelyn. After a time he said, "It narrows here. I'll lead the way." He almost had to run to get in front.

"Dark in here," grumbled Bea. "You really ought to carry a torch, Jocelyn."

He came out of Polly Larkin's Pad into a lesser dark. "Trouble is, Aunt," he called, "I can never remember to buy new batteries." He trudged briskly on.

Now he could see the lights of home. What a lovely phrase that is, he thought. *The lights of home*. Good title for a novel, actually. He began to sketch in the final chapter: reconciliation, happiness, firelight glow? No. Too cloying sweet. Tragedy, then, that was more like it. The lights of home as malign as the will o' the wisp. Nice bit of irony, there. "It is nearer this way, don't you think, Aunt?" he called.

No reply. He'd better wait for her, he thought. She was a game old bird, but after all she was no chicken.

Strange. Not a sound. He began to edge back the way he had come.

And now he heard a faint moaning noise. It came from Polly Larkin's Pad. A thought too terrible to contemplate hit him like a truncheon. It couldn't be! NOT a second time!

He began to run. "It's as black as Egypt's night in here," said Aunt Bea's voice. "And I hate to admit it but I think I'm going to faint with the pain. Pity you haven't got a torch, dear boy."

"Aunt Bea," cried Jocelyn desperately. "Aunt Bea!"

But the rest was silence.

Jocelyn Pentecost had many admirable qualities.

But let's face it, he was not the man to be landed with a large, invisible, and presumably unconscious, Aunt in lonely country and at night. And with absolutely no means of illumination.

The countryside was black and silent. Not a light, not a movement, not a sound.

He didn't panic. His predilection was to sit down, smoke his pipe and think this thing over. But he knew that wouldn't be acceptable behaviour, even if he'd got some matches to light his pipe, which he knew he hadn't.

Then he saw a light, faint and flickering, wobbling along the river road that led to The Cypresses. "Help!" he yelled. "Help!"

The light ceased its erratic movement. "Where are you?" demanded a female voice.

"Here," he shouted.

"Where's here?"

"Polly Larkin's Pad."

"Where on earth is that?"

"Here," he yelled desperately, yet realising in a muddled way that this bellowed conversation had described a complete circle.

But he was relieved to see that the bicycle light appeared to be moving towards him. And now the voice, sounding a little nearer, shouted, "What's the matter?"

"My aunt has had a fall. She was in great pain and now she seems to have fainted. But I can't see a thing."

"Have you got her head between her knees?"

"No. Should I have?"

"Of course you should."

"But I can't even see her knees. Or her head."

The voice said, rather wearily. "Where are you now?"

"Where I always was. In Polly Larkin's Pad."

"Is it Polly Larkin who's fainted?"

"No. Forget about Polly Larkin, for heaven's sake."

"What?"

The light was certainly getting nearer. "Keep on," he called. "Don't change course."

"I haven't got a course. Look, you shout 'help' every ten seconds and I'll try to home in on you."

"Help!" cried Jocelyn, counting one to ten. "Help!" he cried again, counting eleven to twenty.

Great Aunt Bea chose this moment to return from the dead. "What on earth are you making all that noise for, Joss?"

"Help!" shouted Jocelyn, counting twenty-one to thirty. "You fainted," he said, rather accusingly.

"Yes. Sorry about that. But this pain really is hellish."

"Help!" shouted Jocelyn, counting thirty-one to forty. "Where is the pain, Aunt?"

"Ankles, mostly."

"Oh, my God," said Jocelyn. "Help! Forty-one, forty-two – "

He was suddenly bathed in light. And a pleasant voice said, "I say, aren't you Jocelyn Pentecost, the author? I was coming to see you."

"Really? Do I know you?"

"Vaguely. We met in the hospital ward. But you father knows me. I'm Nurse Nightingale. And if you ask me where I've left my lamp I'll clock you."

Jocelyn, deeply shocked, said, "I would not dream of asking anything so obvious or so impertinent."

"Well you're the first man I've met who hasn't. Except your father."

A querulous voice from the darkness cried, "How do you

do, young lady? I'm his suffering aunt."

"Yes," said Miss Nightingale. "We've got to get you moved. Do you think you can walk?"

"I'm damn sure I can't."

"Did I hear the word ankles?"

"Yes."

Miss Nightingale placed her bicycle so that the light shone on Aunt Bea's feet. She felt one ankle, then the other. "Does that hurt?"

"Like hell."

"Hm. Well, I don't think either of them are broken, though I'm open to correction. But they're badly sprained." She turned to Jocelyn. "Has Mr Pentecost Senior still got a wheelchair?"

"Yes."

"Could you go and fetch it, together with an electric torch and bandages and blankets. But, of course, before you do anything else telephone your doctor, say your aunt has suspected broken ankles and is in great pain, and ask him to call at once. OK?"

"OK," said Jocelyn, amazed to hear the hated Americanism on his lips. This girl seemed to have had a bad influence on him.

Miss Nightingale said, "Oh, and leave your jacket. Your aunt will need it."

Jocelyn stripped off his jacket and hurried off, muttering "wheelchair, blankets, bandages, ring doctor, torch, five things; wheelchair, doctor, torch…" Whichever way he did it now he never got more than four things. If he let the fierce Miss Nightingale down he would never hold up his head again.

He burst into the house. "May, I want Father's wheelchair, and bandages and torch – and ring the doctor and – " long pause – "blankets." Thank God. Five things. He'd done it.

But May was staring at him in horror. "Jocelyn. What's happened? Where is he?"

"Who?"

"Gaylord, of course."

"Gaylord? I don't know. Hasn't he come home?"

She looked at him piteously. "But – he's hurt. Where is he, Jocelyn?"

"How is he hurt?"

She almost screamed. "I don't know. You tell me."

"But you said he was hurt."

"I didn't. You said he was hurt." Suddenly she flung her arms around him. "Darling! Tell me what's happened to our son."

"I don't know. I assumed he was at home."

She stamped her foot. "Then why in heaven's name do you want a wheelchair and blankets and bandages? And where's your jacket?"

"And an electric torch and ring up the doctor," he remembered proudly. "For Aunt Bea's ankles," he said. "She needed my jacket for warmth."

"Aunt Bea's ankles?" Her voice was a horrified whisper.

"Yes. She fell in Gaylord's tiger trap. Must say I thought I'd filled it in," he admitted.

"You don't mean Aunt Bea's broken both ankles now?"

"Miss Nightingale thinks they may be just bad sprains."

"Miss Nightingale? How on earth did she come into it?"

"Well, I saw a light on the river road and – and it was Miss Nightingale."

"Oh, God. Jocelyn, you're rambling. And you haven't found Gaylord?"

"Not yet."

"No. You met Flo Nightingale with her lamp, and Gaylord

went clean out of your mind. I'm not surprised."

He remembered something. "Actually she said telephone the doctor first."

May was used to having half a dozen things happening in her mind at the same time. She pulled herself together. "*You* ring up the doctor and tell him what's happened. My version might be a bit garbled. In the meantime, I'll collect the things you want. Let me see, wheelchair, bandages, blankets, torch."

"Correct." He looked at her with admiration. He did wish he'd got a mind like that.

She watched Jocelyn, like Mother Courage, disappear into the night, shoving a wheelchair laden with blankets and bandages. She came back into the lighted house, and sat down quietly to consider the position.

She had been uneasy (but nothing more) about Gaylord's absence. But now that unease had been sharply underlined by the fact that for a few minutes she had thought him injured. In addition to this Aunt Bea had changed, in the twinkling of an eye, from an asset, however tiresome, to a total liability: Father-in-law in one bed, Bea in another, Gaylord adrift, and Jocelyn and this Nightingale woman in cahoots out in the balmy night. And Amanda.

I can't cope, she thought in sudden panic. Suppose Gaylord doesn't appear before bedtime. Suppose I have to nurse both Bea and father-in-law. You're being ridiculous, she told herself. All these things won't happen. But suppose even one of them does? She shuddered.

Now Gaylord was the biggest worry. Ought she to telephone the Police? She didn't want to without seeing what Jocelyn thought. And where was Jocelyn when he was needed? Chatting up a Victorian figment under the stars.

She went in to see her father-in-law. "May," he cried. "Nice to see you. But you look worried."

"Gaylord's AWOL," she said.

John Pentecost looked unconcerned. "Probably out digging more traps for tigers," he said unkindly.

May said, "He doesn't need to. He's caught Aunt Bea now."

He looked at her in amazement. "You don't mean – Bea hasn't gone and floundered into that wretched hole? How absolutely typical."

May said, "I don't think you can talk. You did."

"That's entirely different. Where is the daft creature?"

"Jocelyn's gone trundling off to fetch her back in your wheelchair."

"Has he, by George? And what happens when I need my wheelchair?"

"Father-in-law, you haven't used it for a month."

"That's entirely beside the point. I might need it at any moment. I don't want to have to turf Bea out of it every time."

May said, "Really, you are an impossible old man. Your grandson's missing, your sister's hurt, you and Bea are both going to need a lot of attention, and all you can think about is a wheelchair you no longer need."

He looked like Gaylord after a telling-off. She'd never seen the resemblance before. Suddenly she wanted to hug him but she steeled herself in order to seize this advantage. She said, "So let's get this straight. I'm going to be pretty busy with both you and Aunt Bea on my hands. And I don't want you and her squabbling over your toys as though you were both still five-year-olds. You've a big boy, now, Father-in-law. And I want you to behave like one."

"*I* know Bea. Once she gets her hands on that wheelchair there'll be no shifting her." Then: "Good Lord, what did you say about five-year-olds? May, I wouldn't take that from anyone but you. So don't push your luck, girl."

May said, "Jocelyn's calling. I must go and bring in the casualties." She went out into the stockyard, where stood Jocelyn, a girl with a bicycle, a wheelchair containing an Aunt Bea swathed in blankets. At the same moment a car swept into the yard and Dr Pemberton climbed out. "Hello, May. Where's the patient? Jocelyn wasn't terribly coherent."

"I'm here," came a voice from the pile of blankets. "I'm Jocelyn's Aunt. You must be the doctor. How dedo. My nephew is not good at introductions."

"Right. Let's get you inside, have a bit of light on the scene." Jocelyn seized the chair handles. Miss Nightingale walked beside him, ready to give a hand when they came to the three steps. May said, "I'll lift, Miss Nightingale. I've had lots of practice."

"Quite all right," said Miss Nightingale cheerfully. She chuckled. "I'm a bit younger than you are, Mrs Pentecost."

It was at this (for May, particularly) painful moment that Gaylord shot like a cork from his priest's hole.

He had been getting into even more of a state. But now it was not so much because he was an outcast. It was because it was dark. It was also the realisation that he had been here a very long time and Momma had been calling him and he hadn't answered. Obviously, if he simply appeared now, questions were going to be asked; and the longer he waited the more questions there were going to be. What was needed was a diversion which could occupy Momma's mind while he quietly merged into the landscape. Very humbly he put the suggestion to God that a bit of divine intervention would not be amiss.

To his amazement he almost immediately heard the

sound of an approaching motor. Then, suddenly, he was dazzled by a car's headlights sweeping into the room; and, as suddenly, he was plunged back into darkness.

A moment later the car's engine stopped, and there were voices, Poppa's and Momma's and some other people's.

Gaylord forgot all about being an outcast. He even forgot about merging quietly into the landscape. This was too exciting. He shot out of his priest's hole like an arrow from the bow. "Momma, what's happened? Has Grandpa hurt himself again?"

"No dear. Not this time. It's your Great Aunt Bea this time." Gaylord thought Momma didn't sound very pleased somehow. Yet he had the comfortable feeling that the displeasure was not for once with him.

And, thought Gaylord (a practised Momma-watcher), it must be a serious bit of divine intervention. Because Momma hadn't even asked him where he'd been. "Thank you, God," he remembered to say. And settled down to enjoy the excitement.

May made a mental note that Gaylord was safe, thank God, but that he had turned up at a moment of great activity which meant either that he had the devil's own luck, which of course he always had, or that he'd chosen his moment with exquisite care, which seemed the more likely. Anyway, she promised herself, he's not going to get away with it. Get this little difficulty over, and master Gaylord will be on the carpet, however busy with two invalids she was going to be.

The little procession moved into the house, only to find the way through the kitchen barred by a fierce old bulldog of a man in pyjamas and dressing gown, and carrying a stick which he seemed prepared to use either as a rapier, a cudgel or a staff. "Bea? Who told you you could have my wheelchair?"

"It's not your chair, John. It's the Council's. Says so on it."

"I don't care whose it is. It's not yours, Bea."

"Fiddle de-dee, John. I needed it."

"So did I, dammit. Anyway, you wouldn't have needed it if you hadn't done a belly flop into that hole. Why on earth don't you look where you're going?"

Dr Pemberton said to Aunt Bea, "Don't you pity me, having this dreadful old man for a patient?"

"Don't you pity me even more, Doctor, having him for a brother?"

But John had spotted the rest of the procession. "Why, Miss Nightingale. No one told me you were here. I'm so enjoying your book. Not read anything like it since *The Prisoner of Zenda*."

Miss Nightingale said, "Thank you. Actually that's why I've come to see Mr Jocelyn Pentecost. I've got some news about it. But I'm afraid that will have to wait till we've settled the patient."

Jocelyn pricked his ears up. What possible news could she have about that beginner's effort?

But Miss Nightingale was concentrating on essentials. "Now let me see, the first thing is to get your aunt in bed so that the doctor can examine her. Then I think that if Mr Pentecost Senior would be good enough to stay in his room for the time being, then we could soon get ourselves sorted out."

"Of course, my dear," John said plummily. "Anything that will make life easier for you. But perhaps, Miss Nightingale, you would just be good enough to straighten my bed up a bit before I get into it. A bit rumpled." Courteously he held the door of his room open for her, followed her in. "There is just one other thing, Miss Nightingale. When you've got my sister into bed would you make sure my wheelchair is returned to my room?"

"Certainly, Mr Pentecost." She came back into the hall, addressed May with her glinting smile. "The old gentleman is very anxious to have his wheelchair back as soon as possible, Mrs Pentecost. You will see to it, won't you?"

There was quite a long silence. Then May inclined her head and said "Yes." It was a simple, inexpressive, unadorned word. Yet in some way it said a very great deal.

"Oh, thank you," Miss Nightingale said gratefully. She cocked her head to one side. "Can I hear a baby crying?"

"Oh, damn," said May, who had been trying to pretend to herself for the last five minutes that she couldn't hear Amanda crying. She dashed upstairs, calling over the banisters, "Gaylord, get yourself off to bed."

Gaylord didn't think it would be much use arguing. In fact, he thought arguing could well be counter-productive. He sensed that Momma was at the stage where one word from him might cause a major explosion, goodness knew why, no-one had said anything to her except that nice new lady and it couldn't be that.

Gaylord said to Miss Nightingale, "I'm ever so hungry."

Miss Nightingale called up the stairs, "Your little boy's ever so hungry, Mrs Pentecost. Would you like me to get him some supper?"

"He is capable of getting his own supper," called May.

"Oh, I'll see to it," said Miss Nightingale. She turned to Gaylord. "Now," she said briskly. "I'm Nurse Nightingale. What's your name?"

"Gaylord Pentecost."

"You look like a likely lad. What do you normally have for supper?"

"Honey sandwiches and a cup of hot milk, thank you,

Miss."

"Don't call me Miss. I'm not a confounded schoolteacher. And is that what you'd really like?"

"Yes, please," he said dutifully.

Miss Nightingale waited. She felt more was coming. Gaylord stood on one leg. "Henry Bartlett has baked beans and pop," he announced.

"And would you prefer baked beans and pop?" asked Miss Nightingale.

"I would really. If you don't mind."

"I wouldn't mind anything for you, boy. Right. You get your pop. I'll get the beans."

And now Gaylord was perched at one side of the kitchen table tucking in gloriously and smiling at Miss Nightingale who was watching him from the other side of the table.

It was one of the most rapturous moments of his life. He had always felt deprived when Henry extolled the gourmet pleasures of his baked bean suppers. But it was not just the exciting food. It was eating his supper downstairs, just like a grown-up, in the bright kitchen, with the beautiful blonde Miss Nightingale sitting opposite him. It would be nice, he decided, to marry Miss Nightingale: every night of their lives they would have baked beans for supper, sitting one each side of the table and smiling at each other.

Such thoughts reminded him of the beautiful Circus Lady who had so bewitched him, yet who had so disappointedly failed to be his Auntie Becky. "Miss Nightingale?" he said.

"Yes, dear?"

"Miss Nightingale, you're not the Circus Lady, are you?"

"It seems unlikely, dear. What Circus Lady's that?"

"The one on the flying trapeze."

Disappointingly, she shook her head. "I'm sorry, Gaylord,

I've done a lot of things in my time. But not that."

"She was just *like* you. *And* my Auntie Becky. I was going to marry her, Auntie Becky I mean, but Uncle Peter got in first."

"Oh, bad luck, Gaylord."

"Then I was going to marry the Circus Lady. But if she isn't you and isn't Auntie Becky – ?"

"You're up a gum tree, aren't you dear," said Miss Nightingale, smiling. Not that Miss Nightingale was smiling much at the moment. She seemed, he thought, too busy being aware of everything that was going on about her. A bit like the pilot of Concorde, he decided.

A discordant noise broke in upon these thoughts. Momma came in, carrying an absolutely furious Amanda. And, it appeared, Momma was quite as furious as Amanda. "Gaylord! I told you to go to bed."

"I know, Momma. But Miss Nightingale didn't think I ought to eat baked beans in bed."

"Of course you oughtn't. But you know very well you have sandwiches and hot milk for supper. And you have it *in bed*."

Miss Nightingale rose. "I'm afraid it's my fault, Mrs Pentecost. But you know how much a child likes a change occasionally. I just thought it wouldn't hurt for once."

Don't you tell me what children like, and what wouldn't hurt 'em, thought May angrily. And it was as though Amanda was aware of the anger surging in her mother's body and was inspired by it, for she redoubled her cries and yells. Miss Nightingale said sweetly to May, "Can I relieve you?" Very gently she took the child and cradled her in her arms. Amanda looked at her with loathing, suspicion, doubt, interest, and finally complete trust, and began to coo like any sucking dove. Gaylord said, "Isn't Miss Nightingale good with babies, Momma? You couldn't do anything with her, could you? And you're her mother." He was pleased to have discovered this talking point. He hoped it would take Momma's mind off the undoubted fact that he wasn't in bed. But it didn't seem to. What his mother was in fact saying to herself was: Go, get thee to a nunnery, May Pentecost. As a mother you're a dead loss. This woman is sitting at table with an adoring Gaylord, feeding him convenience foods whose very existence I have tried to keep from him. And he's revelling in every mouthful. And she won over that little traitor Amanda in thirty seconds flat. Yes. I'm right. I might as well go find a good nunnery.

But no. There was still her dear Jocelyn. He wouldn't want her in a nunnery. And I saved him from the wiles of that lovely eighteen-year-old Imogen, so I should manage it with someone no more than ten years younger than myself.

Jocelyn came in, looking cheerful. "You were right, Miss Nightingale. No broken bones. Just two badly sprained ankles." He smiled at her. "Excellent bit of diagnostic work, Miss Nightingale. And your only light a bicycle lamp."

Gaylord said, "Isn't Miss Nightingale clever, Poppa. Knowing what was wrong with Aunt Bea. And just now Momma brought Amanda in and she was yelling her head off, and Miss Nightingale just took her off Momma and she stopped crying immediately."

Miss Nightingale smiled. "Not quite immediately, Gaylord," she said in what May felt was a patronising attempt at modesty.

Jocelyn sat down at the table. "Now, Miss Nightingale, what is this news about your book?" But he was only asking out of politeness and against his instincts. Any news about that book could only be bad. Therefore, embarrassing both for Miss Nightingale and himself.

Miss Nightingale said, "Frankly, Mr Pentecost, I'm here because I need your help."

He looked at the clean-cut young face, the hair of spun gold, the confident yet suppliant expression. He said, just a little warily, "Of course, anything I can do, Miss Nightingale."

"Oh, thank you, Mr Pentecost. I knew you'd help. You see, The Mandrake Press want me to take out twenty thousand words before they can publish my book. And – well, it needs an expert, doesn't it?"

He looked at her in amazement. "You mean – you mean Mandrake are talking of publishing it?"

"Only if I take out these twenty thousand words. They say it's a question of economics rather than any aspersion on my work."

Jocelyn thought: Good God, and was speechless. May said briskly, "Well, it's nothing to do with me, but I don't think you can expect my husband to get involved. It's a tremendous task."

Jocelyn said, "It is, as my wife says, a tremendous task. And one that I think only you can do since it's your book. May I suggest you give up your hospital job and – "

"Oh, I've done that already. I'm not going to miss this opportunity." She was silent. Then she said wistfully, "But I still need help."

When Jocelyn struggled against his own good nature he usually lost hands down. But where his life's work was also involved he put up more of a fight. "I'm sorry, Miss Nightingale, but I have my own books to write."

"I only wanted a little guidance," she said.

"Not even that," he said with a gentle smile.

Bully for you, thought May. And in an attempt to break up the party and save her husband from further appalling cheek she said firmly, "Bed, Gaylord."

Gaylord, having finished the best meal of his life, rose without a murmur. He gave Momma, Poppa and Amanda three rather beany embraces, kissed Miss Nightingale with considerable enjoyment and affection, and went to the door.

And there he paused, to make a considered statement. He said, "I don't think Momma ought to have to look after Grandpa and Poppa and Amanda and me and Messalina and Aunt Bea. It's too much. I bet she won't half be worn out."

"Oh, go to bed," said Momma good-naturedly.

Gaylord said, "I bet Miss Nightingale would stay and help if you asked her."

"I should regard it as a privilege, I assure you," said Miss Nightingale. "But I know you don't need my help."

No I don't, thought May. You'd be helping me while Jocelyn edited your book for you. I know Jocelyn; and I think I know you, my lady. Aloud she said, "I wouldn't think of troubling you, Miss Nightingale."

"Night, night," said Gaylord, and disappeared. Miss Nightingale sighed, and rose. "I must be off, too."

But Jocelyn's slow brain had for some time been gnawing away at a strange coincidence. He had to have it explained. He rose. "I'll come and help you find your bicycle," he said.

"Goodbye," said May. "And thank you for your help, Miss Nightingale."

The two ladies shook hands courteously but without warmth. Jocelyn opened the door, led Miss Nightingale out into the hall. "Why the Mandrake Press?" he asked.

"I thought knowing one of their authors might help."

"You mean – you don't mean you gave my name as an introduction?"

"Yes. Shouldn't I have done?"

"But – you'd only met me in that hospital ward. And I'd only glanced at the working copy of the book."

"I say. You're not cross, are you?"

"I'm not pleased."

"Oh, come on. I thought you'd be glad to have helped a poor girl. And you did help even if you won't do any more for her."

He ignored this. "Have you told my father it may be published?"

"Oh, yes. And he's tickled to death. He thinks it shows his literary judgement is better than yours." She said apologetically, "I don't think that, of course."

They were outside by now. The Milky Way wrapped them in a lacy veil. Yet those teeming suns gave but a feeble light. They groped their way across the stockyard. "Strange," said Miss Nightingale. "I'm sure this is where I left it."

She ran her hands over the wall. "Have you got a pocket torch?" said Miss Nightingale.

"No," said Jocelyn shortly. Dammit, the first thing he'd do in the morning was go and buy a torch.

Miss Nightingale suddenly giggled. "We could use my bicycle lamp if we could find the bicycle. But then we shouldn't need to, should we."

That giggle, in the lonely night, had a curious effect on Jocelyn. It dispelled his irritation and bad temper as a struck match dispels the dark. Suddenly he realised that, since his father's accident, neither he nor May had been much given to laughter. There had been too much sadness and worry in their lives. He looked at Miss Nightingale. Her eyes glittered in the starlight. She was young, unbelievably self-confident. She was beautiful! A line came into his mind: *Dance, and Provencal song, and sunburnt mirth*. He could do with a bit of sunburnt mirth, he thought. He reached out and took her hand. "Careful. These cobbles are slippery." They went on searching, hand in hand, the most natural thing in the world. Jocelyn *did* enjoy it. Be nice, he thought, when Amanda's this age, and can walk so with her old father. It will help me keep my youth.

But, after an extremely thorough search, he had to face the fact that her bicycle had gone. What was the world coming to? Even a remote country farmyard was no longer safe from thieves. "You'll have to stay the night," he said. "We've got plenty of room."

"Goodness, I couldn't put Mrs Pentecost to all that trouble."

"No trouble," he said. "May will be only too pleased." He wasn't going to mention his car. He thought it would be nice if Miss Nightingale stayed.

She pondered. "Tell you what. I'll stay if I can pay for my board with a few jobs in the morning. Washing up and so on."

May had obviously gone to bed. He sat Miss Nightingale down in the drawing room and went to wake May. "Sorry to disturb you, old girl, but Miss Nightingale's stranded. Some blighter's pinched her bike, and I don't like to suggest the expense of a taxi. Which room shall I put her in? Oh, and I suppose she'll need to borrow one of your nighties. Won't be much too big, I should imagine."

Five silent minutes later the bed was made up in a spare room, and draped with May's most glamorous nightie. Then may spoke for the first time. "Right. I'll leave you to see whether she wants a glass for her teeth." She went to bed. It seemed no time at all before she woke again to find Jocelyn sleeping like a simmering kettle beside her, and Aunt Bea calling from her room, in tones of restrained urgency.

She rolled out of bed, pulled on her dressing gown. She

felt an unusual emotion: panic. If the capable Aunt Bea was calling for help, what could she, who had no medical training, do in the hours of darkness? She even longed to waken Jocelyn. But she wouldn't do that. Jocelyn, she knew, had his own worries; though they didn't seem to be losing him much sleep.

She went along to Aunt Bea's room. What did she do if Dr Pemberton's analgesics had had no effect on the poor woman's pain? Or if Aunt Bea's robust nature, weakened by her accident, had succumbed to stroke or heart attack? She tapped on Aunt Bea's door, took a deep breath, and went in.

Aunt Bea said, "May dear, I wonder if you'd mind popping down and feeding Messalina? Just half a tin of Kittycrunch and a bowl of milk. You needn't bother with her vitamin supplement tonight."

"You're quite sure?" said May. "After all, I wouldn't like – "

"Quite, quite sure, dear."

May went downstairs. Messalina was making no attempt to hide her annoyance. She yowled, even more loudly. May said, "Now don't blame me, Messy. In a crisis someone always suffers, and in this case it happens to be you, you toffee-nosed creature."

This reasonable speech did nothing to mollify the animal, who went on yowling. "Oh, shut up," said May, tipping a dollop of Kittycrunch into a bowl, and pouring milk. Messalina stopped yowling, walked over in a dignified manner and sniffed suspiciously at the stuff. "Oh, get on with it," said May, and went back to bed. She felt scared, and depressed. It looked as though Gaylord had been right. May had got everybody on her hands, even Messy. She slid in beside her husband, who woke sufficiently to grab the duvet to him like a Victorian maiden protecting her modesty. May, seeking sympathy, said, "I've been down to feed Messalina."

"Oh good," said Jocelyn. "I heard her holding forth." He tumbled back into sleep.

But May lay awake until dawn, her body in comfort but her mind in turmoil.

Chapter 10

A lovely, early-autumn morning: stillness, and peace, under an azure sky.

Yet, at the Cypresses Farm, everyone was waking to problems.

Gaylord's conscious mind came suddenly together like a completed jigsaw puzzle. And appalled him with its picture of misery to come. True, the shades of the prison house had receded somewhat. But he still faced the dislike of everyone, and especially of Grandpa. He didn't suppose Grandpa would ever speak to him again, ever. Why should he, when Gaylord had done such dreadful things to him?

While he pondered these things there came a cheerful rat-a-tat on his door. And something quite wonderful happened: a breakfast tray with two boiled eggs appeared, carried by none other than Miss Nightingale. "Miss Nightingale," he cried happily. "What are you doing here? Have you come to help Momma look after us all?"

"Nothing like that," she said disappointingly. "It's just that last night – someone stole my bicycle."

Gaylord concentrated on cracking an egg. "Really?" he said at last.

"Really," said Miss Nightingale looking at him rather closely.

"This is a super egg," said Gaylord. "It's got a chickeny taste."

"So I had to stay the night. And I thought it might help your mother if I did a few jobs. Look. When you've eaten that would you like to take your grandfather his breakfast?"

"'Course." Gaylord had planned to give Grandpa a wide berth this morning. But he could deny this wonderful lady nothing. "Fancy someone stealing your bicycle, Miss Nightingale."

"Fancy," said Miss Nightingale. "See you later."

John Pentecost's problems that morning were moral ones. Had he been too hard last night with Jocelyn? And what ought he to say to Gaylord when he met him? After all, children must be made to understand their responsibilities. You can't say, 'you robbed me of months of possible good health, but it's all right, boys will be boys.' On the other hand, you couldn't be too hard when the whole thing had been at worst a piece of irresponsibility. The trouble was of course, that his feelings for his grandson on this fine morning were ambivalent. And John hadn't any time for ambivalent feelings, dammit. He liked to know where he stood. He thought he'd give Gaylord a wide berth this morning, till he'd made up his mind about him.

There was a nervous tapping at his door. "Come in," called John.

The door opened a crack. Gaylord put an anxious head inside. "Can I come in, Grandpa? I've brought your breakfast."

"Yes."

He came in carrying a tray, and made quite a thing of latching the door behind him. Then he turned and faced his grandfather.

And his grandfather faced him.

The silence was a physical weight in the room.

At last: "Hello, Gaylord," said Grandpa.

Another interminable silence. Then Gaylord said, slowly, choosing every word, "I'm sorry about your ageing bones, Grandpa." He watched the old man's face anxiously, and waited.

"So am I," said John.

"It should have been a tiger," said Gaylord at last.

"But it wasn't a tiger," said Grandpa. It was me. Wasn't it?"

"Yes," said Gaylord.

Silence settled again like snow on a winter meadow. "Which was unfortunate," said Grandpa. "Especially for me."

'Yes."

"Unfortunate but not malicious or evil or premeditated?"

"What's that last bit?"

"Thought out beforehand."

"No."

"No." he looked at the young, dejected face; too young, too delicate to carry such a load of remorse. It was not good. "Would you like to go for a walk, boy?"

"Oh, yes, please," cried Gaylord. The tension in the room had suddenly snapped. And John thought: the hell with it. Life's too short. He'll do other things as daft, but he probably won't dig any more traps where I can fall into them. And he'll learn, slowly, bit by bit. We mustn't expect more. "You can push me in the wheelchair," he said, "Provided Bea hasn't already got her hands on it."

But Bea *had* already got her hands on it. And was whizzing round the kitchen in it, bashing the furniture like nobody's business, but nevertheless helping May considerably. (In fact, Bea and the eager Miss Nightingale were dealing with every job in sight. May thought irritably that she'd be better employed doing the *Telegraph* Crossword.)

So Gaylord and Grandpa went for their walk in the good, old-fashioned way, while the river chuckled beside them, and the cattle tore at the sweet grass, or lifted their foolish heads to gaze, liquid-eyed, at these uncomprehended creatures; and the cotton-wool clouds sailed ever onward across the valley like happy little cherubim.

Gaylord and Grandpa talked little. They had no need. They were wrapped in a strange happiness and companionship that Gaylord could not have analysed and the old man couldn't bother to. Was it the fruit of forgiveness and understanding? Or just the product of a late summer's morning? Or was it the benison of youth and old age walking together, content, in the days of their idleness?

And had Jocelyn got problems, this lovely morning? Yes, indeed. (Jocelyn always had problems. On the few occasions when the fell clutch of circumstance wasn't providing any, he usually managed to arrange a few for himself.)

On this morning, they seemed as thick as autumn leaves. Yesterday he had been called a mindless oaf, an unspeakable lout. He had also, indirectly, been called a fool by a neighbour whom surely he had never harmed. He felt eviscerated; empty, drained.

But not resentful. Had he not caused his father suffering and humiliation? It was only fair that he himself should feel humiliation now.

He had been awakened by May hissing through her clenched teeth, "Someone's in my kitchen."

He had listened. Yes. The clatter of tea cups. But now the tea cups sounded as though they were coming upstairs and yes, a tapping at the door. "Mr and Mrs Pentecost, can I come in?"

They had sat up. Miss Nightingale entered, carrying a

morning tea tray adorned with a late rose. She said, "Now everything's under control. Old Mr Pentecost and the little boy have both got their breakfast, but I thought you'd like a quiet cup of tea while Amanda's still asleep."

"That was thoughtful of you," Jocelyn had said appreciatively. May said, "Thank you. I'll be up very shortly." As soon as the door had closed behind her May said, "Jocelyn, we're being taken over. Your books, my kitchen. She's ruthless."

Secretly, Jocelyn had felt that the entrance of morning tea and Miss Nightingale had been like a particularly splendid sunrise. But he sensed that something a little less enthusiastic was called for. He said, "She should have told me she was using my name as an introduction. A bit brash, to say the least. Still, I did appreciate not having to go and make the morning tea for once."

But May was already up. "Where are you going?" he asked.

"To establish my territory," she said. She pulled on her gown, dealt carefully with her face, and then went down to the kitchen.

That was how the morning had started; leaving Jocelyn with the feeling that if he hadn't got rid of Miss Nightingale by midday life wouldn't be worth living.

Writing was impossible. He rose from his desk, strolled across to the window, gazed out at the mellow day. He saw the river, with two distant figures strolling by its edge. Would he and his father ever walk so again, he wondered, in friendship and love?

He saw something else: Reuben Briggs coming up the path: but a new, improved Reuben: an ancient deer-stalker had replaced the inevitable cloth cap; the raincoat looked almost presentable. Reuben, clutching a crumpled newspaper, rang the doorbell. "Oh, good Lord," cried Jocelyn. *What* had Aunt Bea said? "Only one thing I've go to do. Stop him proposing." "Oh, good Lord," he said again. And went downstairs two at a time and wrenched the door open.

Seen at close quarters, there were other improvements. Reuben looked almost spruce. "Brought these for your Aunty," he said shoving the crumpled newspaper at Jocelyn.

"Thank you, Reuben. That *is* kind of you," said Jocelyn.

"Eggs," said Reuben, peering into the house as though looking for Aunty.

"She *will* be pleased," said Jocelyn. "But I'm afraid I can't ask you in to see her. She's had a rather nasty accident."

"Sorry to hear that, Mr Pentecost. Something in the kitchen, was it?"

"No. Outside. Actually it happened soon after you met her yesterday evening."

"Really? Oh, poor lady. How on earth did she do that? Why, you were nearly home, weren't you?"

Jocelyn said, "I'm afraid – she rather fell in the trap my son built for that wretched tiger."

There was a long silence. Then Reuben said, "Mr Pentecost, you're not telling me you hadn't filled in that silly hole?"

"Yes, I had. But I can't have done the job properly."

"Then you're a bigger fool than I thought you were, Mr Pentecost. And that's saying something."

Jocelyn was silent. Reuben said, "She's a nice lady, a lady I respect. And you do this to her. Good day, Mr Pentecost." And he turned on his heel and stumped furiously away.

Twenty-four hours later, Jocelyn thought he was more depressed than he'd ever been. Reuben's angry condemnation had bruised him like iron rods (all the more so because he freely admitted their justice). May was livid because Miss Nightingale was somehow still in residence; and she was growing more livid by the hour. John Pentecost was distant and cool, an unusual state for him. There was no resting place for a literary gent to whom the practical world was a place of alarms and excursions.

Yes, he thought. Fate, plus his own incompetence, Fate had dealt hard with him. Little did he know what the jade had in hand for him now.

He watched the postman coming up the path. He heard the rattle of the letter box. He saw the postman return to the gate, swing himself on to his bicycle, cycle away, diminishing down the river road. He went and picked up the post, carried it to his study.

A circular from a bank, begging him to borrow £7,500 and enclosing an advertisement for a yacht costing, surprisingly, £7,500. A letter, chummily addressing him as Dear Mr Pentecost, assuring him that he, alone of everyone in his district, had been chosen to take part in a competition to win £100,000. A pink, wafer-thin envelope, addressed in block letters to MR PENTECOST JUNIOR, CYPRESSES FARM, SHEPHERD'S WARNING.

He found himself trembling. One of his fears had always been that he would receive an anonymous letter. After all, he thought, an author, revealing himself and his innermost thoughts to thousands of readers, was a perfect target to the envious and the malicious.

Yet why should this nasty cheap envelope, this crude printing appear so menacing? He picked up his paper knife and slit the envelope.

What joy and relief! The envelope was empty.

No. It wasn't. Now he could see a folded piece of rice

paper, covered with tiny printing.

He pulled it out, spread it open on his desk.

It appeared to contain a list, one item of which had been marked with a cross.

He searched in his drawer for a magnifying glass. Now he could see what he was dealing with.

It was a page from the Book of Common Prayer. And the marked item read: *Cursed is he that maketh the blind to go out of his way*.

The Commination Service, he thought. And, sure enough, there it was at the top of the page. A Commination, or Denouncing of God's Anger and Judgements Against Sinners.

He wondered how many people now living had ever heard this service read. Yet it was strong stuff. Someone had cursed him, a Sinner, with the Anger and Judgements of God; and he hadn't minced his words.

It made Jocelyn's flesh creep.

Yet when had he ever made the blind to go out of his way? Was there anything in one of his books that could have made the innocent to stumble? There must be many things. But the question was: what did he do about it? He could not bear to touch either the envelope or the letter. He gazed at them, horror-stricken.

Ten minutes ago his world had been ordered. Oh, he'd had his problems: the need to make things right with his father; to perform the Disappearing Lady Trick on Miss Nightingale; to get back into May's good books; to repent for maiming his aunt, as he had for his father's injuries. How small, how ridiculous all these worries seemed in the face of this sudden, written proof of hatred for that well-loved author, Jocelyn Pentecost!

The letter was stamped for first class mail. Even with his

magnifying glass it was impossible to read either the date or the place of posting.

Then, like the Mills of God, his brain got there in the end. The Book of Proverbs, and now the Book of Common Prayer. The link was too obvious. It was Reuben Briggs who had introduced this new menace into his life. And it was the injury to his aunt that Reuben was cursing him for.

He ought to take that horrible letter straight to the police.

He felt bitterly angry. He had never much cared for Reuben, never even been comfortable with him. And the thought of this man inflicting new fear and torment on him (even though he deserved it, dammit) was outrageous. Reuben deserved to be made to do a bit of explaining.

Then he imagined Reuben, in his mucky clothes, foolishly quoting Flaubert and Goethe to uncaring policemen, or even to uncaring magistrates; Reuben, being mocked and stripped of his little, precious learning by men who had perforce read Flaubert and Goethe at school and never read a word since. No. Reuben was his neighbour. Jocelyn didn't like him. He almost hated him for the fear he had caused him. But he wasn't going to hand him over to his own class for scourging and crucifixion. He could handle this himself.

Chapter 11

John Pentecost returned from another walk flushed with triumph. He had been a couple of miles, wasn't particularly tired, wasn't even in pain. The long days and weeks of exercise and struggle had paid off. God willing, they were now behind him. Oh, he'd still need looking after, still be a bit of a burden, he supposed. Getting upstairs, getting dressed and undressed, in things like that he was going to need help. But when it came to moving under his own steam (or, he hoped, under the Rover's own steam!) then he was his own man once more. It was a moment of intense jubilation.

And, he flattered himself, he'd done the right thing about young Gaylord. Nice lad. Good company. It would have been a pity to let that business of the tiger-trap spoil this grave bond between youth and old age.

Nevertheless, despite this euphoria, as they approached the house he began to behave rather furtively. "Think we'll try to avoid your Great Aunt Bea, boy," he said. "She don't always see eye to eye about the length of my walks. And frankly, dammit, I can't bear to see her playing fast and loose with my wheelchair."

This suited Gaylord down to the ground. Deviousness was meat and drink to the lad. And being devious in cahoots with Grandpa was pure joy. He gave his not inconsiderable mind to the problem. "I know, Grandpa. I'll create a diversion in the kitchen while you creep in at the front. Then you can go and sit in the drawing room and pretend you've been there all morning."

"What a splendid idea," said Grandpa. Five minutes later he had flopped on to his damned hard chair in the otherwise comfortable drawing room.

Almost immediately the door opened. He braced himself for his sister. But was relieved and delighted to find that capable Miss Nightingale looking down at him. "Why, Mr Pentecost, you're back from your walk. But you must be tired."

"A little," he said. (He wasn't, dammit. But a bit of sympathy from a pretty girl wasn't to be sneezed at.)

She made soothing noises. "Can I pour you a glass of sherry?"

"What a splendid idea," said John for the second time in a few minutes. He had an even more splendid idea. "Why don't you pour yourself one and sit and talk to an old man?"

She looked as delighted as a child. "May I? May I really?"

"I do wish you would," he said.

She brought over the glasses and sat next to him, lifted her glass. "Cheers!" Her eyes, over the rim, were brilliant and friendly. "That chair doesn't look very comfortable," she cried. "Let me get you another one."

"Better not," he said. "It's my lumbago chair." She looked at him thoughtfully, then grinned. "I see."

"Sorry about your bicycle," he said.

"Yes. I wouldn't have minded so much if it hadn't made a lot of trouble for Mrs Pentecost."

He said gallantly, "Believe me, Miss Nightingale, it's a great pleasure to have you about the place. And as for making work – why, it seems to me you're being a great help to May.

You sent my breakfast up, both days, didn't you? And the boy's."

"Oh, that was the least I could do. The difficulty is – " She looked suddenly forlorn. "But you don't want to hear my troubles."

"Indeed I do, Miss Nightingale. I'm only sorry you have any."

"Thank you. You're very understanding." She fell silent.

He said, quietly, "Troubles?"

"I don't know how to get home. Without a bicycle."

"I see." He pondered. "Oh, by the way, Miss Nightingale, if you should do my breakfast again – a second rasher would be welcome. Don't think I'm complaining, of course."

She said, "Mr Pentecost, I can't stay another day."

"Why not?"

"I should outstay my welcome. It's – it's impossible."

"Do you think," he said, "you could top up both our glasses?"

"Not mine," she said quickly. "But yours, yes." She did so.

He sipped appreciatively. Lord, it was pleasant: to have chatted with an intelligent and charming woman: pleasant, indeed. And now, he was growing drowsy. What he needed to set the seal on this perfect morning was a snooze in a comfortable armchair. Bea could go hang. He put down his now empty glass. "Miss Nightingale, give me a hand into that easy chair." She did so, willingly and capably. He found her hand as smooth and friendly as his son had done. The chair embraced him. "Night-night," she said softly, as one speaks to a loved child. "Night-night," he murmured. His eyelids closed, fluttered open, closed again. Sleep came, gentle as falling dew, to crown the old man's morning.

"Lunch in ten minutes," said May. "Do you think you could

alert everyone, Miss Nightingale?"

"Of course, Mrs Pentecost." She ran up to the study. "Lunch in ten minutes, Mr Pentecost."

He gazed up from his work as though wondering who she was, what lunch was, and how long ten minutes was. "Wake up, Mr Pentecost," she said briskly. "You must have heard of lunch." She departed. He'd get the message eventually. She ran downstairs again, and into Aunt Bea's room. "Lunch, Aunt Bea. Shall I bring it to you here, or will you come to the dining room?"

"I'll come to the dining room, young lady. No malingerers here. Just give me a hoist into that wheelchair."

"No, you don't," Miss Nightingale said nicely but firmly. "That's Mr Pentecost's chair. You can walk perfectly well if you try."

"The trouble is," said Aunt Bea coolly, "that I don't intend to try."

"Then you get no lunch," said Miss Nightingale, firmly grasping the wheelchair and shoving it into John's room. "Lunch, Mr Pentecost. Got your chair. Heave ho."

They heave ho'd. "Thank you, my dear," said John. "I don't know what an old man would do without you."

"Chocks away," she said. "Take yourself in." she peered out of the window. "Gaylord. Lunch. Straight in or you'll miss it. But wash your hands first."

May, bringing in the joint, was amazed to find everyone perched up round the table. No second and third calls for Jocelyn. No having to wait while Gaylord went to the loo or Grandpa finished his sherry. It really was very impressive.

But it wasn't what she wanted, or, indeed, what she was going to have. It was her kitchen, her menage. Miss Nightingale, bicycle or no bicycle, would be off this afternoon. She wasn't going to impose herself for three nights!

Over the coffee May said, "Now you've been a great help in this crisis, Miss Nightingale. But we can't put upon your good nature any more. I'm sure you'd like to get off as soon as we've finished."

It was a reasonable and carefully prepared speech and so May was quite taken aback by the storm of protest it evoked. Gaylord wailed, "She can't go, Momma."

Jocelyn said, "I'm sure Miss Nightingale would be only too pleased to stay and help for a few days, darling."

May said, "I'm sure she would. But we can't trespass on good nature – darling."

Aunt Bea said, "I feel I'm such a burden. I came to help and I'm an absolute dead loss. I wish you'd stay, Miss Nightingale."

"Well, I don't," May wanted to shout. Instead: "It would be very nice to have you, Miss Nightingale. But I can manage perfectly well, thank you." And to her menfolk she said, "And thank you for all being so concerned about me."

Miss Nightingale said, "I should be only too happy to stay and help you over this crisis. But I do understand, Mrs Pentecost. If, perhaps, Mr Jocelyn Pentecost would be good enough to call me a taxi – ?" She gave him a grateful smile.

John Pentecost was looking very thoughtful. For some time now his brain had been concentrated on the problem of getting his car out without May and Bea sticking their oars in. Now (though sadly it meant losing this splendid girl's company) he saw a way.

He went straight to his room after lunch but he slept little. Very soon he opened one bright eye, and then the other. He picked up the telephone.

"Taylor, has my son ordered a taxi?"

"He has, Mr Pentecost."

"Cancel it, will you."

"Certainly, Mr Pentecost."

John put down the receiver, rubbed his hands together. He was going for a drive! He felt the steering wheel under his palms. He felt the smooth, effortless surge of the engine under his command; the caressing, gliding, floating progress through the countryside. He pulled himself up out of his chair, crossed to the window. "Gaylord," he called softly.

Gaylord looked up from the book he was reading. The conspiratorial quietness was not wasted on him. "Yes, Grandpa?" he whispered.

Grandpa beckoned him inside. Gaylord came in silently through the open window, looked up hopefully at this new, improved Grandpa. Grandpa never used to be furtive like this. Gaylord thought it must be the dread weight of Aunt Bea's presence that had wrought the change. Anyway, it was a great improvement.

He was not disappointed. Grandpa said, "Like to go for a ride, boy?"

"Oh, yes please."

"Right. Tell your father I'll see about Miss Nightingale's transport. Then come and open the big doors so that I can get my car out. Then run and tell Miss Nightingale to join us. But there's no point in mentioning it to Aunt Bea or your mother. They'd only fuss."

"Of course," said Gaylord, understanding perfectly.

"Though why," muttered the old man, "anyone should think Bea fit to drive and not me – it's a mad world. Now. Quietly, boy."

They crept out. Gaylord opened the doors of the big barn. There, grey and dusty, stood the neglected car. John was trembling. With devout fingers he unlocked the driver's door, slipped into the driving seat. It received him as a throne receives its Lord and Master. Gaylord climbed into the back seat. John inserted the ignition key, turned. The engine, with only a token cough of reproach at the weeks of neglect, began to sing sweetly. "Now. Off you go," said Grandpa.

But it was dark in the barn. John switched on the headlights. Gaylord and Grandpa stared.

Brilliantly lit, held in that circle of light, glinting and gleaming, was a bicycle. "What's that?" said Grandpa, absently fiddling with the indicator switch.

"It – it looks like a bicycle," said Gaylord.

"That's what I thought," said Grandpa, peering.

"Yes," said Gaylord.

"Looks like a lady's," said Grandpa.

"It could be," said Gaylord judicially.

"Mmm." Grandpa cogitated. Then: "Oh, well. No business of ours," said Grandpa, staring thoughtfully at his grandson. "But – I think I'll get the car out into the stockyard before you fetch Miss Nightingale."

"Might be a good idea," said Gaylord.

The old man chose reverse, released the handbrake. The car began to move. "Now remember, boy. Avoid your aunt and your mother like the plague. But get hold of Miss Nightingale and tell her the taxi's in the stockyard."

"You bet," said Gaylord. He shut the barn doors. Then he was off like a streak of lightning.

To Gaylord's dismay, Miss Nightingale was in the kitchen saying goodbye to Momma and Aunt Bea. Gaylord hovered. He tried to catch Miss Nightingale's eye. In the end he said, "Miss Nightingale, your taxi's waiting."

"Oh, thank you, Gaylord," she said. "We'll come out and see you off," said Momma.

Gaylord said quickly, "No, the taximan's in ever such a hurry. He says if Miss Nightingale isn't out in one minute he'll have to go without her."

"Oh, well, off you go then," said Momma, without too much regret. Gaylord hurried Miss Nightingale over to the car. "What a nice taxi," said Miss Nightingale as Gaylord courteously opened the front passenger door for her.

"Taxi be damned," cried the driver. "Don't you know a vintage three point five when you see one?"

"Mr Pentecost, I'm sorry."

"So you should be, my dear. Superb car. Get in, both of you. Watch this acceleration." Gently and lovingly he stroked the pedal with his foot. The car glided forward effortlessly. John gave a sigh of deep satisfaction. How many weeks and months was it since he had been wooed forward thus?

Once on the main road he let the needle hover on sixty. Quite fast enough for an elderly gent like him. Then: "Look out!" cried Gaylord. "Whoops!" cried Miss Nightingale. Where a moment ago had been an empty road was now a road filled with a galloping, whinnying, eyes-rolling, hoof-clattering, terrified horse, bearing down on the Rover like the Wrath of God.

John's right foot swung from caressing the accelerator to stamping on the brake. The car felt as though a giant hand had seized it and brought it up short. The animal, with a slight change of course, careered and clattered past the car with an inch to spare. Miss Nightingale touched John's sleeve. "Well done," she said quietly. Then: "Why, what's the matter, Mr Pentecost?"

John writhed in his seat. "My blasted ankle again, dammit. Agony! What the devil are we going to do now?"

Gaylord, bouncing about with excitement on the back seat, gave as his opinion that they were lucky not to have been trampled to death. It was ever so easy to get trampled to death when there were horses about.

Grandpa said, "Agony. I can't drive with this ankle, that's

certain." Despite his pain he turned courteously to Miss Nightingale and said, "I'm afraid, my dear, I shall have to ask you to go and ask the RAC to send us a driver. These cars mustn't be towed in any circumstances."

Gaylord said, "I know, I could crouch on the floor and everytime Grandpa shouted 'brake' I could push the pedal down." He thought it was a super idea.

"Oh, Gaylord, shut up," said Miss Nightingale, laughing.

Gaylord was hurt. He reckoned his friend Henry Bartlett would also have thought it a super idea. Still much as he idolised Miss Nightingale he supposed she was a grown up with the usual grown-up prejudices.

Miss Nightingale said, "I don't know whether I dare suggest this, Mr Pentecost, but I have a licence. If you would be prepared to let me drive you home I would be very, very careful with your beautiful car."

He looked at her in agonised wonder. "Miss Nightingale, of course you may. If you take it slowly, of course. I'll watch the road and be prepared to grab the wheel."

"Oh, thank you, Mr Pentecost. I'm sure we shall manage. Actually, for some years I was chauffeur to Lord Breedon."

"No!"

"Yes. Such a dear old gentleman. Actually, Mr Pentecost, you remind me of him so much. Now. Do you feel that Gaylord and I could help you into the back seat?"

"No."

"Now come along." She ran round, opened the driver's door. "Ups-a-daisy, Mr Pentecost."

"Don't you ups-a-daisy me, young woman." Nevertheless, groaning and muttering he allowed himself to be manoeuvred into the back seat. He sat back, mopping his forehead. Gaylord said, "I bet Momma won't half be pleased to see you back, Miss Nightingale."

Miss Nightingale said, "Oh, I shan't stay, Gaylord. I'll get home somehow." She slipped into the driver's seat. "Now, Mr Pentecost. Ready for take-off?" Gently the car moved forward. She turned for The Cypresses. "Fine," said John. "That's right, Miss Nightingale. Steady as she goes." But he'd got a lot on his mind. Frankly, he'd learnt his lesson. It was back to Taylor's Tip-Top Taxis, after all.

God forbid. Miss Nightingale was handling the car as it deserved to be handled. Miss Nightingale had been chauffeur to Lord Breedon, who must have been a very fortunate fellow. But Miss Nightingale said she wasn't staying.

Why? He asked himself. He suspected it was something to do with that fine woman May. Well, he never tried to understand women. They were kittle cattle, even the best of them.

But though he was the mildest and gentlest of men, he told himself, yet given a choice between Taylor of the Tip-Top Taxis and the late Lord Breedon's chauffeur, it was no time for gentleness. For once he would have to assert himself.

He said, "Miss Nightingale, I want you to turn round, drive to your flat, collect some clothes and things, and then take us back to The Cypresses. I want you to drive my car until I can drive it myself. We'll discuss terms later."

"Super," cried Gaylord.

"Mr Pentecost, I couldn't possibly. Mrs Pentecost – "

"Never mind Mrs Pentecost. I'll talk to her."

"Besides, you're in pain. I ought to get you home."

"That's my worry. You do as I say."

Miss Nightingale did a stunning three-point turn, and was off in the opposite direction. "I really do feel awful," she said.

"No, you don't," said John, surprisingly. "It's what you've

been playing for since the moment you arrived. First with Jocelyn and your book and now with me."

"Well, really," said Miss Nightingale.

"Just don't try to pull the wool over my eyes, young lady. Then we shall get along splendidly."

Miss Nightingale gave him a sideways look and then drive on in silence. John said, "Only one thing I'd like to know. Who hid your bicycle? You or Gaylord?"

"Well, it certainly wasn't me," said Miss Nightingale.

"Oh, look at that Rolls-Royce," cried Gaylord, who appeared not to have heard the question.

They drew in at The Cypresses. Miss Nightingale brought the car to a purring stop, jumped out, and flung open the rear door. "There, Mr Pentecost. Not a scratch on her. Now you wait here while I go and call up reinforcements."

The afternoon was very quiet. A thankful May was putting her feet up. She could relax. Grandpa and Gaylord had gone off for a ride in that taxi. (Do them both good, and give them a chance to renew their old friendship.) Jocelyn was in his study, as always, Bea resting in her room. And best of all, Miss Nightingale was being driven at high speed out of May's life for ever.

What, she wondered, had she really got against Miss Nightingale, apart from her undoubted brashness? Surely it wasn't simply her youth? Or the fact that May's menfolk seemed to like her so much? If I were an inefficient person, she thought, I could be suspected of hating her efficiency. But I'm not. I'm as jolly efficient as she is.

There was sudden uproar. Female voices raised in anger, with Messalina providing a furious descant. What could be happening?

She shot into Aunt Bea's room. Messalina, back arched, was poised on her points like a helicopter ready for take-off, screaming blue murder. Miss Nightingale and Aunt Bea appeared to be fighting over the wheelchair.

Miss Nightingale with a suitcase? What on earth was she doing here?

May took a deep breath. "Will someone tell me what's happening? Miss Nightingale? I thought you'd left ages ago."

Miss Nightingale said, "I did. But Mr Pentecost has injured his ankle again and I came for his chair. He's in great pain."

"She barges in here, dumps her case down on Pussykins, and tries to pinch the chair without so much as a by-your-leave," said Aunt Bea.

Miss Nightingale spun round on her. "Can't you see it's an emergency, you interfering old woman?" she cried.

"How dare you speak like that to a guest in my house?" May's voice was down to a growl. "Really, Miss Nightingale, I must ask you to leave at once."

"I can't accept that," said Miss Nightingale. "It's your father-in-law's house. Isn't it, Mr Pentecost?"

May spun round. John stood leaning against the door jamb, supporting himself on his grandson. He looked ashen and drained. May said, "I don't understand. Father-in-law! Will you kindly tell Miss Nightingale to leave?"

"No," said John. "She's a nice girl and she's taken pity on an old man and she's going to be my chauffeur till I can drive myself."

"She's *not* a nice girl, Father-in-law. She's just called your sister an interfering old woman."

"It's a tenable point of view," said John, coolly.

"Well after that I'm leaving whoever else isn't," said Aunt Bea. "If you can take that about your own sister, John, I'm not staying in the same house."

"Well, you're not having my wheelchair," said John.

May said, "You can't go, Aunt. You're not sufficiently mobile."

"I'm going."

"Then I'm coming with you to see you settled in," said May.

Jocelyn's instinct, hearing the uproar in the room below, was to crawl under his desk and hide. But he knew from experience that this would get him nowhere. He went downstairs and sidled bravely into Aunt Bea's room.

"Is something the matter?" he asked helpfully. Then his face lit up. "Why, Miss Nightingale, I thought you'd left us."

She gave him the brightest of smiles. "Poor Mr Pentecost. It must be terribly confusing for you. But your father's hurt his foot again, so I've brought him home and if you could persuade your aunt to let go this wheelchair I could make the old gentleman more comfortable."

May said, "But – how did you hurt your ankle again, Father-in-law?"

"I braked suddenly."

Gaylord said, "There was an enormous great carthorse, galloping down the road, and Grandpa had to stand on the brake."

May said, "But why didn't Mr Taylor do that?"

"Do what?" asked Jocelyn, who liked to get things right.

"Tread on the brake," cried May in exasperation.

"Who's Mr Taylor?" asked Miss Nightingale.

"Is Aunt Bea really going?" asked Gaylord hopefully.

May almost screamed, "Will somebody answer my question. Why didn't Mr Taylor tread on his own brakes?"

"He wasn't there," said John, verging on the sheepish.

"You mean – you don't mean you were driving his taxi?"

185

"Not exactly," said John.

Gaylord looked anxiously at his grandfather. Momma, it seemed to him, was Getting Her Teeth In.

And if she found out about the subterfuge who'd be blamed, as if he didn't know? Not Grandpa. Not Miss Nightingale. Oh, no.

He gave his mind to concocting a sad story about poor Mr Taylor having one of his funny turns, and Grandpa taking over. But grandpa got in first. "I took Miss Nightingale in my car, May."

"Why?" May said coldly.

"Because I damn well wanted to," said John.

"How extremely foolish," said May.

John said, "And since we are on the subject, May, I've invited Miss Nightingale to stay and be my chauffeur and, if Bea is hopefully going as she says, my nurse. Only doing it for your sake, of course, old girl," he finished rather unconvincingly.

Gaylord thought the room seemed littered with unanswered questions. "Is Aunt Bea really going?" He repeated plaintively.

"Yes, she is," said Aunt Bea firmly.

"And is Miss Nightingale really staying to be your chauffeur, Grandpa?"

"Yes, she is," said Grandpa.

"And is Momma really going with Aunt Bea?"

"Yes, she is," said May.

"Whoopee," said Gaylord.

"And now that that's all settled," said John Pentecost, "I have a few things to say. Jocelyn, May, will you both come to my room, please."

An alarmed silence fell. Such formality was unheard of at The Cypresses. May looked at Jocelyn and found he had gone suddenly pale. Jocelyn looked at May and noted an unusual lack of serenity. The old man opened the door courteously. They passed through, and went into his room, and stood waiting for him, anxious and puzzled.

He hobbled in, seized May's arm. "May, my dear, I rode rough-shod over you then."

"You certainly did," she said, unsmiling. "And then you tried to butter me up by saying it was all for my sake. If you want that girl here to drive you round say so, and we'll discuss it; but don't present me with a fait accompli and then say you're only doing it for me."

"My dear, sit down," he said. "Jocelyn, pour us all a drink for heaven's sake." He turned back to May. "Tell me what you've got against this girl."

May said, aggressively, "I don't like fly-by-nights."

"You don't know she's a fly-by-night. All I'll admit is that she's one of those women who are charming to men, and don't put themselves out much for women. So they're not terribly popular with your sex."

May exploded. "Don't put themselves out much – ? She called your sister an interfering old woman."

John turned to his son. "And because of that innocuous remark Bea's going home and May's insisting on taking her."

"May?" it was a cry of despair. Jocelyn stared at his wife in disbelief. "May! You can't. What about the children?" What about me? he wanted to add, but thought it impolitic.

May said, "I shall take Amanda. You and Gaylord will manage. I should be back in twenty-four hours with any luck."

What if there isn't any luck? Jocelyn wondered.

John's voice became hard and business-like. "May! I want this girl to stay till I can again drive myself. But you're the mistress here. So what do you say? Yes? Or no?"

May was silent. John said, "May, you know the regard in which I hold you. But I do ask you to realise what a change this would make to my limited way of life."

Jocelyn said, "May, if it hadn't been for my folly, Father would be driving himself."

John said, "I hadn't been going to mention that. But – since it's been mentioned, it's a point. Jocelyn did cripple me. You could call it criminal folly."

May remained silent. At last she said, "Between you, you don't give me much choice, do you? Right. You'd better make what arrangements you think fit with Miss Nightingale, Father-in-law."

And she ran out of the room and Jocelyn heard her clattering upstairs. A bedroom door slammed.

Father and son looked at each other. Jocelyn said, "I'd better go."

His father said, "Worst thing you could possibly do."

Jocelyn climbed slowly upstairs. He went into the bedroom. May sat on a small chair, staring at him.

It wasn't a nice stare. It was a hard, hostile stare. "Thank you," she said bitterly. "Thank you very much."

"For what?" he said bleakly.

"For helping your father cut the ground from under my feet."

"I was only trying to be fair. I did cripple him, God forgive me."

"Oh, forget about being fair for once. I'm your wife, remember."

He said, "That doesn't mean you're always right."

She looked at him in amazement. She actually bridled. "It does, as far as you're concerned. Loyalty, my lad. I thought that was one of your cornerstones."

His heart was heavy. He gave a great sigh. "If she's the girl I think she is, she will transform Father's life. And I *was* responsible. It's all true, May."

"True or not – and as for her transforming his life, she's the sort of girl who'll be married to him in a week."

"May, don't be ridiculous. Father, at his age? He's got too much sense."

"No man's got too much sense when a pretty girl's around," she said tersely.

Suddenly she was weeping. "Jocelyn, nothing's ever going to be the same again. You and I quarrelling, a stranger foisted on me, poor Aunt Bea departing in anger. Jocelyn," she wailed, "what's happening to us?"

It was a grim catalogue. And, he remembered, there was an item May didn't even know about yet.

He pulled the pink envelope from his pocket, gave it to her. "That came this morning," he said.

Her eyesight was better than his. She read it, gave him a stricken look. "Who – ?" she said.

"Reuben Briggs," he said.

"Horrible. Has he admitted it?"

He shook his head. "Haven't tackled him yet."

"Then you'd better, hadn't you?"

Had he shown it her, he wondered, in a subconscious effort to get her sympathy. If so, he had failed miserably. "I'll go now," he said.

He stood irresolute, moved towards her. She glowered at him. He changed direction. Went to the door. "See you – later," he murmured. "I'll just – see about this." Then – "Do you have to go, May?"

"Of course I do. Poor Aunt Bea. We've treated her abominably. I must at least take her home and see her settled. If I didn't she'd be on my conscience for the rest of my life. And on yours, I should hope."

She was silent. Wretchedly he pulled the door to behind him.

Chapter 12

He set off for Reuben's cottage, preparing his mind for a thoroughly painful interview. But first into his study to have another quiet look at that infamous letter.

He found the telephone ringing, picked up the receiver. "Can I speak to Miss Nightingale?" said a voice.

"Yes," he said. "Who's calling?"

"Mandrake Press."

"Good Lord," he said. "Isn't that Arthur Mandrake?"

"Yes. Who's that?"

"Jocelyn Pentecost."

"Who?"

"Jocelyn. Jocelyn Pentecost."

"Oh, hello. What are you doing there?"

"I live here."

"Good Lord. I say, can you get La Nightingale? There's an awful lot happening about this ghastly book of hers."

"Ghastly? She thinks you're publishing it."

"Of course we're publishing it. It'll go like hot cakes."

"But you said – ?"

"My dear chap, we couldn't publish old stick-in-the-muds like you if we didn't have a few ghastly bestsellers."

"Thanks very much." He went on to the landing, shouted. She came running. "Mandrake Press," he said, giving her the receiver.

"Ta," she said. "Hello." She listened. Then: "This twenty

thousand words? In ten days? Yes, I should think so." She turned to Jocelyn. "They want me to take these twenty thousand words out in ten days. You will give me a hand, won't you?"

"No, I will not," he said crossly.

She spoke into the receiver. "Yes, that'll be all right. Oh, good." She rang off. "Won't be much of a job," she said. "And I know you'll help whatever you say. You're so good-natured, Mr Pentecost." She smiled winsomely.

"I will not help," he said, in capitals. "And another thing. Don't you think it's rather a cheek to take over this telephone number? You've just given Arthur Mandrake the impression we're living together."

She gurgled with laughter. "Mr Pentecost, what a fascinating idea." But Jocelyn did not reply. He had just seen May go past the open door. That laughter, he thought gloomily, would not help his cause one little bit.

"Teapot's on t'ob," said Reuben, grinning. "Come on in, Mister Pentecost."

The warmth of this welcome quite cut the ground from under Jocelyn's feet. He went in. "Sit you down," said Reuben. He tipped some condensed milk into a cup, wiped the tin with his finger, sucked his finger relatively clean, and filled the cup with a black and virulent brew from the teapot. "Saccharin?"

"Yes, please."

Reuben produced a small brass box, clawed about inside, captured a tablet between two finger nails, and dropped it into Jocelyn's tea. "Always use me old dad's snuff box for sweeteners," he said. He brooded. "Filthy habit, snuff."

"Yes," said Jocelyn.

Mr Briggs settled himself comfortably. "And what can I do

for you, Mister Pentecost?"

Jocelyn would dearly have liked to enjoy the friendliness of this welcome, drink his abominable tea, and go in peace.

But had he not set his hand to the plough? He pulled that frightening letter from his pocket. He said, mildly, "Why did you send me that, Mr Briggs?"

Reuben examined the envelope, turned it over. "Can I look inside?"

"Of course."

Reuben pulled out the sheet, read. "It's the Commination Service," he said.

"I know that. I want to know why you sent it me."

Reuben sipped his tea. "Some good stuff in that Commination Service," he said. "I like straight talking."

"Then why do you resort to anonymous letters? And why don't you tell me why you sent it?" Jocelyn was beginning to feel desperate.

"Because I wanted to tell you how daft I think you are, first not teaching that lad of yours to shut gates, and then crippling first your old dad, and now that nice Anty of yours. Burt I'm only a simple rustic. That old Pray Book says things better. More tea?"

"No, thank you."

Jocelyn rose. "You do realise this is a criminal offence? If I showed this letter to the Police you'd be in very serious trouble."

"Nay, Mr Pentecost. You're the one who ought to be in trouble, after what *you* done." He crossed to the door and opened it. "On your way, Mr Pentecost." He was suddenly contemptuous.

Jocelyn came away. Failure. Reuben had been too clever for him. Which wasn't difficult, he thought miserably. And already the evening was beginning to gather in the grove of trees that hung over Reuben's cottage. And a little wind blew in from the coming winter, stirring the first dead leaves and chilling the heart.

Jocelyn trudged home; and he, who had always so loved walking, now thought what a wearisome occupation it was: picking up one leaden foot, and placing it in front of the other, and so ad infinitum. And at home what awaited him? An angry wife, a father who thought him a fool, and Aunt Bea departing in dudgeon and a beautiful cuckoo bird who was already getting so big that very soon there'd be no room for anyone else inside the nest.

In front of him was the house that held all that was dear to him: his loved ones, his chosen way of life, his books, his comfort, his problems. And it was as threatened as though a thunderbolt hung over it.

There was a light turning in his study. No sign of May downstairs. He ran up to his study. Miss Nightingale was sitting at his desk. A pool of light held her manuscript. She looked up. "Hello, Mr Pentecost. Hope you don't mind, but it's so convenient working up here. I say, twenty thousand words is an awful lot of words, isn't it?"

"Yes," he said shortly. "Do you know where my wife is?"

"In the kitchen as usual, I imagine., I say, you really *will* help me with this won't you? I don't quite know where to begin."

"Page one's a good place," he said. "And now excuse me. I must find my wife."

She said, "You sound a bit edgy to me. Is it because I've pinched your study? I'll clear out if you like."

"Oh, carry on," he said. He dived downstairs. No sign of May. But his father was in the drawing room. Simmering. Bristling. "Jocelyn, there you are. Why the devil are you always missing when you're wanted? May's gone off her head, dammit."

Jocelyn sank into a chair. He sighed. "Where is May?"

"She's driving your Aunt Bea home. Says your aunt's not mobile enough to manage on her own. Well, what about me? Does she think I'm mobile? Charity begins at home, if you ask me."

Jocelyn was feeling a deep hurt. "You don't mean, they've actually left? Without saying goodbye to *me*?"

"Yes. A nightie, two tins of baby food and Amanda." The old man pondered. "It's my belief," he said profoundly, "that she can't stomach my bringing in this bally girl."

Jocelyn sighed again. "Yes. But – not even to let me know."

"Kittle cattle, women," said John. "Even the best of 'em. That's what I always say."

He glared. "I'm not getting rid of Nightingale, mind."

"Did May say when she was coming back?"

"No."

Jocelyn said, "Well, we can't lose May, Father."

"Up to you to talk her round then. Go and fetch her back if necessary. Remind her of her marriage vows. Love, cherish, obey. All that sort of thing."

"I don't think she said 'obey'," said Jocelyn.

"Well that, if I may say so, is typical, Jocelyn. I suppose you accepted some wishy-washy verb like 'honour'. How daft can you get?"

Jocelyn said, "Actually, Father, I don't accept that honour is a wish-washy word. I think it defines the relationship between May and me admirably."

"Oh, yes. For the small change of life, I agree. But – "

"I'd better go and see to Gaylord's supper," said Jocelyn wearily.

"These are super sandwiches," said Gaylord. "You use a lot more honey than Momma."

"Oh good," said Poppa, relieved. His ego could do with a bit of bolstering.

"Why did Aunt Bea go?"

"I think perhaps Grandpa said something that made her cross."

"So she went."

"So she went," said Poppa.

Gaylord mulled this over. "Why didn't Miss Nightingale do my supper?"

Jocelyn said, with a bitterness that did not escape his son, "She's very busy editing her book."

Gaylord was silent, assessing the situation. He didn't think Momma being away was quite as nice as he'd expected. There was a sort of emptiness, as though the lights had dimmed, and a great silence had filled the house. He said, "I bet you won't half be lonely tonight, without Momma. I bet you'll be cold."

Poppa laughed. "I shall survive, Gaylord."

Gaylord wasn't at all convinced. He didn't think Poppa sounded as though he'd survive, or even as though he thought he'd survive. He said, "I'll come in Momma's place if you like, Poppa."

"No thank you," Poppa said, gratefully but firmly. Having Gaylord in bed was like chumming up to an octopus.

Ah, well. Gaylord had offered. He put up a sticky mouth to be kissed. And was suddenly filled with a great pity for this lonely adult. "Night night, Poppa," he said softly, kissing large areas of his father's face.

"Night night, Gaylord," said Jocelyn, making for the bathroom.

When Poppa had gone, Gaylord gave his mind to wondering why Momma's absence was not the splendid thing he had always supposed it to be.

And suddenly he understood. Freedom was the operative word. He was free to wander round the house, even to go outside, and no questions asked. He could do anything, the most dreadful thing in the world; and Momma wouldn't know!

There was only one trouble: he couldn't think of anything really dreadful; and he felt too sleepy to do it even if he could.

And even as he upbraided himself for wasting this golden opportunity, he drifted into sleep...

He awoke to a distant thunder.

He loved thunder. He was out of bed in no time, and in to his father's room. "Poppa, it's thundering."

"Hello, Gaylord," Poppa said wanly. (Did he detect a slight lack of welcome, wondered Gaylord. No, he decided.) He took it as axiomatic that he was always welcome anywhere, at any time.

"Is it funny without Momma?"

"It's bloody lonely," said Poppa, who was feeling sorry for himself and neglected.

Gaylord was deeply touched. He wandered round, making social conversation and fiddling with every object in the room, until Jocelyn wanted to smack his fingers. Then, having cheered his father up, he set off to exercise his freedom.

A light was shining under the study door. He tapped, went in. "Hello, Gaylord," cried Miss Nightingale. (Now she really *did* sound pleased to see him.) "What are you doing out of bed?"

"It's thundering," he said.

"I know." She looked suddenly forlorn. "I'm afraid of thunder, Gaylord. But you'll protect me, won't you?"

Gaylord felt immensely brave. "'Course." And yet, he admitted to himself, he didn't really know how to protect ladies from thunder. He said, "Perhaps you'd be safer with Poppa."

"No, I'll be all right," she said laughing. "I'm ready for bed."

Gaylord was sorry. She'd have been nice company for Poppa; and she wouldn't have been frightened of the thunder. "It'd be all right," he said. "Momma isn't there."

She said, "You funny boy. He doesn't want me."

"He's bloody lonely," said Gaylord.

She laughed, and kissed him fondly. "Now don't you go putting ideas in your father's head," she said. "Or in mine." And she ran into her bedroom.

Gaylord went back to see his father. "Miss Nightingale's afraid of thunder, Poppa, and I told her you'd protect her if she came in here. I told her Momma wasn't here."

"Oh, Good Lord," said Jocelyn, roused suddenly from sleep and gazing apprehensively at the door. "What did she say?"

She said, "Now don't you go putting ideas into your father's head. Or in mine."

"Oh, Good Lord," Jocelyn said again.

"The thunder's getting worse," said Gaylord. "She's ever so frightened."

"Then she'll have to stay frightened," said Jocelyn, with what his son felt was an unusual lack of feeling.

"I told her you were bloody lonely," said Gaylord.

Jocelyn sighed. He said, "Gaylord, stop wandering round the house and go to bed. Off you go."

Gaylord stuck his lower lip out. Here he was, as always,

trying to help everybody out; and everybody, as always, flatly refusing to be helped.

Yet he felt so sorry for poor lonely Poppa. He kissed him fondly, and departed.

Gaylord had been right. The storm was coming nearer. The thunder rattled and grumbled, and now the lightning and the rain were chasing each other down the window panes. Jocelyn sat up in bed. Miss Nightingale, he thought anxiously, would be getting more and more frightened. Then, feeling very foolish, he got out of bed, tiptoed across the room, turned the key in the lock, and went back to bed.

He was deeply ashamed. He read enough modern novels to know that none of his fellow authors would have behaved in so craven a manner. They, red-blooded fellows to a man, wouldn't have locked themselves in. They'd have hung a welcome notice on the door.

And yet? Surely there were still things like honour, and loyalty? Surely he wasn't the only man who would remember an absent wife?

But to lock himself in? Was that where the cowardice lay? Perhaps to leave the door open and confront this beautiful but brash young woman with the Armour of Righteousness? Was that where salvation lay?

What had she said to Gaylord? "Don't put ideas in your father's head. Or in mine?"

Well, he'd certainly put ideas in Jocelyn's head. Puritan upbringing or not, Jocelyn had a very clear idea of what Miss Nightingale would be like under a nightie. But those delights, he knew with all the authority of Calvin and John Knox behind him, were not for him. What are you? he asked himself. A loyal and honourable husband? Or a man so afraid of his brash age that he locks himself in his bedroom?

Being Jocelyn, he strongly suspected the latter.

Eventually, he fell into an anxious sleep. The disagreements with May and his father, Reuben's strange welcome and even stranger dismissal, his curtness with Miss Nightingale, his clumsy self-criticism, all had wearied him. The thunder raged about the house, the rain kettle-drummed on his window, the lightning stormed against his tired eyelids. Yet he slept.

Suddenly he was awake. Someone was tapping gently at his door!

He leapt out of bed, pulled on his old dressing gown (the Armour of Righteousness, he thought bitterly). He hurried over to the door. "Who is it?" he called.

The tapping had grown louder, more insistent. "Who is it?" he called again.

"Me. Nightingale. Can I speak to you, Mr Pentecost?"

He pulled the Armour of Righteousness more tightly about him, and opened the door, certain now, in this moment of truth, of only one thing: that if seduction was on the cards, it wasn't going to be he who dealt them.

But it was soon clear that whatever was on Miss Nightingale's mind, it wasn't seduction. She was clutching the Armour of Righteousness about her even more tightly than Jocelyn. And she looked scared and anxious. "Mr Pentecost, someone's knocking at the front door. And I think they're shouting. I thought – I ought to tell you – in case – you hadn't – "

"Thanks," he said. "I'll go."

"I'll come with you," she said, to his secret relief.

They went downstairs (hand-in-hand, he was surprised to realise). He could hear the knocking now; even, he thought, cries of distress. Who could it be? Surely not May, returning on this night of storm the quicker to be with her forsaken husband?

He unlocked the door, slid the bolts, opened the door a crack.

No sooner was the door open than a small, drenched animal scurried into the hall and crouched by the stairs, teeth chattering, and whimpering with fear. "Poppa, he was horrible. All wet and toothy, and nasty dead eyes, and his fur coat was all sopping." Jocelyn realised it was not the warm summer rain that was making the boy's teeth chatter. It was fear and horror.

Jocelyn peered into the teeming night. Then he shut and locked the door, put his arm round his shivering son. "Who was it? Where was he?"

"Standing in front of the barn door, Poppa. All in the rain."

Miss Nightingale said, "I'll see to Gaylord, Mr Pentecost. He's had a bad fright. If you want to look round outside later, I'll come with you."

"No. You see to the boy. I'm going out *now*."

"Well at least take a coat." She pulled an old raincoat about his shoulders. He set off for the barn, telling himself that even the foolish virgins would not have needed a pocket torch in this weather. The lightning was almost incessant. Every flash illuminated not only the trees and buildings but also brilliant curtains of raindrops. Every tree, every blade of grass was hung with diamonds. It was like standing in an Aladdin's cave of brightness.

Only the black doors of the great barn were unfestooned with sparkling raindrops. He hurried towards it, eager to find what trick of light or darkness had so terrified his son.

Nothing. Or was there? He peered. A greyness in the centre of the black doors? He felt a sudden shiver down his spine.

Now there was a lull in the lightning. He came nearer. Yes, surely, the blackness of those great doors framed something, someone...

Then, a long, continuous flash, peal upon peal of thunder, a tremendous deluge of rain. And the grey, sodden, something or someone seemed to leap towards him in the tempest, its long white teeth glinting in the burst of angry electric fire. Jocelyn gave a strangled cry and flung himself backwards. Now the grey nothingness seemed to be lying on the ground. Jocelyn, despite his horror, stirred it with his foot: the sodden, toothy, obscene remains of a sheep. The next flash showed the dry patch on the barn doors to which the animal had been nailed.

Reuben! he thought furiously. How dare he terrify my son?

Anger was a rare and uncomfortable emotion for him. He could absorb a great deal of hurt when it was applied to himself. But when it affected his loved ones, he was soon emotionally charged. The knowledge that his shoe had kicked that obscenity filled him with a sense of contamination. Savagely he dragged his toecap against the cleansing grass. Then he hurried into the house, sick and helplessly angry. It was two in the morning. Six hours before he could confront that scholarly yet unsavoury sheep farmer with his warped jests. Sleep was out of the question. And anyway, he must comfort Gaylord.

But Gaylord wasn't in his room. "Gaylord," he called softly on the landing.

No reply. There could only be one answer. Gaylord was still in need of care and moral support, and Miss Nightingale had taken him into her room.

He went and knocked on her door.

He heard footsteps. The door opened. Miss Nightingale stood there. She was still wearing the Armour of Righteousness, though now, it seemed, a little less protectively. He was still ready to be angry with anyone. "Where's Gaylord?" he snapped.

She looked at him in surprise. "I put him to bed. He's a brave boy. He'd quite got over his shock. It thought he'd be asleep by now."

"Well he isn't," he said.

"Then he's probably in the kitchen," she said coolly. "If I know small boys."

He made for the stairs. "I'll come," she said.

Gaylord was in the kitchen, enjoying a packet of crisps. "Gaylord, go back to bed at once," cried Jocelyn, amazed to hear the command in his voice. He thought it rather suited him, and imagined he saw a certain admiration in Miss Nightingale's eye. Gaylord thought Poppa sounded like Momma. He was a bit disappointed in him. He said, "I wasn't really frightened at that thing, Poppa."

"Then you jolly well ought to have been," said Jocelyn. Frankly, it had scared the daylights out of *him*.

"Now, bed," said Jocelyn. Gaylord skilfully shovelled the remaining crisps into his mouth and made for the stairs. Jocelyn and Miss Nightingale went with him. Miss Nightingale tucked him in. Then she kissed him goodnight. Jocelyn did the same. "Night-night, old man," he said. "Call me if you have – bad dreams."

They came out. Together they strolled across the landing as he and May had so often done. Miss Nightingale pushed open the door of her room, went in. Jocelyn, absent-mindedly following, suddenly checked, went very red, and said, "Good Lord, I'm terribly sorry. I – just wasn't thinking."

"That's all right, she said. She looked up at him, grinned. She lifted her two white hands, laid one on each side of his jaw. Then she stood on tiptoe and kissed him full on the mouth. "Good-night, you stuffy old thing. Sleep tight," she said fondly.

She lowered her hands. And suddenly both her voice and her expression hardened. "Mustn't do anything to cause darling May any distress, must we dear." And she shut the door with unexpected force.

Chapter 13

Still nearly six hours before Jocelyn could start getting things off his chest.

And there were a lot of things on his chest: one of which was May and another was Miss Nightingale.

How dare May go rushing off like that without even so much as a by-your-leave. He wasn't thinking of her duty to him. But dash it, she'd no business leaving young Gaylord. She wasn't to know Reuben would go finally off his rocker, of course. But the fact remained that he had, and poor Gaylord had had to be succoured and comforted by a stranger. She must come home! As for Miss Nightingale – she'd got to go; and for once he felt angry enough to insist to the old man that he send her packing. He even sat up in bed, prepared to go and have a showdown at four in the morning.

But, he reminded himself, he was a civilised Englishman. Civilised Englishmen chose the time and place for their disagreements with great care. Why, he realised with a shudder, neither he nor his father would have been shaved. It would have been most unseemly.

But he didn't sleep. And he would have been the first to admit that the knowledge that the lovely Miss Nightingale was separated from him by only two doors was a major cause of his wakefulness: that, and the fact that he seemed destined on this coming day to quarrel with almost everyone he knew. It was not a pleasant prospect.

At eight o'clock he rose and bathed, shaved, dressed. At eight thirty he was like a ravening lion, seeking whom he might devour.

Who should be first?

He knocked at his father's door. "Come in," called a cheerful voice.

He went in.

John Pentecost was perched up in bed. The tray across his knees held teapot, cup and saucer, milk jug, a plate of bacon, sausage and fried eggs, and toast, butter and marmalade. The old man said, in a voice charged with emotion, "Look at this lot, Jocelyn. Isn't it splendid, isn't she a splendid woman? Even old May never rose to these heights." He sighed. "Oh, if only I were thirty years younger."

"You'd still be ten years too old for her," Jocelyn said coldly. "Father! Don't start getting maudlin at your age."

"You can't get maudlin about eggs and bacon, dammit."

"I wasn't talking about eggs and bacon," said Jocelyn. "Actually, I've come to ask you to send her away."

The old man nearly tipped up the tray. "Send her away? You must be mad."

"No I'm not." He swallowed. "I'm not prepared to have Miss Nightingale running the house in May's absence."

The old man looked at him shrewdly. "Jocelyn, what's happened to you this morning? Not had Miss Nightingale trying to seduce you, have you?" Jocelyn thought he looked almost envious.

"Of course I haven't," he said indignantly. "But – well, who is she? We know nothing about her."

"I know she's a damn good cook and a damn good driver. That's enough for me."

Something had happened to Jocelyn. He, who was always

so amenable, was finding this new day quite unbearable. And he had the sense to know that it was his own feelings that were tormenting him. He had come in here full of truculent courage. But already he could feel it running out at the heels of his shoes. His father was just too strong a man for him: would have been even without Jocelyn's persistent feeling of guilt over his father's accident.

And now this guilt was suddenly accentuated. The old man jerked suddenly, spilling his tea. He looked contrite. "Sorry," he muttered. "Damned ankles playing up."

"Are they still – very painful?" asked Jocelyn, contrite.

"Yes. It's going to be a long time before I can drive."

"I'm afraid you may be right, Father."

"I know dashed well I'm right." He sat, silent, and Jocelyn realised he was beginning to simmer. Worse. He was coming to the boil. For now he said, "Honestly, Jocelyn. By a piece of irresponsibility worthy of a five-year-old child you break both my ankles for me. I can't walk. I can't drive. And when, entirely by my own efforts, I find an excellent chauffeur, you – " he glared savagely – "you want to send her away and destroy my new-won mobility. You, who are the sole cause of all my misfortune." His voice broke.

Jocelyn crept away, chastened and silent. If it did occur to him that the whole scene had been stage-managed, he very quickly put it away from him. He was a loyal son.

Losing hands down with his father quite destroyed any confidence he had that he could bring May to heel. But he tried.

He telephoned her. Her voice came over the wires, clear, flute-like. "Darling, how lovely to hear your voice!"

Such anger as he had left, abated at those welcoming words. But he would not be mollified. "May, what on earth do you mean by rushing off like that? How soon can you get back?"

"Not for some time, dear. Aunt Bea ran her wheelchair into her own doorpost and badly sprained her wrist. I can't possibly leave her."

He said, "May, listen. Miss Nightingale's taking us all over. It's an impossible situation."

"Well I told you she would if you let her, didn't I, dear? You must stand by to repel boarders."

"It's too late. She's boarded." Carefully he dropped his bombshell. "You were right. Father is talking of marrying her."

There was silence. That's given her something to think about, he told himself. But then there were peals of laughter from the other end. May sounded in the highest of spirits. "You don't mean you believe him, darling?"

"It's no laughing matter," he said grumpily.

"I know it isn't. But then you now he's far too sensible to do anything so foolish."

"Why, you said sense doesn't count when a pretty girl's around."

"It does in this case. It was only a ploy to get me back, wasn't it?"

He wished women didn't all know men so well. Slowly, thoughtfully, he put back the receiver. He was scared. He didn't want another night without May to protect him from Miss Nightingale.

Who next? He certainly hadn't got far with his wife or his father. To be frank he hadn't got anywhere. He'd simply got a veto on any move to get rid of la Nightingale.

He went up to his study to think things over and lick his wounds. But Miss Nightingale was seated at his desk. She jumped up, bubbling over with laughter. "Mr Pentecost, do congratulate me. I've had a proposal of marriage."

He stared at her in amazement. "No!" he groped for words. "What – what did *you* say?"

"Oh, I pointed out the difference in our ages. Said I didn't think it was quite viable. But that of course I was very flattered and should always remember the great honour and so on."

So it hadn't just been a ploy to get May back! "What did *he* say?" he asked, icy cold.

"Oh, that he'd given it very careful consideration, and he'd decided it was me or the shelf, and he thought he preferred me. And he drew a rather moving picture of us both dining every night on baked beans."

A great light dawned. "Good God. I thought – " He dashed out of the study, feeling incredibly foolish, went into Gaylord's room.

Gaylord looked listless and wan. "Hello, Poppa."

"Hello, old man. Have you got over that nasty sheep business?"

"Yes, thank you, Poppa."

"Oh, good." He paused. "And now you're on the shelf, I gather."

"Yes. I can't see anybody waiting for me. Auntie Becky, Miss Nightingale."

"There'll be someone," said Jocelyn comfortingly. He put an arm about his son's shoulders. Childhood, he thought. The problems and fears that haunt us! But nothing to the problems that we adults create for ourselves, he told himself, remembering Reuben, remembering the fraught night that could lie ahead.

He went and saw Reuben…

He went to see Reuben. And as he went his anger mounted

again. There was no doubt about it. This morning his emotions were up and down like a raging fever.

On his way he passed the barn. The sodden fleece, the grinning head, still lay there. Sometime, he knew, he would have to move the sickening thing; or force Reuben to move it? At the moment he felt quite capable of such an unusual *tour de force*. He even found himself looking forward to it.

The wild night had left a morning of unbelievable sweetness. The path that wound up to Reuben's cottage seemed to climb to sunlit uplands where anger had no place. The trees that sheltered the house were as still as the blue sky above them. A column of smoke arose from the chimney as contentedly as smoke from a Red Indian's pipe of peace.

And, standing on a tree trunk, overlooking the placid river valley, was Reuben Briggs. The fact that he seemed totally unaware of Jocelyn's approach enraged Jocelyn almost beyond speech.

"Hey, you, Reuben," cried Jocelyn from a distance.

Reuben turned slowly and stared at Jocelyn. Then he gave his attention back to the river valley. Jocelyn felt about five years old.

Jocelyn came closer. "Reuben! What do you mean by terrifying my son?"

Now Reuben looked him full in the face. "Talking to me, Mr Pentecost?"

"Of course I am."

"My enemies call me Mr Briggs," said Reuben.

Jocelyn faltered. "Am I your enemy?" he asked in wonder. "Why am I your enemy, Mr Briggs?"

"You'd best come inside," said Briggs. He led the way into the cottage. The table was strewn with the remains of breakfast: cold bacon rinds, a half empty cup of tea festooned with fag-ends in the saucer.

Jocelyn stepped gingerly into the porch. "Nay, come on in," called Reuben. Unwillingly Jocelyn moved forward. Reuben, his back to his guest, was now shovelling the detritus of breakfast into the fire. "It's a fine morning, Mr Pentecost," he said affably.

Jocelyn said again, "Why am I your enemy, Mr Briggs?"

Reuben threw a few logs on the fire. "Cold these mornings. Because of what you and yours did to my old ewe, Mr Pentecost."

"But – we've never had anything to do with your sheep."

"Oh yes, you have, Mr P. Didn't teach your son to shut gates. Your son left gates open, ran among the poor old ladies and frightened them out of their wits. Scattered them. One of 'em never returned. Found her weeks later, dead as a doornail poor thing." He gave Jocelyn a look of sudden venom. "You wouldn't think an educated English gentleman would wreak such havoc, would you? But – as I say, Mr Pentecost, I'm only a simple rustic."

Jocelyn didn't want anything more to do with Reuben. Yet he had to behave according to his lights. In spite of all his humiliations he pulled out his cheque book. "How much is a ewe worth?" he asked.

"More than you've got in that fancy cheque book of yours, Mr Pentecost. To me, anyway."

"Please," said Jocelyn.

Reuben's eyes filled with tears. "Get our, Mr Pentecost," he said, "before you make me even more angry."

"Very well," Jocelyn sighed heavily. He put his cheque book back in his pocket. He walked out of the house. He looked back once. Reuben was still staring after him.

Gaylord and Miss Nightingale were washing up together. For disdainful maiden and rejected suitor they looked fairly relaxed. But Gaylord ran to meet him. "Poppa, guess what

– Momma rang up, just to speak to me. She's coming home."

"She is? But – an hour ago she said she couldn't. Did she say why she changed her mind?"

"No." He looked vague. "I just told her about the thunderstorm and about Miss Nightingale being frightened in the middle of the night and me saying Poppa would be ever so good at protecting her and Miss Nightingale saying I mustn't put ideas in Poppa's head or in hers and I told Momma I didn't know what Miss Nightingale meant and Momma didn't answer, she just said she was coming home straight away."

"Thank you, Gaylord," said Jocelyn. He went to see his father. "May's coming home," he said.

"I should damn well think so, too," said John. He glared. "But she's not getting rid of Nightingale; I shall expect your support on that issue, Jocelyn. That's the least you owe me."

Jocelyn's heart sank. It looked like being a lively day, with himself caught once again between the upper and nether millstones. He said, rather desperately, "Father, you've a right to complain every morning of your life about my irresponsibility over the wretched trap. But could we please leave it alone for the moment? You – did say some very hard things earlier about my guilt, remember."

"Guilt, dear boy? What guilt was that?"

"Knowing all these months that I'd crippled you. And that you hated me for it."

His father stared at him in amazement. At last he said, "You know your trouble, Jocelyn. You write too many novels."

It was Jocelyn's turn to stare. "You mean – you didn't think – all those things?"

"'Course I didn't. One of those unfortunate accidents. I don't waste time apportioning blame. Suppose I went and tripped over May's hoover flex. Shouldn't blame old May."

"Why, that's just what she told me," Jocelyn said, awestruck.

Yet surely he was remembering terrible words spoken only this morning: words that in this present context somehow did not ring true: "irresponsibility worthy of a five-year-old child"; "the sole cause of all my misfortune." He said, "You had very different feelings earlier this morning."

"I did?"

"Yes. Irresponsibility, five-year-old child, sole cause of misfortune."

The old man looked interested. "Did I say all that?"

"And much more."

"My dear fellow." John was at his most urbane. "I was simply making a point about something or other. Could have been about Miss Nightingale." Suddenly he gave one of his very rare grins. "You mustn't take me so seriously, Jocelyn."

Jocelyn looked hurt, and cross, and finally managed a smile himself. "You really are – " he said.

But now, a load really had shifted from his mind. His father was walking, would soon be driving. And he, Jocelyn, had spent the summer months beating his breast and crying mea culpa. Now his father had freed him of that load. And May was coming home.

And, as he thought that, all his anxieties returned. May and his father were going to clash as soon as she arrived. And he, Jocelyn, was inescapably cast as Pig-in-the-Middle.

Henry Bartlett said, "Your know that tiger trap, Gaylord?"

"Yes, Henry?"

"It had vandals. Ages ago."

Gaylord looked perturbed. "How?"

"They'd filled it up with soil and flattened the top. I reckon they'd made it so a tiger could walk over it and not be caught."

They walked on, both made speechless by such mindless vandalism. "Perhaps it's the RSPCA," said Gaylord. He couldn't think of anyone else who'd be on the side of Bengal Tigers. "Anyway, if the circus comes next year and a tiger escapes and eats somebody it'll be the RSPCA's fault."

"It won't, Gaylord," said Henry, getting ready to glow with satisfaction. "Because I've repaired it. As soon as I saw the damage I repaired it. It's as good as new now. Perhaps better. I reckon it'd catch the biggest, savagest tiger in the world."

There was a silence. Gaylord said, "*You* repaired it?"

Henry nodded, too full for speech.

"Thank you Henry," said Gaylord. Simple words, but he was deeply touched. Henry, he felt, had, by his prompt action, made Derbyshire a safer place. "Thanks, Henry," he said again.

"That's all right, Gaylord," said Henry.

The telephone was ringing when May walked back into her house. She picked up the receiver: "Shepherd's Warning, 3154."

An alcoholic voice said, "Hello. Is that the Secretary or the girl friend?"

"The wife, actually," said May, and banged down the receiver.

Chapter 14

May was back. And for the moment nothing else mattered. They flew into each other's arms. "Oh darling," she cried. "How marvellous everything looks. I can't believe it's only been a day. Yet I resent every hour spent away from you my love."

"I too," he said. Yet he knew that every lovers' meeting, however ardent, carries seed of discord. In an effort to postpone questions about the thunderstorm, he said, "Something will amaze you: Gaylord proposed marriage to Miss Nightingale."

Her arms fell from his neck. She took a step backward. Her eyes no longer gazed into his. "It does not amuse me," she said heavily. "Neither does Gaylord's story of the thunderstorm. Neither do I enjoy being mistaken for the girl friend the moment I walk into the house. In fact, I find nothing in the least amusing about Miss Nightingale."

He said, "Darling, I think you're exaggerating. She's brash, I know, and pushing; and she plays up to Father. But there's no harm in her."

"No? And Gaylord didn't put any ideas into your head?" She didn't give him a chance to reply. "Jocelyn, I want you to get rid of her."

He said, appalled, "But – I can't, May. Father does need her. And he's already made some sort of arrangement with her."

"Break it," she said.

There was a long silence. Then he said, "But I can't, May. Oh, I realise you might well feel jealous. But I do assure you – "

May said, "Jocelyn, I'm not jealous. But it is time we got back to normal life, don't you agree?"

"In the main, yes," said Pig-in-the-Middle. "But – ?"

"But what?"

For the moment Jocelyn was saved by his father stumping in. "May, my dear, you're back. Settled my sister, have you?"

"Yes. I telephoned Aunt Dorothea. She and Edouard have promised to stay with her for the time being."

"Good." He kissed her fondly. "Nice to have you back, May. But – now you are back I just want to put you in the picture about my chauffeur."

"Now I was just speaking to Jocelyn about that, Father-in-law."

"Really? And what were you saying?"

"I was saying it was time we got back to our old way of life."

"In other words repel boarders and leave the old man to lurch around until he can take the car out for a mile or two on his own. And what did Jocelyn say?"

Jocelyn said, "I said in the main I agreed, but – "

"But what?"

"I hadn't got there," said Jocelyn.

"Hadn't got where?"

"Past the 'but'," said Jocelyn, who went to pieces when chivvied.

"Right. I'll tell you. Miss Nightingale will be my nurse and my chauffeur, on terms arranged between her and myself. You, May, will look after the house and the children and cook for us all as you have so splendidly done over the years.

Jocelyn will continue to do what he has always done – frankly, I've never known what."

Jocelyn said, "Father, I can't allow you to lay the law down to May like this. It's like talking to a paid servant. May's my wife. You – "

"Shut up, Jocelyn," said May brusquely. She sat down the better to face the old man. Her voice rang with fury. "Father-in-law, how dare you speak about Jocelyn like that? He earns every penny I spend on this house and myself and the children. And he earns it by writing good, clever novels that give pleasure and comfort to thousands of readers, that enlarge the lives and the minds of thousands more. He ought to have a medal but he never will. And you, who ought to know better, write him off as an amiable potterer. Father-in-law, I'm ashamed of you, a man of your intelligence."

It was Jocelyn who broke the long silence. "Am I really not an amiable potterer?" he asked in wonder.

"Of course you're not," said May.

This assertion that he wasn't just poor old Jocelyn, whom everyone could and did push around did wonders for his morale. Now he was Jocelyn Pentecost, writer, as well loved as the creators of Mr Pickwick and Mrs Proudie and Long John Silver were loved; whom that fine woman May loved; even, dare he think it, a man with whom Miss Nightingale would not have been averse to a little frolic in the night.

And here was Miss Nightingale, brashly barging. "Oh, sorry everyone," she said, backing out. "I'd no idea – "

"Come in, my dear," cried John. "The very person we want to see." He waved her to a chair. "I've just been explaining to Mr & Mrs Pentecost our plans."

Miss Nightingale sat down demurely. "And Mr and Mrs Pentecost have no objections?"

May said, "Frankly, Miss Nightingale, I have plenty of

objections. I want to bring up my children in my own way, and to have my house, and my husband, to myself."

Miss Nightingale sounded cold. "Are you inferring, Mrs Pentecost, that I am a danger to your marriage?"

"You could put it that way," said May. "Not that I think you would succeed."

Miss Nightingale said nothing. May went on: "But where you might succeed is in involving my husband too closely in your own literary efforts." Her voice rose. "I have protected him for many years from amateur scribblers. And I am not leaving him unprotected now."

"I see," said Miss Nightingale.

"Well, thank goodness that's settled," said John. "Now lets all have a drink."

"Nothing is settled," May said bleakly.

"May, May," John said coaxingly. "It's not like you to make difficulties. What's come over you?"

May said, "A short time ago I answered the telephone. I recognised Arthur Mandrake's voice. He asked whether I was the secretary or the girl-friend." She let it sink in. Then she said, "Do you wonder I make difficulties?"

And that, for the time being, broke up the conference. Pig-in-the-Middle escaped to his study to think things over. But he was faced by a complete impasse. His father wouldn't budge, he knew that. And May had got her teeth in. And May demanded loyalty, and deserved it. And if he didn't offer it, he would sink in May's estimation, and in his own.

And what about Miss Nightingale? She was capable and efficient, she was obviously prepared to serve and nurse his father (something his father badly needed). Even if Jocelyn could send her packing, would that be right? It was a devil of a problem.

He was quite relieved when the telephone rang to take his

mind off his problems.

It was Arthur Mandrake. "Jocelyn, old man, I've a feeling I said the wrong this earlier in the day."

"Your certainly did," said Jocelyn.

"Sorry, old man. I say, do you think I could have a word with the girl-fr—. With Miss Nightingale?"

"Yes," said Jocelyn. We went and called. Miss Nightingale came running. He gave her the receiver. "Arthur Mandrake," he said.

He went downstairs, found May. He said, "Hello, darling."

"Hello," she said.

"It's a – bit of a problem, isn't it?" he said.

"Yes," she said.

"Father does need her," he said.

"And we don't," she said.

If only women didn't make an issue of everything, he thought. Once you made an issue of something it developed the properties of a hot-air balloon, roaring and bouncing about, sometimes belting off God knows where. "It won't be for ever," he said.

"Jocelyn," she said. "I'm sorry and I know I'm being horrible but I don't want her here and I want you to get rid of her."

"I can't get rid of her," he said.

He gave him a look that cut him very deeply: a long, slow, beseeching, disappointed look. "You're letting me down," she said, and as she said it she grasped his hand and held it so tight in both of hers that he cried out.

They heard footsteps clattering down the stairs. Miss Nightingale burst in. "Mr Pentecost, you know those twenty thousand words?"

Jocelyn hadn't thought his heart could sink any lower. But

at these words it did. "Yes?" he said wearily.

"Well, they're going to help me take them out. They've booked me in at a hotel, and they say I shall be busy in London for months. Apparently they're going to hype my book if you know what that means. And help me to write another."

Jocelyn could have said, "It means they're going to spend thousands and thousands deliberately turning your book into a best seller, so they won't have any money left for publicity for chaps like me." But he was a nice man. He said, "Congratulations, Miss Nightingale. It means you've got a best seller on your hands."

"Really? Isn't that marvellous! I say, you couldn't drive me to Ingerby Station, I suppose?"

"I'm afraid not," said Jocelyn coldly.

May said, with an equal chill, "I thought you were going to drive my father-in-law?"

"That wouldn't work. He'd have to get a taxi home. And his precious Rover would be stuck in the station car park."

May said angrily, "I didn't mean that. I meant act as his chauffeur until he can drive himself again. I understood you'd promised."

"Good Lord. I thought after all you'd said you'd be only too pleased to see the back of me."

"I *shall* be glad to see the back of you, Miss Nightingale. But I was just putting in a word on behalf of your conscience, in case it needed my help."

"Thank you. I can look after my own conscience."

"So I see," said May. "And frankly, I was never in much doubt. The poor thing must be on its knees."

Miss Nightingale turned to Jocelyn. Her winning smile was back. "How much is a taxi to Ingerby, Mr Pentecost?"

"About seven pounds," he said.

"Does he take Barclaycard?"

"Good Lord, no. Cash down or you walk, is Taylor's motto."

"Well, isn't this ridiculous. A best seller on my hands, and I haven't even got a taxi fare."

The silence was awful. At last Miss Nightingale said, "I wonder whether it's any good having another look for my bicycle."

Jocelyn said, "No. We searched, remember. Someone had taken it."

"Could have been an inside job," said Miss Nightingale.

"Why, so it could," cried May. "Jocelyn, do let's go and help Miss Nightingale have another look."

"But – " said Jocelyn.

"Please – " said May. They all went out into the stockyard. "We searched all round here," said Jocelyn.

"Did we go in that big barn?"

"No. But it wouldn't be there."

"Worth looking, anyway," said May.

Jocelyn kicked aside that horrible fleece. They went in. It was dark. All they could see was the back of the Rover. "Got a torch?" said Miss Nightingale.

"No, I haven't," said Jocelyn. "And this is a wild goose chase, anyway." A most irritating thought struck him. He could have written a chapter while he'd been helping this hyped female to search. And no one was going to hype *his* book, he could be sure of that.

It was, he realised, the first time in his life that he'd ever felt the sting of jealousy.

From the stockyard came the blood-curdling wail of a police car. But it was only Gaylord. Jocelyn called him. "Gaylord, you haven't see a lady's bicycle anywhere, have you?"

"I don't think so, Poppa." He came into the barn, peered into the gloom. "That isn't one, is it?"

It was. Just in front of Grandpa's Rover. Miss Nightingale went and dragged it out. "Oh you clever boy, Gaylord."

May wished it wasn't so dark. She was trying to see which of the two, Gaylord or Miss Nightingale, was the more surprised.

Gaylord said, "Why does Miss Nightingale want her bicycle?"

"How do you know it is Miss Nightingale's?" asked Momma.

Suspicious woman! "She came on it when she came," he said indignantly. But he was more concerned about another question. "Miss Nightingale isn't going, is she?" He looked close to tears.

May put her arm round him. Miss Nightingale said, "I'll just collect my things." She turned to Jocelyn. "I say, you wouldn't just have a word with the old man for me, would you? Explain things. You know, this hyping business. I really don't understand it."

"No he damn well wouldn't," exploded May. But Jocelyn said quietly, "Yes, I'll speak to him, Miss Nightingale. He's going to get hurt anyway. But I flatter myself I shall hurt him less than you will."

John Pentecost greeted him with, "Where the devil's Miss Nightingale? She's supposed to be driving me in to the dentist's in five minutes."

Jocelyn said, "I'm afraid she won't be taking you, Father. Something rather unfortunate – unfortunate for you, I mean, not for her – has happened. That book of hers: the Mandrake Press are promoting it in a big way. And this – "

But his father was staring at him in amazement and –

could it be? – glee. He slapped his thigh. "Well, damn me. What did I say? Best thing since *The Prisoner of Zenda*. Didn't I? Didn't I? And what did you say? Bloody awful twaddle, or words to that effect."

"I think," said Jocelyn, "you ought to be ringing up the dentist, Father. You can't possibly – "

"Damn the dentist. Really, you literary chaps – "

Jocelyn said, "The point is, Father, they've asked her to go and stay in London and – well, frankly, she's gone."

"I should think so. Know what they're doing those Mandrake people. Why don't you try to interest them in some of your books?"

"They are my publishers," said Jocelyn. "But you see, Father, it means she won't be able to be your chauffeur after all."

"Good God." Jocelyn heard the drop of a metaphorical penny. "You mean – she'll be giving in her notice?"

"Worse that that. She's already pedalling off to literary fortune."

"And you think she won't return?"

Jocelyn shook his head. "I don't think so, Father. The lights of London are very bright. And – I think Miss Nightingale will find plenty of people to fascinate. And to be fascinated by." He sighed. Et in Arcadia ego, he remembered. He sighed again. But only on the threshold, he thought. And in a raging thunderstorm.

The old man grabbed the telephone, dialled. "Miss Rogers, cancel my appointment, will you. I've been sold down the river, 'stood up' is perhaps the modern idiom."

John listened to the reply, put back the receiver. "'Very well, Mr Pentecost,'" he mimicked. "'Thank you for ringing.'" He glared at his son. "The heavens fall, chaos is come; and she says, 'thank you for ringing.'"

Jocelyn said, "I'm sorry, Father. It's an awful blow for you. But – well, May said she was a fly-by-night."

"I knew that without May telling me. But I thought I could handle it."

Jocelyn's heart bled for the old man. He said, "The question is, what can any of us do to help?"

A long silence. Then John said, "I'm afraid, Jocelyn, I've sometimes been a bit critical of your driving."

"A bit," said Jocelyn mildly.

"On the other hand," said John, "you've driven your own car for years."

"Yes."

"And you haven't done a lot of damage," said the old man generously. "Not like my sister Bea, anyway."

"No," said Jocelyn, trying to remember any damage he'd done.

John said, "I think I'd be prepared to let you drive the Rover."

"You would?"

"With myself in the front seat, of course."

"Of course."

"After all, now this bally girl's hooked it, I'm going to be high and dry if you don't."

"Yes," said Jocelyn, wondering whether chaps like Dickens and Trollope ever had to act as unpaid coachmen because they were too good-natured to say no.

"So that's settled," said John.

"Yes," said Jocelyn.

They were silent. Mellow sunlight crept over the window ledge. "Beautiful autumn day," said John. He mused. "Come to think of it, Jocelyn, no reason why you shouldn't have a practice tomorrow. I'll explain things, of course."

"Of course," said Jocelyn, who had just been hoping for a

busy day tomorrow in his study.

"Right. Shall we take the boy?"

"Let's all go," said Jocelyn. "Because we're together again. It'll be a Celebration."

Everything had suddenly come right: May was home, thought Jocelyn, his father had taken the great load of guilt from his mind, he was no longer Pig-in-the-Middle, now that Nightingale had taken herself off voluntarily. Apart from having accepted the post of part-time chauffeur to his father, he hadn't a cloud in his sky.

So why wasn't he on top the world? He didn't know. All he knew was that he was still bloody miserable.

Why do I feel sick and wretched and dispirited and irritable? he asked himself.

It hit him like flash of lightning. Could it be because I am out of kilter with old Reuben?

If it is, he thought, there's nothing I can do about it. Reuben isn't a man you could win round even if you wanted to. Which I don't.

In the meantime, I've still got that horrible fleece to get rid of, confound the man.

He went and got his spade. He dug a hole near the stockyard, tipped the fleece in, covered it over, marked the spot with a cane.

As he smoothed the earth something Reuben had once said recurred to him, "Ain't never cried for a human. Once for a sheep."

Poor devil, thought Jocelyn. And without letting himself think any further he ran up to Reuben's cottage. He burst in. "I've buried your sheep," he panted. "Thought you'd like to know where I put her. Marked the spot. Only a garden cane, I'm afraid."

"Aye," said Reuben. There was a long silence. Then: "Aye," said Reuben again.

"Just thought I'd let you know," said Jocelyn.

"Aye," said Reuben. "Thanks."

Reuben sat on. Jocelyn hovered. Then he turned and ran down the hill, lighter than he had run for weeks and months.

Chapter 15

Gaylord opened the barn doors. John said, "There she is, dear boy. Beautiful, isn't she? Perhaps you'd better let me get her out," he added.

Gently he backed the car into the stockyard. Then they all climbed in, May and the children in the back, John very proprietorial in the front passenger seat, Jocelyn in the driver's seat, very nervous. John said, "Now put that in Drive, take off the brake and ease her gently forward with the accelerator."

Silently the car stole forward at a steady six miles an hour. "Your can take her a bit faster when you get on the open road," said John.

And Jocelyn, to his pride, did. Twenty, twenty-five, thirty. It was exhilarating: swept along glidingly by a superb product of the twentieth century. Eventually he was doing fifty, without his father showing any signs of nervousness. And now they were coming to little hills that climbed out of the valley and on to a sunlit upland. And not even Jocelyn could resist setting this perfect machine at these challenging hills, and soaring up them like a bird. "She's a lovely car," murmured John, enjoying every moment. "And you're not doing too badly, Jocelyn. Considering it's your first time," he added generously.

Jocelyn glowed.

And in the back May nursed the sleeping Amanda, and

held Gaylord to her, and felt a serenity and a peace she hadn't known since her father-in-law's accident. They were together again, the five of them. Oh, they would argue, and misunderstand, but they had fought the good fight and come through, and if they'd done it once they could do it again. And that was a good lesson to have learnt. She called out happily, "Nice to be in the car again, Father-in-law?"

He looked over his shoulder, actually smiled. "You bet, May," he said. And went back to watching the road.

Only Gaylord worried her. Quiet, listless. Surely, she thought, he couldn't really have fallen in love at his age. He couldn't really be suffering the agonies of separation from a departed loved one. "You're very quiet, darling," she said, tenderly rubbing her cheek against his.

"Am I, Momma?" A forlorn, almost despairing, reply.

"It isn't Miss Nightingale, is it?" she asked, greatly daring.

"Sort of," he said.

Her heart ached for him. "In what way, sort of?"

He was silent. Then he said, "Momma?"

"Yes, darling?"

He began running his finger round her palm, that sure sign he wanted a favour. "Momma, what was nice about Miss Nightingale was – "

"What dear?"

"Having baked beans for supper, Momma."

"I see. Is that all that was nice about her?"

"Oh, no," he said.

"What else, then?"

"Coca-Cola," said Gaylord.

She threw her arms around him. "Oh, my darling, you shall have both those."

"Really, Momma?" His eyes shone. Then "All the same, I do wish she'd have married me," he said, back to being forlorn again.

The sun went on shining. The tyres swished happily along the country lanes. The engine crooned and purred. Ahead of them they saw a ramshackle cottage, gaunt and unlovely, but with a rusting metal advertisement on its wall: TEAS WITH HOVIS.

"I haven't seen that sign for years," said May. "Do let's stop."

They had tea in the orchard, gazing down into the sunlit valley, eating homemade scones at a crumbling wrought-iron table, perched on rickety chairs. Gaylord, thoughtfully munching, eyed a nearby swing and a decrepit seesaw. May watched him. Would he, she asked herself, be affronted if she suggested he might still like a swing. Even in his love-lorn state.

Gaylord spoke: "If you sat on the swing, Momma, you could nurse Amanda and I could push you."

"That would be lovely," she said. She went and sat on the swing. Gaylord began to push. Amanda crowed and chortled with delight. Her laughter was infectious.

Soon they were all laughing. Even Grandpa was rumbling inwardly. And the valley of the Trent lay below them like a dish full of sunlight: a long dish wherein lay all their troubles and aspirations and hopes and fears, wherein poor lonely Reuben tended his sheep and pored with limited understanding over old Dusty-ever-so.

And above them the leaves of the apple boughs stirred and danced, and dappled the long grass of the orchard. And Jocelyn held the moment to his heart; knowing it was one of those moments when happiness touches, and blesses, like an angel's wing. And then is gone, perhaps for ever.

Slowly, the swing came to rest. May said, "Now Gaylord, your turn."

But the dark eyes were grave again. "No, thank you, Momma." He wandered off to where a wicket gate led to a field track.

And there he stood, staring. But he wasn't seeing the valley. He was seeing Miss Nightingale bustling off on her bicycle without even looking at him. He was again watching her, as he had watched her earlier that day, go through the gate, and past the bit where the river lapped the edge of the road, her bicycle (and her gold hair) glinting in the sunshine. "Oh, God, let her turn and wave. Just once," he had implored. But she hadn't. She had grown smaller, and smaller, until, tiny, glittering like a falling star, she had disappeared round the last bend.

May said urgently, "Jocelyn, he's gone broody, ten years before his time. Get him on the swing for heaven's sake."

"Oh, ah, yes," said Jocelyn. "Gaylord," he called. "Come and have a swing."

Gaylord turned and looked at him like a somnambulist. Then, slowly, he trudged over to the swing and sat down on its rotting seat. Jocelyn began to push. Gaylord began to swing, gently, deliciously. Or rather, he was the still centre of a crazy world. Everything – Momma, Poppa, the cottage, the sun and sky, the orchard trees, the long valley, the round earth itself, was turning madcap somersaults. While he, Gaylord, sat like a King enthroned, like God himself, at the centre of a whirling universe.

"Higher," cried Gaylord. "Higher!"

Jocelyn pushed, pushed harder. It seemed to Gaylord that he hung poised to shoot into a long blue avenue of sky. "Higher," he cried.

Jocelyn pushed. "Hup," he cried as he pushed. "Hup!"

"Hup," cried Momma. "Hup."

Gaylord was almost sick with laughter. Amanda gurgled

with delight. The old man gazed thoughtfully across the valley which, God willing, would bear his strengthening footsteps into another Spring. May and Jocelyn smiled lovingly.

And the world, this autumn day, was young again.

ERIC MALPASS

THE LAMPLIGHT AND THE STARS

Nathan Cranswick's third child comes into the world on the day of Queen Victoria's Diamond Jubilee. Whilst the Empire celebrates, Nathan's concerns are about his family's future. A gentle and wise preacher, he gratefully accepts the chance to move from the dingy, cramped house in Ingerby to the village of Moreland when he is offered a job on the splendid Heron estate. Anticipating peace and tranquillity for his wife and young family, his hopes are cruelly dashed when their new life is beset by problems from the beginning. A family scandal and the Boer War menace their whole future, but finally it is the agonising choice facing his gentle daughter which threatens to tear the family apart...

MORNING'S AT SEVEN

Three generations of the Pentecost family live in a state of permanent disarray in a huge, sprawling farmhouse. Seven-year-old Gaylord Pentecost is the innocent hero who observes the lives of the adults – Grandpa, Momma and Poppa and two aunties – with amusement and incredulity.

Through Gaylord's eyes, we witness the heartache suffered by Auntie Rose as the exquisite Auntie Becky makes a play for her gentleman friend, while Gaylord unwittingly makes the situation far worse.

Mayhem and madness reign in this zestful account of the lives and loves of the outrageous Pentecosts.

ERIC MALPASS

OF HUMAN FRAILTY
A BIOGRAPHICAL NOVEL OF THOMAS CRANMER

Thomas Cranmer is a gentle, unassuming scholar when a chance meeting sweeps him away from the security and tranquillity of Cambridge to the harsh magnificence of Henry VIII's court. As a supporter of Henry he soon rises to prominence as Archbishop of Canterbury.

Eric Malpass paints a fascinating picture of Reformation England and its prominent figures: the brilliant, charismatic but utterly ruthless Henry VIII, the exquisite but scheming Anne Boleyn and the fanatical Mary Tudor.

But it is the paradoxical Thomas Cranmer who dominates the story. A tormented man, he is torn between valour and cowardice; a man with a loving heart who finds himself hated by many; and a man of God who makes the terrifying discovery that he must suffer and die for his beliefs. Thomas Cranmer is a man of simple virtue, whose only fault is his all too human frailty.

ERIC MALPASS

THE RAISING OF LAZARUS PIKE

Lazarus Pike (1820–1899), author of *Lady Emily's Decision*, lies buried in the churchyard of Ill Boding. And there he would have remained, in obscurity and undisturbed, had it not been for a series of remarkable coincidences. A discovery sets in motion a campaign to republish his works and to reinstate Lazarus Pike as a giant of Victorian literature. This is a cause of bitter wrangling between the two factions that emerge. For some, Lazarus is a simple schoolmaster, devoted to his beautiful wife, Corinda. For others, who think his reputation needs a sexy, contemporary twist, he is a wife murderer with a deeply flawed character. What follows is a knowing and wry look at the world of literary make-overs and the heritage industry in a hilarious story that brings fame and tragedy to an unsuspecting moorland village.

SWEET WILL

William Shakespeare is just eighteen when he marries Anne Hathaway, eight years his senior. Anne, who bears a son soon after the marriage, is plain and not particularly bright – but her love for Will is undeniable. Talented and fiercely ambitious, Will's scintillating genius soon makes him the toast of Elizabethan London. While he basks in the flattery his great reputation affords him, Anne lives a lonely life in Stratford, far away from the glittering world of her husband.

This highly evocative account of the life of the young William Shakespeare begins the trilogy which continues with *The Cleopatra Boy* and concludes with *A House of Women*.

ERIC MALPASS

THE WIND BRINGS UP THE RAIN

It is a perfect summer's day in August 1914. Yet even as Nell and her friends enjoy a blissful picnic by the river, the storm clouds of war are gathering over Europe. Very soon this idyll is to be swept away by the conflict that will take millions of men to their deaths.

After the war, the widowed Nell leads a wretched existence, caring for her husband's elderly, ungrateful parents, with only her son, Benbow, for companionship and support. But Nell is a passionate woman and wants to share her life with a man who will return her love. Meanwhile, Benbow falls in love with a German girl, Ulrike – until she is enticed home by the resurgent Germany.

This moving story of a Midlands family in the interwar years is a compelling tale of personal triumph and disappointment, set against the background of the hideous destruction of war.

1535529R0

Printed in Great Britain by
Amazon.co.uk, Ltd.,
Marston Gate.